# TO SPELL WITH IT

## A MOONSTONE BAY COZY MYSTERY BOOK FOUR

### AMANDA M. LEE

WINCHESTERSHAW PUBLICATIONS

## ONE

"**You** can't be serious."

I cracked into my crab leg and fixed my boyfriend Galen Blackwood with a dubious look. He had an odd sense of humor sometimes and it was clearly on display now.

"Oh, I'm serious." Galen dumped steak sauce over his rare steak to cover the pooling blood — he knew it gave me the heebie-jeebies — and took a swig from his drink. "It's a big thing and it happens every seven years or so. They change locations."

I stared hard at him. I was convinced he was playing with me. "A cupid convention. We're actually having a convention for cupids in Moonstone Bay?" There was no way that could be real. "Does everyone whip out their bows and arrows for it?"

He regarded me with solemn eyes as he cut into his steak. "I'm not messing with you."

"This is like the time you told me that trolls lived under the bridge, right? I went looking for a troll because I wanted a photo and it turned out that the only thing that lives under the bridge is some local guy who likes to drop his pants and flash women. I guess he was sort of a troll."

Galen's expression darkened. "I told you I would handle that. I didn't know he was still doing that. No one purposely goes down there, so there haven't been any reports for some time."

"I don't want you arresting him." I meant it. "He just caught me by surprise. I wasn't even sure what I was looking at until I saw him move his hand." I mimicked the movement, causing Galen's eyes to light with mirth.

"Stop that." He reached out and slapped my hand down before scanning the restaurant's waterfront patio to make sure nobody was looking. This was the sort of place men took women when they wanted to score, so absolutely no one was looking at us because they were too busy staring at their dates. "You can't do stuff like that until we're alone."

I caught the double meaning of his words and rolled my eyes. "Please. I could make you back down from that super-fast if I wanted."

"How do you figure?"

"I'd dress up like a cupid and wear nothing but a satin diaper and shoot arrows at you."

He snickered at my roundabout way of bringing the conversation full circle. "I'm not lying to you, Hadley. We're actually having a cupid convention. It's a weeklong event and ... it often gets out of control."

I narrowed my eyes and stared hard at him. I was determined to get him to admit he was lying. When he didn't as much as blink I started to wonder if he could be telling the truth. "I don't understand," I said. "How does that work?"

It was hard for me to admit when I was confused. In fact, I, Hadley Hunter, was almost never confused. I was proud of that fact. Even if I ran off half-cocked in the wrong direction, I was rarely confused about it. That's a good thing, right?

"Are you asking how the conference itself works?" Galen asked as he broke a breadstick and handed me half. In a moment of weakness I'd admitted that I believed the calories didn't count in bread ... and pie ... and cake ... and candy ... if someone shared the item with me. He'd found my logic confusing, but embraced it all the same. Since then, he ordered the fattening item and gave me half. I didn't feel healthier physically, but I did in my head. That's all that mattered.

I nodded as I bit into the bread and moaned. "Oh, this is buttered goodness. I want to date this breadstick it's so good."

"I guess I know where I stand." He offered me a wink to let me know he was joking and leaned back in his chair. "Do you really want to know about the cupid conference, or are you just digging your heels in because you like to argue?"

That was a loaded question. "I really want to know."

He waited.

"And I might be digging my heels in a bit," I added. "I'm curious. I can't help it. What do cupids have to conference about?"

"Being a cupid isn't what you think it is."

"No?" I'd given this a lot of thought since I found out my new friend Booker — no last name — was a cupid. Moonstone Bay was full of paranormal creatures. Galen, for example, was a wolf shifter. My new best friend Lilac Meadows (yes, that's her real name) was a half-demon who could turn her hair red and make her eyes shoot lasers. Okay, I'm making that last part up. During a fight several weeks ago, though, that's exactly what I thought she was going to do. Her eyes turned red and fiery and she shot fireballs from her hands while fighting with a local cult. She was really impressive. But it was the cupid in my life that was cause for concern. "What is being a cupid like?"

Galen heaved out a sigh. He was used to me asking questions about paranormal beings. It had been happening since I landed on the island months before. He was usually open and honest about things because he figured that was the best way to placate me. The cupid stuff clearly had him on edge, though.

"Are you going to tell me?" I pressed.

"I don't necessarily know all the ins and outs of being a cupid," he admitted after a beat. "I didn't grow up in that world."

"There's a cupid world?" This just kept getting better and better. I dug into the crab shell for meat and yanked it out with the tiny fork provided. "I can't wait to hear about this."

"I don't know how much I can tell you. I don't know much about cupids."

"You're friends with Booker," I pointed out, enthusiastically dunking my crab in butter. "Did I mention how good the food is here? Yum."

He smiled indulgently. "I'm glad you're enjoying yourself. I figured you would love the seafood."

"Why haven't you brought me here before?"

"Because it's expensive and I'm a public servant."

I slowed my chewing and frowned. "I can help pay."

Instantly, the expression on his face switched from amusement to regret. "That is not what I want. I brought you here because I knew you would like it. Dinners on the beach are going to be harder to come by because our stormy season begins in a few weeks."

I'd heard other people in town talk about the stormy season. I assumed that meant tourists stopped coming. The storms were apparently intermittent, so that wasn't the case. Moonstone Bay was the premiere paranormal vacation destination fifty-two weeks a year. That was essentially drilled into my head now.

"I can still help." I meant it. I wasn't yet working — I'd inherited a lighthouse several months ago from a grandmother I didn't know and had been settling in since leaving the mainland — but I had savings. I could definitely help swing dinner, no matter how expensive it was. "I want to help."

"Knock that off." Galen made a face and inclined his chin toward my plate. "Eat your crab. I've got dinner covered."

I made a mental note to think hard and long this week about exactly what I wanted to do with my life. I was having a great time on the island. It already felt like home. Just because I had a guaranteed place to live, though, didn't mean I'd be able to slide by without getting a job. It was becoming more and more of a necessity. I simply had no idea what I wanted to do. "I'll cook you dinner tomorrow to make up for this," I promised. "We don't have to eat out all week."

"I'm sorry I brought it up," Galen muttered, rolling his neck. "Let's talk about something else."

"I thought we were talking about cupids."

"Right." His eyes momentarily glazed over. "Like I said, I don't have a lot of information regarding cupids. All I know is what they've made public and, frankly, that's not much. They like to be mysterious."

"You know Booker, though," I pressed. "All you have to do is ask if you're curious."

"I do know Booker. He's not the talkative sort."

"He talks to me."

"Only because you chase him around and pepper him with inane questions until he gives in. He basically agrees to answer them because it's that or listen to you whine for hours."

"I don't whine." I grabbed a new crab cluster and went to town. "I think that's a horrible thing to say about the woman you spend every night with."

His gaze turned sexy and his grin widened. "I have very specific plans for you tonight."

"Oh, yeah?" I wasn't surprised. Galen wasn't always talkative, but he never hid his intentions. "I'll happily play that game once you tell me about cupids. Why do they need to have a conference? I mean ... do they work? Do they really shoot people with arrows? Do they make people fall in love?"

"That was a lot of questions for one breath."

"I can't help it. I'm curious."

"Well, I guess I can answer some of it though I'm not an expert by any stretch."

"You've already mentioned that."

"I just wanted to remind you." He cracked another breadstick and automatically handed me half. "Booker and I weren't exactly close in high school. You already know that."

"Yes, you were in constant competition to see which of you could bang more cheerleaders. I'm well aware."

He chuckled at my airy response. "I would much rather bang you, honey." He made a face immediately after uttering the words. "That didn't sound as bad in my head. I apologize."

I waved him off. "Forget it. I started it."

"Yeah, well, it was still weird. Anyway, our paths crossed a time or two. His mother and my mother had a lot in common."

"You mean the mother I still haven't met?"

He ignored the question. "Occasionally we would get stuck at island events together and I got to see his mother in action," he continued. "Booker was never all that interested in being a cupid. Apparently there are classes you have to take — chemistry and psychology classes — and you're expected to pass some big test."

"So, it's like becoming a lawyer," I suggested. "You have to learn thirty million things and then pass the equivalent of the bar exam."

"I ... well ... I was going to say that it was nothing like that, but it is kind of like that."

"I'm smarter than I look." I tapped the side of my head, causing him to laugh.

"You're too smart for your own good sometimes. As for cupids ... they have a specific job to do. They're in control of love. There would be no happiness without them."

That sounded like a steaming pile of crap. "But ... how do they control love? I mean ... they don't shove two people together and force them to have feelings." The mere thought was enough to have my blood running cold as I regarded Galen. We fell for each other quickly. Some would say it was almost magical. I didn't like the idea of someone else being behind that. "I mean ... we're not together because they wanted us together, are we?"

He must've realized what I was worried about because he quickly covered my hand with his. "It doesn't work that way. Cupids do influence emotions, but you're in charge of your own destiny. Basically cupids smooth out the wrinkles. Most of them serve as therapists — I'm not kidding — and they help that way."

That didn't make much sense. "What did they do before therapists existed?"

"Caused wars."

I knit my eyebrows. "What?"

"I shouldn't have said that." He held his hands up in a placating manner. "The truth is, cupids weren't exactly beloved back in the day. You know that whole Helen of Troy thing? She was the woman who had an older husband and had an affair with a younger prince who happened to be his enemy. A cupid caused that because he was bored."

I worked my jaw. "But ... I thought that was a myth."

"Most myths are based in reality. Helen of Troy was a real woman. A cupid served as the king's right-hand man and he counseled Helen and the king for years. Legend has it, one day the king ticked him off and he decided to 'inspire' another young prince because he wanted to see what would happen. What happened was that two sides warred and a lot of people died."

"And that's true? You're not making that up to mess with me, are you?"

"You need to stop assuming people are messing with you. I like a good joke as much as the next person, but I'm only messing with you twenty percent of the time. The other eighty percent, well, I'm being perfectly serious."

I didn't have a ledger in front of me, but I was convinced he was messing with me a good fifty percent of the time. "So ... why are they having a cupid conference? Do they have it every year?"

"There is a cupid conference every year, but it hasn't been held here in a long time. This is a special conference with mandatory attendance unless you have a medical excuse, and they only have those every seven years or so. I was trying to think about the last conference we had here, but I can't really remember the exact date. It was a wild event."

"Wild? Do they run around shooting each other with their bows and arrows? What? I could see that happening. It's like when people chase each other with guns after bonfires. Oh, don't look at me that way."

His expression was stern. "I don't know who you've been hanging around with, but that gun thing is not normal."

"I didn't say it was normal. It's a Michigan thing."

"Then remind me never to visit Michigan." He rolled his neck and watched as I attacked my cheddar mashed potatoes. "Cupids are notorious for not getting along ... with each other and outsiders. They can influence the emotions of others if they exert their powers in a negative manner. I don't believe Booker does that — and I would arrest him if he did — but you might be in for a rude awakening if you decide you're going to spend a lot of time with the cupids."

"What makes you think I'm going to spend a lot of time hanging out with the cupids?"

"I've met you ... and you have time on your hands. What else are you going to do the next few days?"

I didn't like his tone. "I've been considering getting a job."

He didn't immediately react, but I saw the flash of interest in his eyes before he shuttered it. "Oh, yeah? Where are you thinking of getting a job?"

"I have no idea. I'm not qualified for anything on this island. What do you think I should do?"

"Oh, I'm not answering that question. I'm not an idiot. You should do whatever you want to do."

I made a face. "I'm honestly asking your opinion. I need to do something. My savings will last only so long. Plus, well, I'd like to be a productive member of society. All I've done the past few months is wander around and get into trouble."

"You've also snagged the most attractive man on the island," he added. "Don't sell yourself short there."

"Ha, ha, ha." I rolled my eyes. "I need to figure out what I want to do. There must be something I'm good at."

"I'm sure you're good at a lot of things."

"I want a career, not just a job. But I might take a job simply to keep myself busy."

He ran his tongue over his teeth as he regarded me. "May I make a suggestion?"

"Is it going to annoy me?"

"I hope not."

"Okay. Lay it on me."

"I think you should take a week to really think about what you want to do," he started. "Make a list. Do that two-column thing. Have a list of pros and cons. You don't want to be miserable while you're

here. I don't want you to be miserable because that means you'll be more likely to leave."

I was taken aback. "I have no intention of leaving."

"Not now. If you're unhappy working, though, that might change. I would prefer keeping you happy."

"Oh, that's cute." I offered him a saucy grin. "You can make me happy later."

"Now we're talking."

"With a massage."

His grin only widened. "I was thinking we could take a walk along the docks before heading home. It's a nice night and we can burn off some of this food before calling it a night."

"You want to walk?" I could think of a hundred different activities I would rather do. "I guess."

"Some of the cupids are expected to come in on this evening's ship," he offered.

I perked up exponentially. "Why didn't you just say that? I'm dying to see these cupids in action. I'm still not sure what they can and can't do, but I'm definitely willing to watch and learn."

"Somehow I knew you were going to say that."

"I'm nothing if not predictable."

## TWO

*G*alen was the tactile sort. He was also easily amused, which meant we spent the next hour laughing as we bought ice cream and held hands on the dock. When the cruise ship finally docked, I was awestruck.

"No way!"

He grinned as he used his napkin to dab at the corner of my mouth. I loved ice cream beyond reason, but it melted fast in Moonstone Bay's infamous humidity. "Do you like it?"

"It's ... got huge hearts on it."

"It does at that."

"There are arrows through the hearts."

"There are."

"No fat babies in diapers with bows and arrows," I noted, disappointment getting a foothold. "That's a little sad."

"You know the babies-in-diapers thing isn't real, right?"

"You don't have to ruin everything." I licked my ice cream. "I like the idea of Booker floating around with a bow and arrow when he was a toddler."

"Only you would find that image comforting," Galen muttered. "Still, I thought you would want to see the ship."

"You have no idea." I moved to one of the benches at the side of the dock and sat, Galen wordlessly joining me. We'd been together for a few weeks but he already recognized the things that excited me. "How many cupids are coming to town?"

"Seven-hundred."

"Seven-hundred?" I was flabbergasted. "Wow! Is that ... all of them?"

"Do all humans go to conferences?"

"No, but ... I thought maybe it was a thing."

"I already told you that it's mandatory. I should've explained it was mandatory for working cupids and they only need one representative from every family. Not everyone is a working cupid."

He settled on the bench and draped one arm around my shoulders as he continued eating his ice cream. "Remember when I told you that the conference hadn't been held here for a bit? Well, there's a reason for that. There's been a power struggle brewing in the cupid ranks for a very long time."

I had no idea what to make of that. "A power struggle?"

"That's what I said."

"But ... what do cupids have power over?"

"I already told you. They can affect moods and influence relationships."

"But ... you also said it came down to free will," I remembered. "You said we have control over our own destinies."

"We do. I don't think I'm explaining this very well." He licked the ice cream dripping down his cone and changed tactics. "If I were a cupid, I could use my magic to try to make you fall in love with someone," he explained. "If you were open to that suggestion, you might willingly embrace it. If not, then you can fight it."

"Can the cupid overpower you?"

"Technically."

He definitely wasn't explaining it well. I had the feeling that was because there was something he was desperately trying to keep from me. Now to figure out what that something was. "Have cupids ever forced humans to do things they didn't want to do for sport?" I played

a hunch. I would've gotten to it eventually, but I decided to push forward now because I couldn't wait.

He sighed. "I should've known you would sniff that out."

"Yes, I'm like a dog that way." I finished my cone and wiped the corners of my mouth. "You might as well just spill it. I'm going to find out eventually."

"By peppering Booker with questions until he answers them."

"Or just ask Lilac."

"I had not considered that." Conflict, obvious and stark, flitted over his features before he regrouped. "Okay, I'll tell you. But I expect you to keep it to yourself."

"Who am I going to share it with? The only people I know on this island probably already know."

"You can't ask Booker about it."

That didn't sound like something I would agree to. "Why not?"

"Agree or I won't tell you."

I hated being backed into a corner. "Maybe I would be better off chasing down Lilac and asking her. She wouldn't make me agree to anything."

He lowered his voice. "Agree."

"Fine. You can have your way. I won't mention it to Booker." I didn't add that I wasn't opposed to working a conversation to my benefit, to the point Booker had no choice but to mention it to me. "Tell me."

He looked around as if making sure nobody was eavesdropping and then continued. "The last cupid conference held here was about fifteen years ago. I would have to look up the exact date. Booker and I were in middle school."

"You're dragging this out to excruciating levels. What happened?"

"It was ... ugly." He took on a far-off expression. "Cupids can affect moods. They're not supposed to and most have honed their skills. There's a strict licensing board if you want to work as a cupid these days. As with anything else, there's bureaucracy."

"Okay."

"There are several powerful cupid families," he continued. "They're

kind of like dynasties. That might not be the right word but it's the only one I've got."

"And?"

"And Booker is a member of one of those dynasties. His mother is a powerful force in cupid circles. When he refused to join the profession it was a big deal. He got a lot of grief for it."

"You're still not explaining what happened at the last conference. You're stalling."

"I'm not stalling." His lips twisted as he shot me a pointed look. "I'm laying the groundwork. These family dynamics are important."

"Fine. Carry on." I was rapidly losing interest in the conversation. I pushed for him to answer, though, so I could hardly back away now. "What happened?"

"These dynasty families get special treatment in the cupid hierarchy."

"You have to be born a cupid, right?"

"You do, and they're very particular. Only full-blood cupids will do. If you're a half-breed, well, you're out of luck."

I didn't like the sound of that. "Basically you're saying they're judgmental jerkwads."

He smirked. "You have a way of breaking things down to the basest level. Have I ever told you how much I enjoy that little trait?"

"No, and you're stalling again."

His smile slipped and he made an exasperated sounded deep in his throat. "There was a battle at the conference. A small but extreme insurgent faction argued that half-breed cupids should be given the same standing as those who were full-blooded."

"I would agree with that. You can't control your parents. Trust me. If that were possible, I would've stopped my father from dating people the same age as me a long time ago."

He moved his hand to the back of my neck, to where I carried my tension. He was well aware that I had issues with my father. He'd yet to meet the man, but I could tell he was dreading it. "When I say there was a battle, I mean it got physical. Ten cupids died."

My mouth dropped open as I swung my eyes in his direction. "No way."

"It happened." He turned glum. "I obviously wasn't sheriff back then because I was still in school. I heard stories, though. Nobody was arrested because they refused to rat on each other."

"Even though the sides hated each other?"

"There are multiple sides in cupid wars. Even those who agree in principle still find reasons to fight with one another."

"They sound like a fun group."

"They're ... interesting."

"If things were so bad the last go-around, why did you agree to let them have a conference here again? Why not simply ban them and make your life easier?"

"I don't have control over that." His lips twisted into a sneer. "The DDA banned them. It also lifted the ban."

Ah, the Downtown Development Authority. Most communities had one. Apparently Moonstone Bay's was made up of omnipotent hell beasts who could make virtually anything happen with a snap of their fingers. I'd yet to meet anyone on the authority, but I was dedicated to making it happen. "Did they give you any reason why?"

"No, and I'm nervous." He wasn't ashamed to admit he was fearful. That was only one of the things I liked about him. It ranked right up there with his muscles, eyes and the way he kissed. What? I'm not totally shallow.

"Is there anything I can do to help?" The offer was heartfelt. I was new to the community but I had magic of my own. Sure, I was still getting used to the fact that I had magic — to say nothing of learning how to wield it correctly — but I was more than willing to jump into the fire if he needed help dousing the flames. "I'll do whatever I can."

He briefly lowered his forehead to mine. "That's a very nice offer. It's probably best if you steer clear of this one. You can hang around Booker, but beware the others. Don't volunteer anything about yourself."

"I thought they could control minds."

"Oh, geez. You're going to fixate on this the entire time they're here, aren't you?"

He wasn't wrong.


**WE SPENT AN HOUR WATCHING** the cupids arrive. Most of them disembarked from the ship in small groups. A few parents with toddlers pushed strollers or carried infants. There were no children, though, and I found that suspicious.

"Are they not allowed to bring kids to this thing?"

Galen, who was buying a bottle of water from one of the kiosks, arched an eyebrow. "I don't know. Why do you ask?"

"Because I've only seen children under the age of two or so. I'm guessing they don't want kids around in case they go to war again. There won't be any underage sacrifices this time. Wait ... were there any last time?"

"I don't know. It's a good observation, though." He cracked the bottle, downed a quarter of it and then handed it to me.

I wordlessly took the bottle and drank. Moonstone Bay's humidity was absolutely brutal. I watched the steady stream of passengers as I hydrated, my mood picking up when I recognized a familiar face.

It was Booker, and he wasn't alone. He pulled a huge suitcase on wheels behind him while a tiny woman — I swear she couldn't have been more than five feet tall — talked nonstop at his side. She wore a powder pink suit with heels and an extravagant hat that would've been "out there" at the Kentucky Derby.

"Well, well, well." I couldn't contain my excitement. "What do we have here?"

Galen followed my gaze, his eyes lighting with mirth when he realized who I was studying. "Oh, well, this should go over well." He cleared his throat to get Booker's attention and then took a step forward. "Hello, Mrs. Pitman. It's been a long time."

Mrs. Pitman? The name meant nothing to me, but I watched the interaction all the same.

"Ah, young Galen. I've told you repeatedly to call me Judy."

"I was never allowed to call adults by their first names when I was a kid," Galen countered. "My mother would've tanned my hide."

"Well, you're an adult now." She extended her hand in greeting. "You turned out to be a handsome boy, didn't you? I knew you would."

I pursed my lips as I shifted my eyes to Booker. He looked as if he would rather be anywhere but the middle of the dock watching his mother fawn over Galen. "Your last name is Pitman?"

He scowled. "It isn't."

"I took the name of my third husband," Judy volunteered. "Booker kept his father's name, although I have no idea why. That man never did anything for us that I can remember."

"Well, great," Booker muttered. "You've been here exactly five minutes and you're already complaining about Dad. I can tell this is going to be a terrific week."

Judy's expression turned dark. "What have I said about your attitude?"

"Which time?"

Judy rolled her eyes and focused on me. "And who are you? You have a familiar look about you but I can't quite place you."

"Oh, I'm Hadley Hunter."

Judy screwed up her face in concentration. "I'm sorry, my dear. I can't remember you. Did you and she run around in high school together, Booker?"

"We did not." Booker found something interesting to stare at on his hand, refusing to make eye contact. "We were definitely not in high school together."

"Hadley didn't grow up on the island, Judy," Galen offered hurriedly. "She's a relatively new transplant."

"I see." Judy was more standoffish now as she peered down her nose at me. "And why did you decide to move here?"

"Because a grandmother I'd never met left me the lighthouse," I answered. "It's not every day that you get left a lighthouse, so I wanted to check it out."

"The lighthouse?" Judy's lips flattened. "Then that would mean ... ."

"She's May Potter's granddaughter," Booker supplied. "Wesley is her grandfather."

"Right. That makes sense. That would mean Emma was your mother."

"Yes, ma'am."

"I knew your mother a bit." There was no warmth to Judy's words. "She was never a fan of the island. She couldn't wait to get away."

"Well ... I guess." I never knew my mother. She died during my birth. There was nothing I could say about her because I knew absolutely nothing about her life. All I knew is that her body was returned to Moonstone Bay after her death and now she got up — along with the other bodies in the cemetery — and walked around the walled-in space every night. Sometimes I sat on a blanket and watched her for hours. Other times Galen came to collect me because he said it wasn't good to spend so much time wondering how different my life would've been if she'd lived. I understood where he was coming from, but that didn't stop me from imagining a multitude of different paths.

"Hadley never met her mother," Galen volunteered, his arm going around my waist. "If you had issues with Emma, it's not her fault. Hadley didn't know her."

"Did I say I had issues with Emma?" Judy took on a petulant tone. "I was simply making an observation."

"Yes, she was simply making an observation," Booker echoed. "You're imagining that snotty thing she does that everyone else picks up on."

I had to press my lips together to keep from laughing at Judy's dark expression. She obviously wasn't happy with her son's attitude. As with everyone else, though, Booker didn't care what she thought. He was his own man.

"Is there a reason the line isn't moving forward?" another voice interjected from behind Judy and Booker.

Judy was already scowling when she turned to face the woman waiting to pass. "Darlene." Her voice practically dripped with hatred. "Is there a reason you can't go around us?"

Darlene wasn't much taller than Judy. She was much plumper,

though, and could've taken Judy down with mass alone. She had dark hair that was pulled into a pretty bun — complete with curling tendrils that escaped to land beside her face — and she wore a printed floral skirt and matching top. She looked as if a greenhouse had exploded and all that was left was her outfit.

"You're in the middle of the walkway," Darlene insisted. "If you must have a conversation you need to move to the side and keep the walkway clear. Everyone knows that's the rule."

"What rule?" Judy made a face. "I've never seen any such rule."

Galen leaned closer so his lips brushed the edge of my ear when he whispered. "This would be an example of the warring families I was talking about. Judy is in charge of one. Darlene is in charge of the other. They hate each other."

I'd already figured that out.

"We can move over here," Booker suggested, giving the oversized suitcase a tremendous heave. "It will be fine."

"We most certainly will not move." Judy held her ground and glowered at the other woman. "We're not in the wrong. All she has to do is move around us. If she's not smart enough to do that, well, it's frankly not our fault. She can sit there and stew."

"It's not a question of intelligence," Darlene argued. "It's a question of manners. Those with good breeding know not to take up the center aisle when fraternizing with ... locals. I always knew you had poor breeding."

She said "locals" like my father would've said "off-brand liquor." It was clear she believed herself above almost everybody, including — or perhaps especially — us.

"You're right," I said to Galen, keeping my voice low. "This is like a soap opera."

"And it's only going to get worse." He brushed his hand up and down my back before giving me a nudge with his hip. His intent was obvious. "Why don't we get out of your way and you can both make your way to the hotel?" he suggested.

"That's a fabulous idea," Booker drawled. "The faster I get my mother away from here, the better."

"She's not staying with you?" I couldn't hide my surprise. "That's kind of sad. How will you spend time together?"

He pinned me with a harsh look. "We'll spend as little time together as possible. That's how we like it. In fact ... ." Whatever he was about to say died on his lips when a scream from down the dock cut him off.

Next to me, Galen immediately tensed as he lifted his nose and started scenting for enemies. I was still getting used to the fact he could do that. The scream was frightening enough that it sent chills down my spine, but I still couldn't help wishing for a catastrophe so I could escape the Judy and Darlene Chronicles.

I got my wish. When I realized several sets of eyes had moved to a figure at the top of one of the dock posts my blood ran cold and I forgot the sniping I'd witnessed. The man was too far away for me to make out his features. All I knew is that he climbed to the top of the post, extended his hands as if he thought he could fly and then leaned forward as if to take flight.

He couldn't fly.

I cringed when he hit the ground. The sound echoed throughout the entire area, bouncing off the water and causing my stomach to threaten revolt.

While I worked to keep the contents of my stomach intact, Galen was already moving. "Stay here," he ordered as he and Booker ran in the direction of the man. "Don't go wandering around. I'll be back as soon as I can."

And just like that, he was gone ... and I was stuck with Booker's delightful mother and her arch nemesis. This evening had certainly taken a turn for the worse.

# THREE

*M*y heart hammered so loudly I hoped it would drown out the hard-headed women. I didn't get that lucky.

"Well, that was a nice welcome," Darlene said dryly. "I'm so glad we came back to this hellhole."

"Oh, like it's the island's fault," Judy groused. "The island didn't make him do it."

"I didn't say the island made him do it." Darlene's tone was withering. "This isn't *Lost*. There's no strange man living in the foot of a statue making people do things."

That reminded me of something. "I think *Lost* is on Netflix. Galen and I should watch it together. I haven't seen it in forever."

Slowly, as if they were both remembering I was present, Darlene and Judy tracked their gazes to me.

"Or I could go catch up with the guys and see what's going down," I said hurriedly. I had no interest in seeing a body ... especially one that had fallen from a great height. That horror, however, was more welcome than listening to the two cupids shade one another. "You guys should wait here."

"Are you with the police?" Darlene asked primly.

"No."

"Then I don't believe I have to answer to you." She gripped the handle of her suitcase, which was exactly the same size as Judy's monstrosity, and gave it a tug. "I'll go where I like."

"Fine. Knock yourself out." I was happy to get away from the women and practically ran to the body. A small crowd had already gathered around Booker and Galen, who were kneeling next to the fallen man and talking in low voices.

"How did he die?" I asked as I leaned over Galen's shoulder.

He lifted his eyes to mine and arched an eyebrow. "Really?"

That was a stupid question. Of course, I only realized it in hindsight. "I don't mean it like that. I just ... did he fall or jump?"

"You saw him for the same amount of time I did. I have no idea."

"He looked as if he was trying to fly," I offered. "Did you see the way he spread his arms? I thought maybe he was a cupid and they really could fly."

Booker made a strange noise. "You think cupids can fly?"

"Just because I haven't seen you do it doesn't mean it's not possible. Since I came to the island a lot of things I thought were impossible turned out to be normal ... at least for this place. I mean, I watched Lilac's hair go red — and not Madison Reed red either — and she magically kicked the butts of an entire cult. I definitely didn't think that was possible."

Galen worked his strong jaw back and forth. "Didn't I tell you to stay back with the other women?"

"Yes, but my sanity — and your love life — require me not to follow those orders."

It was a serious situation, but his lips quirked. "Thanks for the warning." He was grim when he turned back to the body. "I did see him hold out his arms, but I can't be sure that he wasn't trying to balance himself. It's not as if the glimpse I got of him was complete. It was fast."

"I'll say." I hunkered down for a better look. Surprisingly, his head wasn't splattered all over the docks as I'd anticipated. "Why didn't his

head crack open like a melon? My father always warned me that would happen if I ever fell off our balcony when I was out there playing."

"Your father sounds like a joy," Booker noted. "My mother used to say things like that, too. Then she would follow it up by saying, 'Now go and play in heavy traffic.' If you haven't figured it out yourself, she's the devil."

"Oh, I figured it out." That went without saying. "What's her deal? Have you tried taking her to a doctor to see if she can have that huge stick removed from her rectum?"

"Hadley." Galen's voice was low and full of warning.

I was in no mood to be chided. "What? It's not as if Booker hasn't noticed what a pain she is. He doesn't care."

The sound of someone — obviously a woman — clearing her throat behind me caused the hair on the back of my neck to stand on end. "Oh, geez. She's right behind me, isn't she?"

Booker appeared more amused than Galen when he nodded.

"Oh, well. It's not as if we were going to be best friends anyway." I flicked my eyes over my shoulder and found Judy glaring at me. "I bet you're glad I'm dating Galen instead of your son, huh?"

"I'm not glad you're dating either of them," she fired back. "You have a lot of May in you." She spoke about my grandmother as if she'd known her well. I found that interesting, especially because I was just getting to know her given the fact that she hung around after her death in ghostly form.

"Is that a bad thing? From what I can tell, May was well loved around here."

"May was definitely loved," Galen agreed. "As for whatever you two have going on over here, it'll have to wait. I need to call the medical examiner and then question witnesses. You might want to go home, Hadley. I'll be a few hours."

That was one possibility. The other was that I stay and help. It would allow me to see more of the cupids, and I wasn't keen on going home alone after witnessing a man fall to his death. "I would rather stay here. I mean ... if that's okay."

He studied me for a moment and then nodded, sympathy washing over his features. "That's fine. You can help me question the bystanders. You might be of some help there."

"I fail to see how," Judy sniffed. "I'm pretty sure she doesn't know the meaning of that word."

"Come on, Mother," Booker said wearily, exhaling as he stood. "I'll take you to your hotel and then come back."

"Why would you come back? We have a lot of catching up to do."

"Why do you think I'm coming back?" He sent me a wink as he crossed in front of me. "Oh, don't start kvetching, Mother. I was just joking. Kind of."

I watched him go with a mixture of amusement and pity. I'd never had a mother so I didn't know if such interactions were normal. Most of my girlfriends in high school yelled and screamed at their mothers something fierce. They seemed to outgrow that by the time they hit their twenties, though. Given Booker's mother's attitude, I was surprised he hadn't yet killed her and stuffed her body in a chest to sink at sea.

"What are you thinking?" Galen asked when he realized I was lost in thought.

"I was just thinking about mothers."

"Because of Judy? I wouldn't spend too much time basing assumptions on her. She's not a normal mother. Heck, she's not a normal anything."

"What's your mother like?"

"Here we go." He rolled his eyes to the sky, as if pleading with a deity to smite him so he could change the subject. "I told you that I will arrange a meeting between you and my mother as soon as it's possible. Why can't that be enough?"

"It's fine." I wasn't in the mood to argue. There was a dead guy between us, after all. "Let's start interviewing people." I took a moment to study the man's profile. There was blood under his nose, which suggested to me he'd broken it during the fall. "Do you know him?"

"Actually, I do. His name is David Fox. He went to school with me and Booker."

I was taken aback. "Was he a friend?"

"I wouldn't say that."

"Was he an enemy?"

"He was ... not the sort of kid I wanted to hang around with. He grew into the sort of man who was easy to ignore."

That was a roundabout way of answering the question. "Meaning?"

"Meaning he was from a very wealthy family." Galen kept his voice low as he dug in his pocket for his phone. "His mother is one of the wealthiest women on the island."

"So ... he wasn't on the ship?"

"I don't believe so. I guess it's possible he was off island and returned on the ship. I doubt it, though. His family would more likely charter a private helicopter to get him home."

"Tell me how you really feel." I poked his side. "You had to have another reason to dislike him besides the fact that he was wealthy. You don't seem the sort to make fun of someone for being poor. Making fun of them for being rich is just as bad."

"You never met him. He refused to wear the lacrosse jerseys provided by the school because they weren't made of organic fabrics."

"Okay, he was a total douche. Why would he jump?"

"We don't know that he did jump."

"We don't know that he fell either," I pointed out.

"We don't know anything," he stressed. "I'm placing a call to the medical examiner. Once that's finished, we need to cordon off the area. After that we can start questioning the people who were around at the time he took his swan dive."

"I'm looking forward to that."

"The oddest things entertain you."

"Which is why I'm dating you."

He blew me a kiss and then dialed. "This is not how I saw my night going."

.  .  .

24

**CASS DOHERTY WAS THE** first person we interviewed. I knew his face, but I couldn't remember ever talking to him. He was often in Lilac's bar on the main drag and I recalled a raucous round of karaoke coming out of him on occasion. That was pretty much the only thing I knew about him.

"You were working at the time he fell, right?" Galen had a small notebook out and was jotting down information. "Did you see him before he climbed the post?"

"What is that post, by the way?" I was suddenly curious as I glanced toward the top of the item in question. "Is it a telephone pole?"

"It used to be," Galen replied. "Now it's just kind of … there. We buried all our lines several years ago because of trouble we had during hurricane season in 2015. The power doesn't always stay on during storms now, but it's much better."

"Oh, well, that's a relief."

"Back to David," Galen prodded. "Did you see him before he was on the pole?"

"I did, but it was only for a second," Cass replied, rubbing his chin. "I remember because I was surprised to see him out here. The Fox family has their own private yacht club on the north side of the island. They're never down here."

"They're not," Galen agreed. "Do you think he was on the ship?"

"I don't think so." Cass appeared to be puzzling it out. "I'm pretty sure he came from that direction." He pointed toward the opposite side of the dock. "He was over by the bait store."

"Why would he be at the bait store?" Galen queried. "I've never known him to fish."

"He certainly wasn't dressed for fishing," I added. "He was wearing an expensive suit."

"I don't know why he was there," Cass answered. "I didn't see him buy anything. I only noticed him a few minutes before people started screaming and pointing. I saw him wandering around. I noted it because it was weird. That was it."

"Okay. Thanks for your time." Galen inclined his chin toward the bait shop. "That's our next stop."

I wrinkled my nose as we closed the distance. I was well aware of what the shop sold. That was the precise reason I didn't want to get up close and personal with the owner. Galen either didn't notice the odor or didn't care, because he swaggered straight up to the counter and fixed the older man, who looked to be wearing some sort of rubber overalls, with a tight smile.

"Hey, Harry."

"Hey, Galen." Harry had spark plugs for eyebrows and a craggy smile. "What are you doing out here today? I didn't think you enjoyed night fishing."

"That's not on the agenda for today."

I was confused. "You fish?"

He slid me a look. "I'm an islander. We all fish. You have to turn in your Moonstone Bay Man Card if you don't participate in the island pastime."

I couldn't tell if he was kidding. "Have you been fishing since we got together?"

"A time or two. You don't usually notice that I'm out here because I take my lunch hour to get a few casts in."

"I guess you learn something new every day," I muttered.

He flicked the end of my nose. "Why? Do you want to go fishing with me one day?"

That sounded like pure torture. "I'm good. I don't want to intrude on your man time."

He snickered. "I'm shocked that fishing isn't on your to-do list." He turned back to Harry. "I'm sure you heard about David Fox."

"I heard people whispering," Harry confirmed. "I didn't really believe it was him until just now. I can't believe he jumped like that."

"Are you sure he jumped?"

"I saw him. I didn't know it was him at the time, but I saw him when he got up there. I could hear him, too."

"He was speaking?" Galen cocked an eyebrow. "Did you hear what he was saying?"

"He said he was going into the light."

"Were those his exact words?"

"Yeah. He said 'I'm coming to you, to the light. I'm almost there.' Then he waved his arms like a lunatic and fell headfirst into the dock. That's going to be a mess to clean up, I bet."

"His head didn't crack open like a melon," I offered helpfully. "It shouldn't be too bad."

Galen shot me a quelling look and shook his head as Harry snickered.

"I like her," Harry announced. "She reminds me of May."

"That seems to be the general consensus today," I agreed blandly. "I'm not sure if I should take that as a good or bad sign."

"Good," Galen and Harry answered in unison.

Galen tapped his pen tip on the notebook to regain Harry's attention. "Did you ever see David hanging around here any other time? I mean ... did he spend time out here?"

"Not that I recall. That's why I was surprised when I heard it was him. I thought for sure the gossip had to be a mistake."

Galen thanked Harry for the information and then led me to the edge of the dock where we stared at the setting sun. "It's looking more and more like a suicide."

I studied his profile. "You don't seem convinced."

"Maybe it's because I can't figure out what that guy had to be depressed about. He had loads of money, every toy he could dream of, and never had to work."

"Things don't make a person happy."

"The right things do." He swooped in and gave me a quick kiss before pulling away. "I'm going to talk to a few other people, but I'm pretty sure this is going to turn out to be a suicide. It's not as if anyone else was around to force him to do it. His mother will fight that determination, but I can't worry about that."

I chewed my bottom lip. "You're worried about telling her, aren't you? Do you think she'll break down?"

"I don't know how she'll react. I've only met the woman a few times. None of those meetings were exactly warm and cozy."

"Do you want me to go with you?"

"Not for this one." He rubbed his hand over my back before prodding me forward. "Come on. I'll take you home and then head out to talk to David's mother. I should be back before you even get into those comfortable sleep shorts I love so much. You know, the ones with the cute little ruffles?"

I rolled my eyes. "Those aren't girlie ruffles. They're ... womanly ruffles."

"I'm glad you clarified that for me."

"I just wanted you to be aware that I don't wear girlie ruffles."

"Good enough." He brushed his lips over my forehead and slowed his pace so he could talk to the medical examiner, who was toiling over David's body. "I'm taking Hadley home and then heading out to talk to his mother. I don't want her to hear it from someone else."

"I pity you having to go out there, but I'm glad I'm not the one making the call."

Galen's lips turned down as he started to move me away from the body. Something caught my attention before he could steer me away. "What is it?"

"Do you smell that?" I lifted my nose, causing him to chuckle.

"You hate when I do that."

"You briefly look like a scary wolf when you do it. I look cute when I do it."

"I guess I can't argue with that." He grinned as I sniffed again. "What's the deal?"

"Seriously, can't you smell that?" My stomach revolted at the scent. It made me feel lightheaded and weak in the knees.

He mimicked my earlier motions and shook his head. "I don't smell anything. Am I supposed to smell something?"

"I don't know. I ... it's weird. Are you certain you don't smell anything?"

"I honestly don't and I have a pretty engaged sniffer." He tapped his nose for emphasis. "What do you smell?"

"It's like ... rancid honey." I didn't know how else to describe the overpowering scent. "I can't believe you can't smell that."

"I think you've had a long day and we should get you out of here." He locked me against his side and dragged me toward the parking lot. "Let's get you home. I'm sure the lighthouse will smell the same as always."

I certainly hoped so. Romance would be out of the cards if this kept up. Vomit is never sexy.

# FOUR

*G*alen made sure to give me a lingering kiss before dropping me in front of the lighthouse. He promised he wouldn't be long, that the drive would take longer than the notification, and I waved him off while managing to hide my anxiety.

I was agitated. I couldn't quite put my finger on why or when it had started. I glanced over my shoulder as I completed the walk to the front door — Galen didn't leave until I was inside — and studied the group of bushes to the east side of the property. Did I sense something there? Not really. That didn't stop me from feeling as if someone was watching me.

The feeling didn't last long once I was inside. There, I found my grandfather Wesley playing Monopoly with my dead grandmother. They seemed to be getting along this evening, which was a welcome sight. When they were first reunited after my grandmother's death they'd spent weeks arguing. Since I put my foot down about privacy and respecting the feelings of others they'd saved the fights for Wesley's property and the pleasant conversations for mine.

"You look tired," May noted as I threw myself in the chair across the way. "Did you and Galen have a fight?"

"Why did you jump to that conclusion?" I was legitimately curious. "Can't I be tired for other reasons?"

May and Wesley exchanged looks that weren't lost on me and I groaned as I pinched the bridge of my nose.

"Ugh. This day seems endless," I complained.

"Let's go back to the beginning," Wesley suggested, the game forgotten. He was trying to be a more hands-on grandfather. That wasn't easy for either of us because I was a grown woman who had only recently met him, but we were both doing our best. "Did you have a fight with Galen?"

"No."

"Then why isn't he here? You two have been attached at the ... hip ... for weeks. You haven't spent a night apart in as long as I can remember. Why has that suddenly changed?"

"We're not spending the night apart. Something happened after dinner." I filled my grandparents in on what happened at the dock. When I was finished, they were more puzzled than excited. "He had to drive out to some mega-mansion to inform David's mother about his untimely passing."

"That's too bad." May made a clucking sound and shook her head. "I didn't know David well. He always struck me as ... well, to be truthful, he always struck me as something of a ponce. He thought a lot of himself and expected others to bow down. That doesn't mean I wanted him to die."

"What about his mother? Galen seemed worried about seeing her. He didn't come right out and say that, of course, but I could tell by the look on his face."

"Cora is ... not the easiest woman to get along with," May hedged. "She has a certain reputation on the island."

"You know you're allowed to gossip as much as you want now that you're a ghost, right? No one will stop you and the worst has already happened, so there's nothing to worry about."

She shot me a quelling look. "I'm not averse to a little gossip. It's just ... Cora is going through something terrible. I don't want to kick her while she's down."

"She won't even know you're kicking her. I'm just looking for some information."

"I can see that." May mimed touching her finger to her forehead, a gesture I was sure she carried over from life, and shifted from one ethereal foot to the other. She had several nervous mannerisms. I recognized a few from my repertoire, which I found amusing, because we didn't meet until long after she was dead. "I've known Cora for a number of years. She's a good twenty years younger than me, but she always has been imperious."

"Her family managed to buy a huge piece of Moonstone Bay in the 1940s," Wesley volunteered. "They slipped in at the exact right time. I think they bought something like a hundred acres for around fifty-thousand dollars."

"And that's cheap?" I wasn't familiar with real estate prices. I'd never owned as much as a townhouse. I always rented.

"That's unbelievably inexpensive," May confirmed. "One acre on the water now would go for a good two-million dollars."

"Even without a house?"

"Yes. I believe Galen explained not long after you inherited the lighthouse how real estate is at a premium on the island. Everyone wants to own something, but there's not enough property to be had."

He had gone into great detail about that not long after I moved to Moonstone Bay. It played into my grandmother's murder, because the man who poisoned her wanted to inherit the land she owned. Now, instead, I was the proud landowner of a vintage lighthouse, which meant I was in the middle of Moonstone Bay's wacky politics. "You both owned property. Does that mean you're as revered as this Cora Fox?"

"Well, we do fine financially," Wesley countered after a moment. "I do quite well and I'm happy where I am. My property isn't adjacent to the water, though. There's not as much of a premium on it."

"The lighthouse is different," I mused.

"It is," May confirmed. "This property could make you a million-aire several times over if you wanted to sell it."

My eyebrows migrated up my forehead. "Seriously?"

"Yes." May looked worried. "I hope you won't do that."

"I have no intention of selling the lighthouse." I meant it. "I consider it my home now. It's just ... interesting. This property the Fox family owns makes them like island royalty. I wondered why Galen was so fidgety when he realized who was dead."

"Galen probably understands that Cora is the type who will lash out and blame him," May explained. "If she's hurting, she's willing to hurt everyone around her until they're as miserable as she is."

"Still, she's in mourning," I argued. "She's allowed to be upset. It's her son, after all."

"He is most definitely her son," May agreed. "Cora has numerous faults, but I've always believed that she loves her children."

"How many does she have?"

"Just two, I believe. David and a girl. The girl left not long after high school. I didn't blame her, although at the time there was a lot of chatter. David was the favored child and got all the attention. She was an afterthought and her parents treated her as such."

"Galen didn't mention anything about a father," I pointed out. "Where is he?"

"Ashton Fox is technically still married to Cora, but in name only," Wesley supplied. "He lives on the mainland. I think in some ritzy community in southern Florida. Cora lives here. They rarely see each other. Ashton is notoriously open about running around with young women on the mainland and Cora pretends she doesn't hear the whispers. It seems to work for them."

I had my doubts that could work for anybody, but who was I to judge? "Well, it's just incredibly sad." I pushed myself to a standing position. "I'm heading up to take a bath. Galen will probably be another hour or so. You can finish up your game."

"That's okay." Wesley shuffled forward and gave me a kiss on the cheek. He was a sweet man with a gruff exterior. He'd gone out of his way for me several times since I'd arrived, and we were forging a legitimate bond. "We can take the game out to my place. I just wanted to see how you were doing."

"Things were good until David decided he could fly," I offered. "I

got to see the cupids arriving for their conference. That was entertaining, especially when Booker showed up with his mother."

May lifted her head, her eyes going wide. "Judy is back on the island?"

Oh, well, that was interesting. May didn't look any happier with the turn of events than Booker did. "She is. Galen said this is the first conference they've had here in, like, fifteen years or something. He's on edge."

"I don't blame him." Wesley snapped a photo of the game board with his phone before packing up the money and houses. "The last cupid conference here turned into a bloody massacre."

"He might have mentioned that."

"Cupids can't behave themselves." He made a face. "They're jerks most of the time. They play with people's emotions for sport."

"Most of them don't do that," May corrected. "Only a few of the bad apples play games that way, and the cupids are diligent about weeding them out."

"They're also diligent about covering up for them," Wesley argued.

"Well, that's kind of true." May looked uncomfortable as she shifted her attention to me. "Cupids are an acquired taste, my dear. Not all of them are trustworthy. Be careful around them."

"What about Booker?" The question was out of my mouth before I thought better of it. It didn't matter what they said. I trusted Booker implicitly. I didn't expect that to change.

"Booker is not cut from the same cloth as the rest of them," Wesley replied. "He pulled away from that little cult of personality a long time ago. He doesn't want anything to do with their shenanigans."

That was good news.

"Booker is a good boy," May interjected. "Sure, he's a bit of a Romeo and enjoys romancing as many women as possible, but in his heart he's a good boy. You don't have to worry about him. He's loyal to a fault."

"I wasn't really worried about him," I admitted. "His mother is another story. She has so much attitude I'm surprised it isn't spurting out of her ears."

"Judy is ... a horrible woman," May said after a moment's contemplation. "She was always strict with Booker, demanded certain things of him. That came back to bite her when he was old enough to make his own decisions and opted to shun the cupid coalition. She was mortified, but refused to give up her leadership position. Booker's insistence on being his own man weakened her position. Everyone knows that."

"I sensed a bit of tension between them," I said.

"Judy loves her son. I have no doubt about that. She would love him more if she could control him."

"Well, I'm glad he's not the type who blindly follows orders. I kind of like him the way he is."

"We all do."


**IT WAS ALMOST MIDNIGHT BEFORE** Galen let himself into my bedroom. I'd fallen asleep waiting for him, my e-reader open on my chest. I felt him slide into the bed next to me, his warm skin touching mine, before I actually registered his presence.

"Hey." I was sleepy and it took everything I had to stay coherent. "Are you okay?"

"I'm fine." He kissed the ridge of my ear as he spooned behind me. "I'm sorry it took so long. Cora completely fell apart. I saw it coming, but ... she was difficult to deal with."

"Did you tell her you think it was a suicide?"

"I did and she called me the dumbest man alive. She said David would never commit suicide and I should be stripped of my badge and title – and forced to work as a janitor at a bathroom for men who can't aim – because I dared suggest such a thing."

I thought about what May and Wesley told me. "She can't make trouble for you, can she?"

"She's a rich woman. She can make a lot of trouble if she sets her mind to it."

"Are you afraid?"

"Right now I'm tired." He kissed my cheek. "Go to sleep. We can talk more in the morning."

"Okay, but I thought you were going to wow me tonight. This is a disappointment."

He poked my side. "Neither one of us is up for wowing. I'll carry out my duties in the morning."

"That's cheating, but ... whatever."

"Yeah, yeah, yeah." He let out a heavy breath. "I kind of felt sorry for her," he added after a beat. "She believes money can buy anything. It can't buy her son's life back. That realization will eventually crush her."

"You've done everything you can do."

"I guess."


**I SLEPT HARD. MY DREAMS,** often tumultuous, were weirder than normal. I was trapped in a dark house, no lights other than the ambient moonlight – which seemed brighter than normal – filtering through the windows.

I didn't recognize the house. It was big, cavernous really, but all the windows were open and a terrific cross breeze blew strong enough that my hair whipped back and forth as I tried to find my way through the corridors.

I called out occasionally for those I knew. I wanted to find Galen most, and yet, instinctively, I recognized he wasn't in the house. I had no idea where he was, but he wasn't close. That realization left me unsettled.

I kept searching for a long time, to the point of exhaustion. Eventually the dreamscape faded and I was plunged into darkness.

When I woke the next morning, I was flat on my back and Galen's head was propped on his hand as he watched me sleep. His expression was unreadable and it threw me.

"Did I drool or something?" I wiped at the corners of my mouth as he chuckled.

"You didn't drool." He leaned forward and kissed my forehead. "You did, however, sleepwalk."

Whatever I expected him to say — most mornings he's flirty and handsy — that wasn't it. I furrowed my brow and vigorously rubbed the sleep from my eyes as I regarded him. "Get out. I don't sleepwalk."

"Last night you did."

"But ... no way!" I had no idea what I was supposed to say. "Why would I suddenly start sleepwalking out of nowhere?"

"I don't know." His fingers were gentle as they brushed my morning-mussed hair from my face. "Yesterday was stressful. I don't know much about sleepwalking, but I'm betting stress triggers incidents."

"Are you sure you didn't just dream that I was sleepwalking?"

"Why would I dream that?"

"I don't know. Why did I dream about having a pet hippopotamus in the lighthouse several nights ago? Dream logic makes no sense."

"You were sleepwalking." He was firm. "I didn't know what to do. I once read that you shouldn't wake sleepwalkers because they could accidentally hurt you or themselves due to surprise. I followed you around for a bit and didn't say anything. It was weird."

It sounded weird. "Did I do anything interesting? I mean ... I didn't get naked or anything, did I?" I lifted the covers to check and was relieved to find I was still in my pajamas from the night before.

Galen let loose a low chuckle. "No. Were you dreaming about getting naked?"

"No." I thought back to the dream. "I was dreaming about being lost in a really big house. I remember that. I kept calling for you ... and Lilac ... and Wesley ... and even Booker. No one came, though."

His eyes were sober as he smoothed my hair. "I'm sorry I didn't come to you."

"It's my subconscious. I very much doubt there was anything you could do about it."

"True enough. I'm still sorry."

"Well ... ." I broke off and chewed my bottom lip. "You don't think it's dangerous, do you? The sleepwalking, I mean."

"I don't know. If you're upset I could take you to the hospital. They might be able to run a few tests."

That sounded like the worst possible way to spend a day. "I think I'll pass."

"I thought you might say that." He rubbed his nose against mine before rubbing my lips with his. "You didn't do anything but walk to the window. You looked out at the water for a long time."

"My eyes were open?"

"Yes."

"That's creepy."

"I still think you're adorable." He gave me another kiss and rolled on top of me. I had no doubt how he wanted to start the day, and I was fine with it. I wanted to shake the dregs of the weird dream. "I tried talking to you after a few minutes. I asked you to go to bed and you just sort of turned around and did it. I was relieved."

"I guess maybe watching David Fox plummet to his death affected me more than I realized," I mused, my hands moving to Galen's strong back as he rubbed his stubbled chin against my cheek. "Are you feeling romantic?"

"I don't know. You tell me."

I laughed, delighted, when he kissed my neck. "If you do a good job, I'll make you breakfast. How does that sound?"

"Like a challenge. You know how much I love a challenge."

I did indeed.

# FIVE

$\mathcal{I}$ went all out for breakfast, whipping up blueberry pancakes and bacon. Galen was smug when I slid his plate in front of him.

"I take it I met your lofty standards."

"Ha, ha." I flicked his ear before sitting across from him at the large kitchen table. He'd already poured me a mug of coffee, so I dove right in and started with the caffeine. "Is it wrong that I'm still worried about the sleepwalking?"

He shifted his eyes from the newspaper he was flipping through — Moonstone Bay had its own publication, although there wasn't much hard news to cover — and focused on me. "I'm not joking. If you're worried about it, I can take you to the hospital to have you checked out."

"I don't want to go to the hospital if it's nothing." I felt slow and stupid. "I've never done it before. It seems weird to happen out of the blue like this."

"Well, I'm not a doctor, but I would guess seeing David die the way he did was traumatizing. I've seen things like this before and I was traumatized by it."

"I guess." I doused my pancakes with syrup. "I'm just confused because I've never done it before."

"How do you know? You didn't remember doing it last night. You only know because I told you. There's a chance you've done it before and simply didn't realize it."

I hadn't considered that. "Oh, well ... huh. Maybe I should call my father and ask."

Galen struggled to keep his face neutral ... and failed. He wasn't my father's biggest fan. Even though they'd never met, Galen was convinced my father kept me from May and Wesley as a child — which was true — and he was slightly bitter about it. "Are you sure he would know? I didn't get the feeling from the stories you told that he was a hands-on father."

"He wasn't a bad father." I meant it. "He came to most of my school events and made sure I never wanted for anything when it came to clothes and shoes."

"That doesn't make him a good father."

I sighed. "He was limited in some respects. He did his best. My mother dying the way she did crippled him. He's never dug out from beneath the mountain of grief he lives under. In some ways I feel sorry for him."

Galen grumbled something under his breath that I couldn't quite make out. If I had to guess, it was something akin to "I don't feel sorry for him," but it ultimately didn't matter.

"Let's not talk about my father," I suggested, sipping my coffee. "What are you going to do today?"

"I have to check in with the medical examiner. I want an update on David."

"You still think it was a suicide?"

"I do. I have to be sure, though. That's why they pay me the big bucks."

"What about after?"

"After I will probably be hotel hopping to make sure none of these cupids are getting out of hand. I would rather head off any potential fights."

"That makes sense."

He reached over and squeezed my hand. "What about you? What are you going to do with your day?"

"Well, I was thinking that I would head over to Lilac's bar and start some brainstorming about what sort of job I want. I can't be a woman of leisure forever."

"I don't know. I think you're good at it."

"No matter how good at it I am, I absolutely want to work. I just don't know what I want to do. Do you have any suggestions?"

His eyes lit with wicked intent.

"Not that, you pig." I threw a piece of bacon at him, which he deftly caught and slid into his mouth. "I want to do something I can be proud of."

He hesitated as he swallowed. "Everything you do is something to be proud of," he said finally. "A job isn't status. Who you are is what's important. I happen to like who you are a great deal."

The words were simple, but they sent a jolt of warmth straight to my heart. "Thanks."

"You're welcome." He turned back to his breakfast. "As for the sleepwalking, give it a day or two. If it doesn't return I would assume it was a fluke. It's not every day you see a guy plummet to his death. That had to be disconcerting."

"Yeah. You have a point."


LILAC'S BAR WAS PACKED. It was barely mid-morning, so I couldn't wrap my head around why the place was so full. Then I realized that most of the people sitting at the tables and telling raucous stories were cupids. I recognized them from the boat the previous day.

"I take it cupids like to day drink," I noted as I slid onto one of the stools at the bar. Lilac was on the other side vigorously shaking a martini mixer. "This is probably good for you, huh?"

"It's good for the bar," she replied. "But they're terrible tippers. It's not good for me personally." She said the words loudly and I couldn't help glancing over my shoulder to see if some of the assembled cupids had heard. Two of them tipped their drinks in her direction.

"You obviously don't care about being nice to them," I offered. "They don't seem offended by what you said."

"They don't care." She upended the shaker into a glass, a purple concoction I'd never seen before swirling out.

"What is that?" I leaned closer, intrigued.

"That is a plum martini. Shaken, not stirred."

I smirked. "Is it good?"

"They're okay. I think Judy just likes having purple drinks." Lilac plopped the glass on the bar and whistled, catching me off guard.

Booker, who I didn't realize was in the bar, appeared at my elbow and snagged the drink. He made a face when he saw the color. "She's just messing with me to mess with me now."

I pressed my lips together to keep from laughing at his horrified expression and watched as he delivered the drink to his mother, who was determined to be the center of attention and didn't as much as acknowledge him. When he returned, he hopped onto the open stool next to me and buried his hands in his forearms.

"I hate my life," he whined.

Pity stirred as I patted his wrist. "Once, when I was in high school, my father made me wear leggings underneath a skirt because he thought it was too short and I would entice the boys to grope me if I didn't cover up. He actually had the leggings delivered to school and I was pulled out of class to put them on."

Booker lifted his head and narrowed his eyes. "What does that have to do with anything?"

"I'm just saying that you don't have the market cornered on embarrassing parents. There's no need to get worked up."

"Oh, geez." He covered his eyes again. "I just want this week to be over."

I was amused despite my pity for him. "I don't know. Your mother has a lot of spirit. What's not to like about that?"

"You've met her." Booker rested his chin on his palm and his elbow on the bar. "You didn't spend two minutes with her before you ran to join us next to a dead body. Don't pretend she's normal."

I could never pretend that. "I'm not saying she's normal." I risked a glance at the woman in question and frowned when I realized several of the younger women sitting at the table — in fact, all of the women below the age of forty — were staring at Booker with wistful expressions. "She's memorable. You have that going for you."

"I'm pretty sure that's not a good thing." Booker wasn't the whining type, so his tone amused me. "I just want her to go home."

"Where does she live?"

"Tampa. She likes warm weather but doesn't want drug dealers living on her street. *Miami Vice* taught her there are drug dealers on every corner in that city so now she lives in Tampa."

"Is that bad?"

"No. I wish she would move to Canada or something, though. I think that's a much more comfortable distance."

"Oh, poor Booker." I laughed at his hangdog expression. "There's no reason to get worked up. She'll be here only a week, right? After that she'll be gone again and the island will be yours."

One of the women at the table, a lithe blonde with legs that went on for miles and sparkling blue eyes, edged her way to the bar. Booker and I were the only ones sitting at it, so she had plenty of room. She managed to arrange herself so that she was practically in Booker's lap when she snapped her fingers to get Lilac's attention.

"I would like a gin and Dubonnet," she announced.

"We don't have Dubonnet," Lilac replied. "I have tonic water and can throw in a splash of grenadine if you like."

The woman made a face. "That's not the same thing."

"Definitely not. They both taste like crap, though, so they're kind of similar."

The woman's eyes darkened. "Gin and Dubonnet is what the queen drinks."

"Well, the queen's not here."

The woman made an exasperated sound deep in her throat. "I'll have violet gin and tonic."

43

"We don't have violet gin either."

"Oh, geez!" The woman was clearly feeling dramatic. "Do you have anything good?"

"No." Lilac's temper flashed hot and fierce, and I noticed a ripple of color run through her hair — red, like the red I saw the day the cult attacked — but she covered quickly. "If you don't like the drink selections, you could always go to one of the other thirty bars on the strip."

"Oh, trust me. I would rather be somewhere else."

"Dani, don't be a pain," Booker's mother ordered, breaking off in mid-conversation and focusing on our small group at the bar. "I told you that your fancy drinks wouldn't be available. You said it would be fine. Order a martini and be done with it."

"Yes, Mrs. Pitman." Dani turned sour. "I'll have a plum martini, too."

"Great." Lilac offered up a sardonic eye roll and grabbed the martini shaker. "You can have a seat. I'll have Booker deliver it when it's ready."

Dani perked up and nodded as Booker glared at the smirking bartender.

"Why did you tell her that?" he asked once she returned to the table.

"Because she only ordered a drink to be close to you," Lilac replied. "She's got the fever. We both know it."

I was officially intrigued. "What's the fever?"

"It's that thing women come down with when they can't stop from throwing themselves at him."

"Oh." I was familiar with the fever. I hadn't seen it in action until a few weeks ago. Er, maybe I had and I simply didn't realize it. Either way, as a cupid, Booker exuded some sort of musk that made him utterly delicious to women. I was apparently immune. I was thankful for that. "Aren't they all cupids? Shouldn't they be immune to you, too?"

"It's a different kind of fever," Booker said dryly, pinning Lilac with a dark glare. "Don't encourage them. You know how much I hate it when stuff like this happens."

I was still struggling to catch up. "I don't understand what you guys are even talking about. Are the cupids attracted to you as much as human women?"

"Everyone is attracted to me." He offered up a wink but it wasn't nearly as playful as it would've been on a different day. "The attraction comes in a variety of degrees."

"Right." I nodded in thanks when Lilac slid an iced tea in front of me. "So, I'm actually here for a reason."

"I heard about David Fox," Lilac supplied. "I didn't know him well so I don't have a heckuva lot of information. This wasn't his sort of establishment. He spent all his time in the private bar at the yacht club."

"That wasn't what I was talking about. Galen thinks he killed himself. He's waiting for a report from the medical examiner, but right now it looks as if he climbed that big pole and tried to fly."

"Really?" Lilac wrinkled her forehead. "I wouldn't think he would have a reason to off himself. I mean ... he was rich. He obviously didn't have to worry about money. Why would he want to end things rather than soldier forward?"

"Money isn't everything," I reminded her. "Although, that's actually the reason I'm here. I didn't come about David at all. As for him, depression is a real psychological malady. It's possible he was clinically depressed."

"I guess. I still don't see what he had to be depressed about." Lilac grabbed a towel and started drying glasses. "You said you're here about money? I'm not sure I have much to loan you. I have a few hundred bucks if that will help."

My cheeks flooded with color, embarrassment washing over me. "Oh, no. I wasn't talking about that. I was talking about a job."

"You want to work here?"

I considered the question for a full half-second before shaking my head. "Our friendship wouldn't survive that."

"Probably not," she agreed, laughing. "I still don't understand what you're getting at."

"I need a job." I was matter-of-fact. "I need somewhere to go when

Galen takes off in the morning. It was fine to take a bit of time off to settle and get accustomed to my new surroundings. It's time to move forward."

"And you need a job to do that?" Booker lifted his head, scowling when one of the women at the bigger table next to us waved and giggled. "I hate that. Why do they have to keep doing that?"

"I thought you liked it when women threw themselves at you," I said.

"Not these women. I wouldn't date another cupid if I was marooned on an island and the only choice was her or my hand."

I scowled. "That was a bit of an overshare."

"Well, it's how I feel." He forced his attention back to me. "What are you qualified to do?"

That was a good question. "I don't know. I could work in a law office or something. That sounds boring, but I understand court information thanks to my father."

"I think you'll melt down being trapped in an office all day," Booker countered. "Have you considered opening the lighthouse and allowing people in for palm or tarot readings?"

The suggestion was ludicrous. "I don't know how to do either of those things."

"May does. She volunteered her time doing both at festivals throughout the years. Ask her to teach you."

"I can't do that. It's not a real job."

He snickered. "If you make money at it, it's a real job. Besides, you could work a few hours a day doing readings and make bank. Then you can read on the beach the rest of the time. That's the best sort of job."

"He's not wrong," Lilac agreed. "In fact, if you don't want to open the lighthouse to people — which I totally understand, because that makes for a lack of privacy — we could set up a table in here for you. I bet it would draw in more drinkers and benefit both of us."

The suggestion seemed out of the realm of possibility and yet a small voice in the back of my head was already gushing that it was a good idea. "Do you really think May could teach me how to do it?"

Lilac shrugged. "It's worth a try. This is a paranormal island. You don't have to hide who you are. It makes sense to play to your strengths. Magic seems to be your biggest strength these days."

"Yeah, but ... ." I trailed off, uncertain. "I have to give it some thought," I said after a beat. "I'm not sure I'm comfortable opening myself up like that."

"Definitely give it some thought," Lilac agreed. "If you don't want to do that, you could always join Booker's team and be a jack-of-all-trades."

Booker stuck out his tongue. "I'll have you know not just anyone can do the things I do. It takes training and talent."

Lilac rolled her eyes. "Whatever. Oh, hey, another chick is coming this way for a drink. Twenty bucks says she rubs her boobs against you."

Booker buried his face again. "Will this torture never end?"

I laughed along with Lilac, but my mind was already elsewhere. The idea of giving readings had never crossed my mind. Now I couldn't seem to shake it. Was that actually an option for me? I was intrigued, but unsure.

I needed to talk to May ... and Wesley ... and Galen. I also needed to search my heart. I said I wanted a career, not a job. Could this be my career?

## SIX

*I* still had the idea jumping around in my head when I exited the bar. I was almost outside before a hand shot out in the vestibule and grabbed my wrist, causing me to bite back a shriek and fix the tiny woman standing next to the cigarette machine (I didn't even know they still made those until I came to Moonstone Bay) with a dark look.

"Mrs. Pitman, you really should announce yourself before grabbing someone." I managed to contain my anger, but just barely. I had to remind myself that she was Booker's mother and it would do more harm than good if I jumped all over her.

"I didn't mean to startle you, dear." She talked like a kindly woman in her fifties, one caught between parenthood and living the life of a grandparent, but there was something I didn't like in her eyes.

"Well, you did." I forced a smile, although it was flat and hard. "Can I help you with something?"

"I just have a question for you."

"Then I'll try to answer it."

"Fabulous." Her lips spread into the approximation of a smile, but it was much more akin to a sneer. "What's the deal with you and my son?"

The question caught me off guard. "I'm sorry? There is no deal between us. We're friends."

"Just friends?"

This I could deal with. These weren't the questions of an evil mother. A normal mother would dig into the business of her child. Television and Hallmark movies had taught me that. "I'm dating Galen."

"That doesn't mean you're not keeping my boy on a string, too."

"Actually, it does." I didn't like what she was insinuating. "I happen to care about Galen a great deal. I care about Booker, too. He's just a friend, though. He's never been anything other than a friend."

"He seems fond of you."

"Really? I think he tolerates me."

"No, he laughs at the things you say and acts interested when you talk. That's not normal for him."

"Well, no offense, but how do you know what's normal for him? I was under the impression that you didn't see him very often."

Her eyes narrowed to slits. "Who told you that? Did Booker tell you that? I may live on the mainland, but that doesn't mean I don't take an interest in my son."

I held my hands up. "I just meant that he doesn't talk about you much." I realized after the fact that was the wrong thing to say. "I mean ... most guys don't sit around talking about their mothers. That's a downer of a conversation. He doesn't not talk about you any more than anybody else would not talk about their mother."

"Uh-huh." She lifted her chin and I got the distinct impression she was trying to look down at me even though I was a good six inches taller than her. "Just be careful around my son. The last thing he needs is a broken heart. I hope that you understand."

Boy did I ever. The woman had made herself more than clear. "I promise not to break Booker's heart."

"You should probably stay away from him," she added. "I have big plans for him this trip. You'll mess with those plans."

I thought back to the women at the bar who couldn't stop

watching Booker with moony expressions. "I bet I know exactly what plans you have for him."

"Good. Then we don't have a problem." She turned to leave. I should've let it go, but I never met a problem I didn't want to make worse by opening my big, fat mouth.

"He doesn't want the life you seem to want for him," I volunteered. "Why can't you just let him be who he wants to be?"

"That's not what a parent does. Now ... move along." She made shooing motions with her hands. "Now that you're gone, Booker will have no choice but to join us."

"He'll still have a choice."

"Not if I have anything to say about it."

I was feeling down — and a little hacked off — when I left the bar. Judy Pitman may be small, but she was a mountain of energy to contain. I didn't know what to make of it. I was simply glad to be free of her.

A second dose of annoyance waited for me at the curb. Darlene stood staring at my purple golf cart — a gift from Wesley — and making a series of faces that would've been welcome in a mime act.

"Oh, geez," I muttered under my breath, pinching the bridge of my nose. This day kept getting worse. "Can I help you with something?" I asked when the woman didn't immediately turn in my direction even though my shadow crossed hers.

"I certainly hope so." She turned a blinding smile in my direction, one that could've skinned a squirming cat, and held out her hand. "I'm Darlene Metcalf. I don't believe we've had the pleasure of meeting."

I took her hand, but only because it was expected. "I'm Hadley Hunter, and we did meet last evening."

"I don't recall that."

"No? I was standing on the docks with the sheriff, Judy Pitman and Booker when you came up and pitched a fit about people getting in your way."

"Oh, *that*." She offered up a dismissive wave. "That had nothing to do with you and everything to do with Judy. She's a nightmare."

"Oh, yeah?"

"Definitely. Kind of like this golf cart. Who paints a golf cart purple?"

I raised my hand. It was hard not to take offense at the woman's tone, but that didn't stop me from doing just that. "It's mine."

"Did you paint it purple?"

"Actually, yeah. It was peach before that. I happen to like the purple."

"Yes, but ... it looks like some tacky accessory for one of those witches you see on television. I mean ... you could sell goods out of it for heaven's sake."

That's when it hit me. I didn't have to read people in the lighthouse or take up space in Lilac's bar. I had a golf cart and could take my talents wherever I wanted, including house calls or meetings on the beach. "Oh, wow."

"You're finally seeing the color for what it is, aren't you?" She looked hopeful.

"No, but I have an idea." I dropped my purse in the passenger seat. "Was there something else that you wanted?"

"Actually, there is." She looked uncomfortable about broaching whatever subject she had on her mind. "You see, I'm not familiar with Moonstone Bay. I've been here a few times, but it's not my home."

"Oh, yeah? Where do you live?"

"Aspen."

That would explain her expensive outfit. She was on an island, but dressed in clothing trimmed with fur. The clothing made her stand out ... and not in a good way.

"Well, that's a bummer," I offered after a beat. "I guess you must like Aspen, huh?"

"It's a beautiful area, filled with those who ... understand good taste. I mean, don't get me wrong, Moonstone Bay has some beautiful sunsets. The island itself is hardly high class, though. No offense."

No offense? She had to be kidding. I was hardly a native, but there was nothing about that statement that couldn't be offensive. "You could always leave," I suggested. "You don't have to stay in a place you obviously hate."

"The conference won't be held for several days."

"And it's necessary you attend?"

"It is."

"Why?" I decided if the woman was going to insist on taking time out of my day to play me — and make no mistake, she wanted something from me — then I could at least dig for the information Galen was unable to give me. "What happens at a cupid convention? I'm not prying or anything. I'm genuinely curious. I'm not even sure what cupids do."

"I heard you were tight with Booker. What does he do?"

"Odd jobs, the occasional cult fight. Sometimes he drives me around when I'm frustrated and need to vent."

Her expression twisted into something I couldn't quite identify. "He does odd jobs? That's not the way Judy makes it sound at the annual events."

I sensed trouble. "I can't speak for Judy or Booker. All I know is that he's been ridiculously helpful to me since I got here. He's a good man."

"Good in what way?"

I knew what she wasn't coming right out and asking. "Good in the sense that he treats me very well and we're friendly. I'm not interested in him the way you're suggesting. You don't need to get your panties in a twist about it."

"I'll have you know that I never get my panties in a twist."

"Sure. Whatever." I moved closer to the cart. "If you don't mind, I should probably be going. I have some things to do."

"Oh, really? And what things do you have to do? You're a witch without a job."

Something sizzled in the back of my brain as I slowly straightened and turned. She didn't exactly shrink in the face of my anger, but it was obvious she was regretting what she'd said. "Perhaps that came out harsher than I intended."

"Perhaps," I agreed, squinting one eye and raising the opposite eyebrow. My father told me it was my "do what I say or else" look. He was the only one who ever adhered to it, though, and he was rather hit or miss when it came to carrying out my bidding. "How do you know what I am?"

Darlene fidgeted, smoothing the front of her blouse before attacking her hair. She kept her eyes averted as she stammered. "Oh, well, I think someone told me. I can't be sure."

"Since very few people on this island are aware of what I am, I have trouble believing that. I very much doubt you're in tight with those in the know."

"Well ... I make it my business to find out everything I possibly can before I visit a place." She finally got up the gumption to meet my gaze again. "I'm not going to apologize for checking into you. I've had private investigators working this island for two months. You might not have heard, but several years ago we had a conference here that went very wrong."

"I've heard."

"You're dating the sheriff. Of course he would tell you." She said it to herself more than me, but I got the gist of her intent.

"It seems you really have been doing your homework," I noted, frowning. "Why would you care about me if you're here for a cupid convention?"

"I asked for a list of the ten most powerful beings on the island as part of my check. You were near the top with a big, fat asterisk by your name."

I had no idea what to make of that. "Why the asterisk?"

"The gentleman I hired said you'd only recently come into your powers and that you could be something special. He said it was too soon to tell."

"I see. Who else was on his list?"

"Does it matter?"

"I would like to know."

"Some half-demon who owns a bar. The sheriff himself. Booker."

"And what do you plan to do with this information?"

"I don't plan to do anything with it," Darlene replied, her irritation coming out to play. "I simply wanted to make sure that I wasn't walking into a trap."

"What sort of trap would be waiting for you?"

"I see you don't know Judy very well." She clucked her tongue. "That woman is the worst. She's the devil in Chanel. I mean ... that woman would make her own mother want to hide her in a closet she's so obnoxious."

"There seems to be a lot of that going around," I drawled.

"Yes, well ... ." She moved her hand to my arm and smiled. "I can tell you're a good girl, though. You only use your powers for the right reasons." She frowned and moved her hand a second time. "A very good girl."

Something pinged in the back of my head and somehow I understood what she was doing. It amused more than aggravated me. "Are you trying to get a reading on me? If so, I've found that doesn't seem to work when it comes to cupids. I'm apparently immune to your charms."

"I ... no. That's preposterous." Her cheeks flooded with color. "I'm not trying to read you. Why on earth would you say anything of the sort?"

"Because you're not good at hiding your intentions." I exhaled heavily and shook my head, my eyes moving toward the beach. It was a rough-surf day. The waves were crashing into the beach with breathtaking frequency. Even the diehard islanders who liked to surf the big ones weren't out. Despite that, a man in a suit padded across the sand. He appeared to be walking directly toward the water. "It doesn't matter. There's nothing I can do to help you."

"There's one thing." Darlene was a woman used to getting what she wanted. She wasn't about to back down now simply because I was seemingly uninterested in whatever plot she was cooking up. "You were just inside. I saw you leave. What can you tell me about what's going on in there?"

"You'll have to spy on Judy yourself," I replied, my eyes still on the man in the suit. He didn't seem to be slowing as he approached the water. In fact, he appeared to be speeding up. "What the ... ?"

Agitated, Darlene followed my gaze. "What is he doing?"

"I don't know. I ... ." The man plunged into the water, shoes and suit jacket in place. He didn't even jerk when the first wave hit him. Instead, he steadfastly walked forward and began sinking deeper.

"Son of a ... !" I swore viciously and broke into a run. "Get Booker," I yelled over my shoulder. The order was meant for Darlene, but I doubted she was listening. Even if she heard me, the odds of her helping were slim.

I hit the water quickly, doing my best not to gasp as the cold waves rocketed against my shins. I had to slow my pace as I followed the man into the surf. He was up to his chest now, but he kept walking. I was breathless when he disappeared beneath the water. My heart started hammering when he didn't resurface.

"I can't believe this," I gritted out before diving under an incoming wave. Aurora, one of the sirens who lived on the island, had been giving me swimming lessons. She said I was a marginal swimmer at best, and I thought it was smart to increase my level if I didn't want to be clutching a flotation vest every time Galen took me out on a boat.

I surfaced and sucked in a breath before immediately diving under another wave. By dipping beneath them I kept from being rocked backward, but I wasn't nearly as good at it as Aurora.

One more dive and I was on top of the man. He was unconscious, floating face down. I wrapped my arm around his waist and turned him so his nose and mouth were out of the water and then put my arm around his neck so I could tug him.

When I turned back, the distance to the shore seemed insurmountable. I had no idea I'd swam as far as I did. The waves weren't helping and even now I fought them at regular intervals to get the man to safety. I could see people gathering on the beach — Darlene and Judy among them — but it was only when I saw Booker thrashing through the water toward me that I found any measure of relief.

"What are you doing?" he barked when he caught up to me. "You could've been killed out here. Didn't you see the beach warnings?"

I rolled my eyes as I blinked the saltwater out of them. "I didn't plan it. This guy just wandered in. It was as if he wanted to drown. I don't even know if he's alive."

"Here. Give him to me." Booker took the man from me and placed his ear to his mouth. "He's breathing."

"What should we do?"

He was incredulous. "What do you think? We're going to swim back."

"I get that. It's just ... ." Suddenly, I felt really tired. "It's a long way back."

"It is, but I can't carry you and him. You need to swim with me."

"Don't wait around for me if I fall behind."

"Don't fall behind." He was beside himself. "Galen will kill me if I don't come back with you, so it won't matter if I make it back to shore and you're not with me. Just ... steady strokes. Duck your head under the waves. You know what to do."

I did. I simply needed to make my body acquiesce to what my mind readily commanded.

# SEVEN

*I* was exhausted when we finally hit the beach. It seemed the swim took much longer than it should have. My arms and legs trembled even though I wanted to rejoice at the feeling of sand under my feet. The waves kept crashing, pitching me forward as one especially vicious wave took my legs out from under me. A set of strong arms caught me.

"Galen?" I had never been so happy to see anyone in my entire life. "It's you."

"Yeah, it's me." He tugged me up even though all I wanted to do was lie down and rest my legs. "What were you thinking rushing into the water like that?"

"He was going to drown."

"Better him than you." His eyes momentarily fired and then he heaved a sigh as he curbed his temper. "We're going to talk about your self-preservation instincts a little later. Until then, here's some water." He pressed a bottle into my hand and led me to a bench in the sun. "Are you cold?"

"I'm okay. The water isn't cold. It's just ... wild."

"Which is the reason we posted 'no swimming' signs," he muttered.

"I heard that." I was in no mood to be chastised. "I did the best I could. I couldn't just let him drown."

"I know." He put his hands over my wet hair and kissed the top of my head. "I'm not ranting to make you feel bad. It makes me feel better."

"How?"

"Because if I'm yelling that means I'm not thinking about what could've happened to you. I mean ... you do understand about tides, right? You could've been dragged out to sea and we never would've found you."

"Wouldn't you have just sent Aurora out to find me? She's found me in the middle of the ocean before."

He extended a finger. "Yes, but you can't rely on stuff like that. You need to be more careful."

"I'll get right on it."

"You'd better." He grabbed a towel from a passing hotel employee and wrapped it around my shoulders. "You need to sit here while I check on the other guy. I'm going to have to take a statement from you on record."

He sounded equally thrilled as I felt at that.

"Awesome," I said blandly. "After that, can we get some lunch? I'm starving."

"Something tells me you're going to get your way on this." He gave me one more squeeze before moving over several feet and kneeling next to Booker. A paramedic was waiting for Booker when he hauled the man to shore and he immediately started working on the unconscious man as the weary cupid collected his breath.

"What did you see?" Galen asked him.

I waved to get his attention. "You didn't even ask what I saw yet," I reminded him. "Shouldn't I get top-billing?"

His lips quirked, telling me he'd lost the battle with keeping his amusement at bay. "I'm talking to Booker first, smartie. I will be with you again shortly. Drink your water and rest."

"Yeah." Booker shot me a pointed look. "You're lucky to even be alive. There were a few tense moments during that swim back where I was afraid to take my eyes off you."

"Don't tell me things like that." Galen made a face. "The mere thought is going to crush me like you wouldn't believe."

"Oh, you're just lucky you weren't there. It was terrifying. She needs to become a stronger swimmer. I thought I was going to have to leave Mark to his fate and go after her."

Galen's gaze sharpened. "Mark? Do you know him?"

"As a matter of fact, I do. Mark Earle. He's a high-ranking cupid who is about my age. We were always pitted against each other at events when we were growing up."

Booker's tone told me what he thought about that. "I take it you didn't like him?"

"We never got a chance to like or dislike one another." Booker was grim as he dragged his hand through his dark hair. "We were never going to be friends, because our mothers wanted us to be winners at all costs."

I slid my eyes to the beach where people had started to gather. Judy was one of them. Galen had two deputies keeping people back. Booker's mother looked as if she was about to spit nails. "Your mother is a trip. I thought my father was bad — and he is — but your mother is way worse."

"My mother is proud of being worse." He rubbed his forehead and watched as the paramedics checked Mark's vitals. "I came in at the tail end of things, Hadley. You were already in the water and giving chase. It was right before he went under. Did he say anything?"

"I didn't hear him utter a word."

"Then how did you know to go after him?" Galen asked. "How did you know what he was going to do?"

That was a good question. "I don't know." I shrugged. "I was in front of the bar. I had just finished up with Booker's mother, who very sternly warned me to keep away from you, in case you're curious, and came outside to find Darlene standing next to my cart. I was lamenting my bad luck when he caught my attention.

"I knew the beach was shut down because I saw the signs on my way in," I continued. "I thought it was weird to see a guy in an expensive suit walking straight toward the water. I don't know how to explain it. I read his body language, I guess. I was looking for a reason to get away from Darlene anyway. I thought saving a life fit the bill."

"Very cute." Galen flicked the end of my nose. "What were you talking to Darlene about?"

"Forget that." Booker was incensed. "What were you doing talking to my mother?"

"She was waiting for me in the vestibule when I left," I protested. "She wanted to make sure that I was aware I wasn't good enough for you. She has big plans for you, by the way. That's why all those women are throwing themselves at you."

"I'm well aware." Booker's already dark eyes went almost went opaque. "I can't believe she said that to you."

"I told her I was seeing Galen, but she was convinced that I was keeping you on a string, too. She said that's why you spent all your time in the bar talking to Lilac and me instead of looking at the prime pieces of female flesh she brought for you. I added that last part. She was thinking it pretty loudly."

"She was thinking it?" Galen cocked his head to the side. "You read her thoughts?"

"I picked up on the ones she couldn't let go of," I corrected. "You know I can't control any of that. It comes willy-nilly. As soon as I can make it happen at will, you'll be the first to know."

Booker snickered, genuinely amused. "She has you there."

"Shut up," Galen snapped. "You're lucky I'm even talking to you after you were hanging around with my girlfriend at the bar in the middle of the day."

"Oh, trust me. I would much rather be working than hanging out at the bar, but I don't have any control over my life when my mother is around. You know that."

"I well remember." Briefly, Galen looked as if he pitied Booker. He shuttered his emotions quickly, and focused on me. "And what about Darlene?"

"Well, that's what was even weirder," I admitted. "She was waiting outside. She said she knew I was a witch — I swear I didn't tell her — and she wanted to talk to me about my powers."

Galen and Booker exchanged conflicted looks.

"We're talking my mother's nemesis, Darlene, right?" Booker asked after a beat.

I bobbed my head.

"I wonder how she knew Hadley was a witch," Galen mused.

"I asked her that. She said she hired private investigators during the run-up to the convention because she wanted to know who was a danger to her. I thought that was weird, but she seemed to believe it was perfectly normal."

"Private investigators?" Galen straightened. "Did she say who?"

"No. I didn't know that was important."

"I don't like hearing that our people are talking out of turn."

"I asked who else was on her list," I added. "She said both of you were on it ... along with Lilac. She didn't make it all the way through all the names."

Booker furrowed his brow. "What list? I'm confused."

"The list of creatures that could be a risk to her."

"And she put you on the list?" Galen asked.

"Along with you, Booker and Lilac. Yeah."

"Huh." Antsy, Galen ran his hand along his jaw as he thought about the bomb I'd just dropped. "I guess it's not altogether out of the realm of possibility that she really was trying to protect herself."

"I wouldn't trust anything Darlene says or does," Booker countered.

"Are you sure you're not just saying that because she's a super villain in your mother's comic book?" I teased.

His expression remained dark. "Listen, I wouldn't trust anything my mother does either. That doesn't mean Darlene is trustworthy. Together or apart, they're both manipulative jerks."

I risked a glance at the congregated looky-loos and had to bite the inside of my cheek to keep from laughing at Judy's expression. If I didn't know any better, I would assume she'd heard what Booker said.

"I don't trust either of them," Galen said calmly. "We need answers, though. I don't know this guy, but I'm guessing it's not normal for him to walk into choppy waters and try to drown himself."

As if on cue, the man who had just been prone on the beach suddenly bolted to a sitting position and looked around. "What am I doing here?" His voice was rough.

"We were just about to ask you that." Galen hunkered down in front of Mark and fixed him with a flattened smile. "My name is Galen Blackwood. I'm the sheriff on Moonstone Bay. I don't suppose you could tell me why you were walking in the water even though the beach is closed?"

Mark was handsome. He was blond and fair, chiseled cheekbones. I tended to trend toward darker and brooding, so he did nothing for me on the physical front. I could see why he would attract women, though. He had a certain ... something.

"I most certainly didn't walk into the water," he argued, annoyance lighting his features. "That's the stupidest thing I've ever heard."

"I've got witnesses who say the exact opposite," Galen countered.

"Then they're lying."

My mouth dropped open. "Hey!"

Galen held up a finger to silence me and kept his attention on Mark. He seemed fascinated by something in the man's eyes. "Multiple people saw you walk directly into the surf. You kept going even though people tried to stop you. You were unconscious by the time Hadley found you."

Mark worked his jaw. "I have no recollection of that. How do I know you're not making it up?"

"What would be my rationale for that?"

"I've heard horrible things about this island." Mark made a face. "I didn't want to come here. It's dangerous. Mrs. Pitman insisted, though, and she always gets her way. There's a rumor going around that she wants to thin the ranks so she can take over more management positions on the council. I guess this is how she plans to do it."

I flicked my eyes to Booker and found him staring at Mark with open contempt. "Mrs. Pitman wasn't anywhere near you when this went down," I said. "You were completely alone."

"That's neither here nor there." He appeared to be the type who wouldn't accept blame, so I wasn't surprised when he denied everything. "I'm sure it was her."

"You're sure, huh?" Booker's voice was edged with fury.

Slowly, Mark tracked his eyes to Booker. It was as if he was seeing the man for the first time. "I should've known you would be part of this. You're always standing up for your mother, aren't you?"

"Not even close," Booker shot back. "I have no interest in taking up for my mother. But she was nowhere around when this happened."

"Oh, really? And how do you know that?"

"Because he's the one who pulled you out of the water," Galen answered, folding his arms across his chest. It was obvious he didn't like Mark, not even a little. He might've had issues with Booker at a few random turns — they liked to compete with one another, after all — but he was loyal to Moonstone Bay's favorite cupid son. "You'd be dead if it weren't for him."

"I hardly think that's true," Mark sputtered, his gaze bouncing between faces. Finally, he landed on me. He must've figured I was his best shot at hearing what he wanted to hear. "That's absolutely ludicrous, right?"

I shook my head. "I tried to pull you out," I offered. "I chased you into the water. I didn't have the strength to swim back with you. Thankfully, Booker saw me struggling and swam out to help. The rest of your brethren stood on the beach and watched. He was the only one who lifted a finger."

"Don't get too excited," Booker chided when Mark timidly looked toward him. "I only went into the water to make sure Hadley was okay. I would've left you."

I didn't believe that for a second. "You would not have left him."

Booker ignored me. "She insisted I bring you back. I did it for her, not you."

Galen cleared his throat. He was obviously uncomfortable. "We need to know what happened right before the incident, Mr. Earle. What can you tell us? I mean ... were you trying to harm yourself?"

"Certainly not." Mark was scandalized as he shook his head. "I would never do anything of the sort."

"Then something had to happen to compel you into the water."

"I ... ." Mark worked his jaw and descended into silence, his mind clearly busy.

From the sidelines, a distinctly female throat-clearing caught everyone's attention. I was surprised to find Darlene standing there when I turned.

"You're supposed to be behind that line," Galen ordered, pointing.

"I understand that." Darlene was calm. "I think I might have some information for you."

Oh, well, this was bound to be good.

"And what information is that?"

"I was in front of the bar when it happened," Darlene explained. "I saw everything."

"So did Hadley," Galen pointed out. "We already know what happened."

"Yes, but I was standing with her and I believe I know what propelled poor Mark here into the water."

Galen's forehead wrinkled. "You do?"

Mark mimicked his expression. "Yeah, you do?"

She nodded, solemn. "I think it was a spell of some sort, a curse."

I'd been thinking the same thing but hadn't wanted to give my suspicion voice until I thought it through better.

"We've basically already figured that out," Galen offered.

"It's not just that," Darlene added hurriedly before he could outright dismiss her. "I'm pretty sure I know who cast the curse."

"Oh, yeah?" Galen appeared largely disinterested but cocked an eyebrow all the same. "And who is that?"

"Her." Darlene crooked her finger in my direction. "She's a powerful witch."

Galen scowled. "She didn't do this. She raced out into the ocean to save him."

"I was standing next to her," Darlene said soberly. "I felt the power emanating from her. She definitely had a hand in this."

Even though I was innocent my cheeks burned. "I did not have a hand in this."

Galen rested his palm on my shoulder, his fingers gripping lightly. "You'd better have proof to back up that accusation."

"I know you don't want to believe it because she's your girlfriend, but it's true. She's an evil witch."

I worked my jaw, a million insults and threats on the tip of my tongue, but Booker sent me a quelling look before I could unleash my fury.

"Hadley has done nothing but help the people of this island since she arrived," Galen argued. "She is not a suspect. She risked her life to save this man."

"Even though I wouldn't have needed saving if it weren't for her," Mark added solemnly. "She's the reason I almost died."

"Two minutes ago you were blaming Judy Pitman," Galen snapped.

"Oh, I still think it was her." Mark was serious. "I think she hired this witch to take me out because she has an agenda."

Galen was beside himself. "Well, that didn't happen."

"It didn't," Booker agreed. "That won't stop Mark and Darlene from spreading that rumor, though. That's how they operate."

"I'm just trying to be a concerned citizen." Darlene laced her fingers together in front of her. "I'm doing my civic duty."

"I'll show you civic duty," Galen muttered as he took a threatening step in front of her.

Booker intercepted him with a hand to his chest. "That's what they want," he warned, his voice low. "They want to make you look deranged so no one will take you seriously and they can manipulate the situation. Don't give them what they want."

"We only want the truth to be known," Darlene countered serenely. "If there's a dangerous witch on the loose, the people of Moonstone Bay should be aware. They could be next."

I felt sick to my stomach. "You're all kinds of demented, aren't you?"

Galen slid his arm around my waist. "Ignore her. Don't feed into her nonsense. She can't touch you."

Darlene made a clucking sound with her tongue. "I just want everyone to be safe and get along. Is that too much to ask?"

# EIGHT

*G*alen's anger was palpable, but he managed to hold it together. The paramedic insisted on transporting Mark to the hospital so a doctor could sign off — something Mark was bitterly against — but Galen put his foot down. Once Mark was gone and Darlene was secured back with the other voyeurs, he turned his full attention to me.

"You shouldn't be here."

The simple statement crushed my spirit a bit. "Sure. You don't want to be seen with the evil witch. I get it."

"Knock that off." He lightly gripped my shoulder and gave it a small rub. "I don't care about that. I'm worried about you. I don't want you out in the open like this with Darlene plotting against you."

That's what it felt like. She was plotting. I felt stupid for not realizing the lengths she was willing to go to from the start. "I didn't do this," I offered quietly."

He turned his eyes to me, surprised. "Of course you didn't. I don't think you're capable of doing this."

"Because I can't control my magic?"

"Because you're you," he answered quickly. "You're not the type to cast spells to kill people. You might only be learning how to control your magic right now, but I know you. You're a good person."

"I kind of want to do evil things to Darlene. I don't think that makes me a good person."

He chuckled, clearly amused. "I want to do things to her, too. I can't focus on that right now. She played us both extremely well. I have to be careful. Otherwise she'll have legitimate grounds to complain to the DDA."

The DDA again. I was so sick of hearing about it. "She can't hurt you, can she?"

"Not over the long haul, no. She can cause short-term damage, though. That's exactly what she's trying to do."

"Do you think she caused this?"

He looked taken aback by the question. "I hadn't really considered it up until now. I guess it's possible. She was present for both instances." His gaze was weighted as it tracked to the woman in question, who appeared to be having a great time hamming it up with her cohorts as they watched the show. "I'll see if I can pull some information on her. I don't know a great deal about her."

"What should I do? I mean ... I want to help."

"I know you do." He stroked his hand down the back of my matted hair. Thanks to the sun it was almost dry, but I had no doubt it was lacking in the style department. "We'll talk about that tonight. I think you should get out of town for a bit this afternoon while I feel things out."

"Out of town? Should I hop on a boat and ride to Miami for the day or something?"

"I thought maybe you could visit your grandfather."

I hadn't even considered that. But it made sense. Wesley lived miles outside the city limits. If any place was safe, it was his farm. "I guess I could do that. You don't want me to stay out there all night, do you?" The thought caused my stomach to flip.

"Absolutely not." He leaned over and gave me a quick kiss. "I'm not banishing you. I'm simply trying to figure out what's going on. I don't want you to be a target while that's happening."

"I guess." I exhaled heavily and met Darlene's triumphant gaze across the beach. "I really want to punch her in the head with a brick."

He snickered. "We'll consider that option later. For now, I'll feel better knowing you're in a spot where no one can get at you."

"Okay. But if I have to listen to Wesley and May argue all afternoon I expect you to fawn all over me when I get back tonight."

"Your wish is my command."


WESLEY WAS SURPRISED TO SEE me. Once I told him what went down, though, he became agitated.

"Sit down," he ordered as he poured me a glass of lemonade. "I know Galen has probably already handled this part of the conversation, but what were you thinking following a strange man into the ocean on a day like today? You could've been killed."

I hunkered lower in my chair. He had a lovely sitting area on his front porch, with beautiful views in every direction, but all I could see now was his disappointment. "I wasn't really thinking about it at the time," I admitted. "I just didn't want to be the sort of person who sits around while another person drowns."

He sent me an exasperated look. "I understand. Still, you could've been hurt."

"Booker followed me out. He had to swim back to shore with the unconscious guy. I had it relatively easy compared to him."

"Yes, well, thank the Goddess for Booker. Now there's a sentence I never thought I would say."

I shot him a look. "You like Booker. I've seen you interacting before. Don't bother denying it."

"I have no intention of denying it." Wesley twirled his straw in his lemonade and stretched his legs out in front of him as he got comfortable. "I think he's the best cupid I've ever met. But he's still a cupid."

"I don't know anything about cupids. Everything I've asked Booker since finding out his deep, dark secret has earned an eye roll or a laugh. Like, for example, apparently they don't shoot random people with love arrows."

Wesley snorted, genuinely amused. "I bet you've been drilling him with a bunch of questions like that."

"I can't help it. I'm curious. I want to ask Lilac about being half-demon, too, but she's been sort of quiet since that whole thing went down."

"I can't help you with Lilac." Wesley turned sober. "That's her story to tell when she's ready. She's a good girl and she's earned the right to tell you about her past in her own time."

That seemed fair. "What about Booker? Will you tell me what you know about cupids?"

"Absolutely. As much as I like Booker, I think it's important for you to know what you're dealing with since you seem to have been targeted by one of the fringe groups. Now, where should I begin?"

"I don't know. How much of the story is important?"

"What do you already know?"

"That cupids can affect moods and even make people act out of character. I think I might be immune. Other people claim Booker smells like pie and cookies, but I don't smell a thing when I'm around him."

"Really?" Wesley looked intrigued as he shifted in his chair. "Your grandmother was mostly immune to cupids, too. There were occasions — when she was fighting off an illness or just waking up — when she could fall under Booker's spell. Once they realized it was happening, they turned it into a game."

I was horrified by the thought. "Booker used to try to seduce May? That's so ... gross."

"Hey, your grandmother is a handsome woman. She always has been."

"I'm saying it's gross because she's my grandmother and he occasionally flirts with me to annoy Galen. I'm not saying it's gross because of her age."

"Fair enough." He smirked at my discomfort. "He didn't flirt with her *that* way. It was more that he tried to influence her plans for the day. If she wanted to garden, he tried to make her believe she wanted to cook him prime rib. It was simple things like that. Fun things."

"Oh." I furrowed my brow as I concentrated. "You're basically saying that cupids can make people do things that go against what they truly want."

"Not exactly," he hedged. "If a cupid were to try to convince you to do something horrible — like murder someone, for instance — your inner morality will be the guidepost. You're not a murderer, so you won't acquiesce."

"But, let's say I have bad tendencies. What if I really did want to kill someone but I managed to tuck those feelings away until a cupid came along and took advantage of me? Would I be compelled to kill under those circumstances?"

"You'd be more likely to kill," he confirmed. "Would you be compelled? I don't know. I've never heard of that happening."

"The thing is, I'm not asking just because I'm curious. That man today was compelled to enter the water. He didn't remember it. In fact, he was so full of himself he accused us of messing with him. He didn't strike me as the sort to kill himself.

"And, yes, inherently I know there is no 'sort' of person who is more likely to commit suicide," I continued. "It's just ... he's full of himself. He thinks he's above others. He was adamant he would never harm himself."

"And you're asking if a cupid could make him do what he did." Wesley turned thoughtful. "I don't know. I think, like anything else, you would already need to play host to those instincts to make it happen. Only someone predisposed to suicide could be forced to take his or her own life."

That made sense, at least on the surface. "What about other cupids? I mean ... can one cupid force another to do something?"

"Why do you ask?"

"The man who almost drowned himself today was a cupid. He's from one of the groups that has standing in the cupid community."

"Huh." Wesley took on a far-off expression as he gazed at the woods surrounding his property. "That right there is a good question. I'm not sure how to answer it. What does Galen think?"

"Galen has his hands full because that horrible woman accused me of cursing Mark to commit suicide. He couldn't get me out of town fast enough."

"That doesn't sound like Galen. He wants you by his side more often than not. Heck, he wants you by his side ... and on his lap ... and snuggled up on the couch with him ... and sharing a patio lounger ... much more than I'm comfortable with."

I laughed at his hangdog expression. Wesley had made no bones about the fact that he was struggling with the idea of being a grandfather to an adult woman. His instinct was to protect me. I was capable of making my own decisions, so that didn't always go over well. "It's not that," I explained. "It's this woman. Darlene Metcalf. I think she might be the devil."

"Darlene?" The expression on Wesley's face was almost comical. "Oh, geez. Don't tell me she's back. I thought we'd seen the last of her."

I was confused. "Back? The way she made it sound she hasn't been to the island in a number of years."

"That's true."

"I was under the impression that she visited only that one time as well. I mean ... wasn't she part of that entire cupid conference that went down the tubes and resulted in a bunch of people dying?"

The expression that flitted over Wesley's face was ugly. "Oh, she was definitely a part of that. I was knee deep in that scene, too. Your grandmother insisted on getting involved. No one could figure out what happened, who killed who, and she was determined to find answers."

"Did she?"

"Obviously not. No one was ever arrested."

"I wonder if what happened at that conference has anything to do with what happened today," I thought aloud. "Maybe that's why Galen was so keen to send me away. He's usually fine keeping me with him even if it doesn't look professional. He was practically gassing up the golf cart himself this afternoon to get rid of me."

Wesley arched an eyebrow, amused. "I think you're taking this personally when that's not how it was meant. Galen wants to protect you above all else. He may be a pain in my posterior when it comes to the public displays of affection, but I never doubt his loyalty to you.

"As for why he sent you away, I think that's fairly obvious," he continued. "He wants to keep you safe. You're in a unique position right now. Darlene has set her sights on you. Judy has marked you as a possible thorn in her side. That's on top of the fact that you're seemingly immune to the cupids."

"What does that have to do with anything?"

"The immunity? It's a big deal. If you can't be influenced, that would make you far more attractive to certain cupids. Booker, for example, has always wanted a woman who loves him for who he is, not how he smells."

I chewed my bottom lip. That made sense. "Because then he's assured it's real."

"Exactly. I'm surprised he didn't go after you."

"I'm with Galen."

"Which is probably the only thing holding him back. You have to remember, Galen and Booker grew up together. They were in constant competition. Galen had his nose out of joint because Booker kept stealing his girlfriends. Booker had his nose out of joint because Galen had a natural charm that worked wonders on the girls and he didn't need to utilize magic tricks to give himself a leg up on the competition. They were both insecure thanks to the other."

"I'm pretty happy with Galen," I offered. "I really don't want to be part of some weird *Gossip Girl* love triangle. I'm pretty sure I'm too old for that."

Wesley chuckled. "I don't think you have to worry about that. I've seen you and Galen together. It's obvious you're right for each other. Booker might enjoy needling Galen, but he has no interest in hurting you. Making a play for you would result in three people being hurt. Besides, I don't know that he feels anything but friendship from you. I simply assume that the fact that you're immune to him would serve as an aphrodisiac of sorts."

"Good to know." I went back to pouting about my afternoon. "I still don't understand why Darlene turned on me the way she did. It's not as if I thought we were going to be best friends or anything, but it came out of nowhere."

"Not nowhere. Darlene has always been this way. Ever since she was in school she's been the devil's mistress. That's what I used to tell your mother when she would come home crying from school because of something Judy and Darlene did to her."

I was beyond confused now. "Wait ... what? Darlene lived on the island?"

"She spent the first eighteen years of her life here. As soon as she reached adulthood, she couldn't escape fast enough."

"Darlene made it sound like she was a visitor," I argued. "She never mentioned living here."

"She probably wouldn't. This island is considered Judy's jurisdiction in cupid circles. Darlene would never admit to living under Judy's thumb. That's not how she plays the game."

I had no idea what to make of the new information. "I wonder if Galen knows that."

"I'm sure he does. He grew up on the island. He heard the warring Buchanan sisters stories as often as the rest of us."

It took my brain a few minutes to catch up. "Who are the Buchanan sisters?"

"Judy and Darlene."

"Wait ... you're saying they're sisters?"

"Of course they're sisters." Wesley snorted in delight at my expression. "Judy is the older sister by eleven months. She's higher in the hierarchy. Darlene couldn't have that, so she married a man who was higher in the cupid hierarchy than Judy's first husband. They're basically neck-and-neck for dominance ... and they're also part of separate families now thanks to Darlene's marriage."

I was completely flabbergasted. "But ... how did I not know this?"

"Darlene and Judy hated each other as kids. They weren't close. I can't ever remember them being close. Even when they were young — we're talking kindergarten and first grade — they went out of their way to screw with one another.

"They were always in the market for other kids to join with them," he continued. "Your mother made the mistake of thinking Judy wanted to be her friend in third grade and helped her pull a prank on Darlene. It had something to do with a yellow dress. I can't remember.

"Anyway, Darlene had an absolute meltdown and threatened to kill your mother for turning on her," he added. "For weeks, your mother was too afraid to walk to school by herself. I had to pick her up and drop her off. It got so bad she had to get on medicine because her stomach was so upset."

I'd never heard the story. And, picturing my mother making herself sick over two vipers when she was only a child made me wish Wesley hadn't dusted it off. "I knew I disliked both of those women. This is so ... gross."

"It's definitely gross." Wesley was grave. "If you ask me, Galen did the right thing. He sent you out here to make sure you were safe. He knew I wouldn't let either of those hussies on my property to do you harm. He's much smarter than he lets on when he makes those growling noises he thinks I can't hear and chases you through the yard."

I laughed despite myself, the statement lightening the mood. I had a feeling that was his intention. "Well, I'm stuck here for a few hours anyway. What do you want to do?"

"How do you feel about a horseback ride through the fields?"

"I've never really ridden a horse before."

"You'll be fine. I have a gentle mare. It will give you something to focus on other than the cupids."

"That's probably exactly what I need."

"I figured. Come on. Finish your lemonade and then we'll get you suited up. You might as well have some fun while you're out here."

# NINE

*I* texted Galen when I was about to leave so he would know when to expect me. He sent back some weird kissing emoji that made me laugh — which was probably his intention — and then gassed up my cart before heading out.

Wesley packed a box of snacks in case I got hungry during the drive home. It was only a thirty-minute drive, but he was nothing if not a diligent grandfather.

"That's a pie," I noted when I realized what was at the bottom of the box.

"I'm glad to see you can identify food," he drawled.

I ignored the sarcasm. Apparently I came by it hereditarily. "I can't eat an entire pie on the way back to the lighthouse. I mean ... I'm good, but I'm not that good."

His eye roll was pronounced. "That's for after dinner tonight. My cook made three pies. I can't eat them all myself. I gave one and a half to the workers, kept a few slices for me, and this is for you."

"Really?" I was charmed by the gesture. "That's nice. What kind is it?"

"Blueberry."

"I love blueberry pie."

"Good. Then you can eat that instead of playing games with Galen tonight. You'll do your grandfather proud by focusing on the pie."

I didn't have the heart to tell him that I would share the pie with Galen and that eating it would probably involve one of the games he was loath to talk about. He'd been good to me all day — I had pain in my backside from the slow horse ride through the property to prove it — and I didn't want to disappoint him.

"Thank you." I rolled up to the balls of my feet and pressed a kiss to his cheek. "This means a lot to me."

His cheeks colored with embarrassment. "It's just a pie. I didn't even bake it."

"No, but you're taking care of me all the time these days, even when you don't realize it. Between the golf cart and this ... ."

"It's just a pie."

I ignored him. "I wish I'd had the chance to know you when I was younger."

"You're only saying that because you know I would've spoiled you rotten."

I flashed a smile, mostly because I knew that's what he was going for, and nodded without hesitation. "Is that such a bad thing?"

"I wish I'd had the chance to spend time with you, too." He squeezed my hand. "You'd best get going. The cart has lights but you're not going to beat the sunset back. I should've sent you home sooner."

"It's not so bad. What could possibly happen?"

He graced me with a dark look. "I believe you've been attacked once before on this road. I don't want it to happen again. In fact ... maybe I should drive you back."

"And leave the cart here?" I was horrified at the prospect. "No way. I love that cart. It's the best gift anyone has ever given me. Now that it's not peach I don't look like I'm driving around in a vagina either."

His mouth dropped open. "I can't believe you just said that ... and to your grandfather. That is just horrible."

I grinned and wiggled my hips. "Hey, if you have to live with the visual, so do I. I'll be fine. Trust me."

"Text me when you get home. I'll feel better."

"Yes, sir." I honored him with a saucy salute and then hopped behind the wheel. "I'll talk to you later. Don't worry about me. I have everything under control."

**I WAS TEN MINUTES FROM TOWN** when darkness fully descended. A sunset on an island is truly majestic and I had a beautiful view for an extended period. Once the sun dropped, though, it was gone. The rosy glow that burned the horizon followed within five minutes. After that, I was truly lost in the darkness.

Somehow I had forgotten that there were no streetlights on the rural highway that led to Wesley's house. I saw a few lights twinkling in the distance beckoning me, but it was dark.

The cart was quiet. Galen, Booker and Wesley spent a lot of time fixing it up after I received it. Booker painted it and Galen spent hours grunting under the hood. He was shirtless when he did it, so I was fine with the display of testosterone. That's probably sexist, but I don't care. The man looks ridiculously good when he's sweaty and topless.

I still wasn't used to the sounds of the country. In Michigan, I lived in the city. I grew accustomed to ambient noise — humming streetlights and electrical wires, heavy traffic, even police and rescue vehicle sirens — and I didn't notice until it was all stripped away exactly how desolate the country feels when you're alone.

I wished Wesley hadn't reminded me of the attack I'd faced not long after I'd moved to the island. I was in Booker's van that night. He'd loaned it to me, and I almost melted down when a huge animal tried to make me an evening snack. Galen showed up that night. He shifted into a wolf and cast my entire belief system into tumult when I realized paranormal creatures really existed. He hunted my attacker for a long time, and the moments I was left alone, stranded, not knowing what was about to happen, were some of the worst of my life.

That's what I thought about now as I scanned both sides of the road for signs of movement.

I'm a horror movie fan. That's to my benefit and detriment, depending on the occasion. On one hand, I'm not afraid of random noises and often check upstairs to make sure I'm still alone with little prompting. On the other, I know the terrible things that can happen and my imagination has a tendency to get ahead of me. There's a reason I'll never go camping ... or live next to an ancient burial ground ... or try to bring a monster out of my dreams. That way lies death, bloody and cruel.

Two weeks ago, Galen and I were bored during a rainy Saturday and watched five *Friday the 13th* movies in a row. That was probably a bad idea, because all I could picture now was a crazy person behind a hockey mask, hiding in the bushes and armed with a machete.

It was probably a self-fulfilling prophecy when I heard a loud noise in a stand of trees up ahead. It was so loud I couldn't mistake it for my imagination. Instinctively, I removed my foot from the gas pedal and let the cart coast to a stop. My heart hammered as I stared into the trees, searching for movement. Even though a variety of shifters lived on the island — I was still holding out hope to see a shark shifter — an animal would've been a welcome sight. I was hoping for something innocuous, like a raccoon or a deer. Heck, I would've taken a snake at this point.

There was only blackness.

I pressed the tip of my tongue against the back of my teeth and internally chided myself. There was no reason to get this worked up. I was almost home, for crying out loud. All I was doing by stopping in the middle of the road was delaying the trip.

Still, something inside wouldn't allow me to continue. It was as if I had an inner danger alarm and it was shrieking furiously. It spoke to me, and it said, "Don't be an idiot." Because I was nervous I made a series of popping sounds with my lips. I needed something to drown out the sound of my heart.

That's when something finally moved. It was a shadow, and it didn't shift much, but I definitely saw it move in the darkness. It was as if someone was readjusting, perhaps moving from one foot to the other to remove the weight from one hip to the other after standing motionless for a lengthy period.

My throat clogged as I briefly pressed my eyes shut. Then I realized that closing my eyes when a foe was directly in front of me was pretty much the stupidest thing I could do. When I snapped them open again, the shadow appeared to be gone.

"Hello?" I called out, my voice barely a whisper. I cleared my throat and tried again. "Hello? Is anybody out there?"

No answer. I didn't really expect one. If I was stalking someone in the woods after dark, the last thing I would do is speak and alert them to my presence. The terror was so much more effective when there was no answer.

I fumbled in my pocket for my phone. My hands shook when I hit Galen's name on my contact list. He picked up on the second ring, sounding cheerful.

"What's up, Sugarpop?"

As far as nicknames go, that wasn't a favorite. It was hardly worth worrying about now. "I think someone's watching me."

He was all business. "Where are you? Are you back in town?"

"I'm still on the highway, a few miles out. I heard a noise and I slowed down. I swear I saw someone."

"What do you see now?" I heard him moving and starting to breathe heavier. It sounded as if he'd grabbed his keys.

"I don't see anything, but I can't make myself move. It's as if something is stopping me."

"Hold tight." He was grim. "I'm on my way."

"What if it attacks?"

"Then you'll have to protect yourself. You shouldn't have waited so long to leave Wesley's. You know what time the sun sets."

Agitation, hard and bright, rolled through me. "Is that really what you want your last words to me to be? A freaking admonishment? Thank you so much."

"Calm down. I'm on my way. I'll go with full lights and sirens.

You'll be on your own for a few minutes. You'll have to fight if it comes to it."

This was hardly the first time I'd been forced to use my magic. I was still getting used to it, of course, but the power had come through in a pinch more times than I could count. "Please hurry."

"Keep the phone on. Keep the line open."

"I can't do that and have both of my hands free."

"Put the phone on speaker and then place it on the passenger seat. Don't drive unless you have no other choice. Your instincts are telling you something. If they don't want you to move forward, there's a reason for it."

That sounded perfectly plausible. Still, my mouth was dry and my heart felt as if it was about to pull an *Alien* larva and split my chest. "Okay. I'm doing it."

"I'll be right there with you the entire way." He sounded calmer than he probably felt. His truck roared to life on the other end of the call and momentarily drowned him out. When he returned, I knew he was already on the road and heading toward me. "Tell me what you see," he instructed.

"I ... um ... ." I couldn't see anything. I could feel something. Whoever had been near the trees to the front of me had somehow managed to circle back and was now behind me. "Oh, no."

"Hadley, what?" Galen sounded as if he was about to have his own heart attack.

I wasn't much of a fighter. Sure, I got into the occasional hair-pulling contest in high school. That was normal for females fighting over boys and status, though. This was something else entirely.

I sensed more than saw a weapon of some sort coming directly at me. My magic sprang to life even as I ducked, and a wall of some sort — teal and sparkling — popped into existence and cut off the weapon before it could strike me. The noise that followed was loud, as if two vehicles collided. The wall held true, though, and allowed me to suck in a breath and survey my surroundings.

Somehow, and I still wasn't sure how, I'd erected some sort of force field that surrounded the entire cart. The shadow — and even though the force field was illuminated, I couldn't make out a face — hammered away with what looked like a hatchet of sorts. The assault was relentless, but the shield held.

The noise was enough to make me sick to my stomach. With nothing better to do, I buried my face in my hands and attempted to block the unrelenting sound that sickened me to my very core.

GALEN GOT TO ME IN SEVEN minutes. That meant he probably ran both lights in town and broke every speed limit on the island. The shadow fled minutes before he arrived. I could see the lights coming in my direction. Apparently, so could my would-be assailant.

"Hadley!" He was mystified when he hopped out of the truck and approached me. He looked leery. "What is that?"

"I don't know." I shrugged. "I don't know what it is. It just sort of happened."

"Did you do that?"

"Yeah. When whoever it was jumped out from over there and tried to hack me to death."

He worked his jaw. "Well ... that's impressive." He flashed a tight smile. "Can you make it go away?"

"I don't even know how I put it up!"

"Take it down a notch." He grinned despite the situation. We were separated by only a few feet, but the barrier glowed as bright as airport lights. It made me feel as if we were miles apart. "I think if you calm yourself, suck in a breath and do some of that yoga stuff you'll calm down and the bubble will just kind of dissipate."

That was easy for him to say. "What if it doesn't? What if I have to live in here forever?"

"That won't happen."

"Will you wait for me?"

"Are you asking if I'll date a woman who lives in a bubble? I'll have to give it some thought." His smile broadened. "You're in control of this. All you have to do is take in a breath and ... exhale." He moved his hands for emphasis. "So, exhale."

I did as instructed, even though I felt ridiculous, and after a few minutes of steady breathing I closed my eyes. Just having Galen close was enough to calm me, and when I opened my eyes again the shield was gone. The only thing between us was his amusement.

"It's not funny." I slapped at him as he drew me close for a hug.

"It's a little funny." He stroked the back of my head and glanced around. "Which way did the guy run?"

"I'm not sure it was a guy. It was hard to tell in the light and ... well ... he or she wore some sort of mask, which is weird, because I couldn't get Jason Voorhees out of my head right before it happened."

"I knew I shouldn't have let you watch those movies," he grumbled, brushing his lips over my forehead before pulling away. "Stay here while I check things out."

"Wait." I stomped my foot as I climbed onto shaky legs. "You can't just leave me. I've been through an ordeal."

"I can't take you into the ditch where I might fight your attacker."

I jutted out my lower lip. "There's strength in numbers."

He cocked an eyebrow and then snickered. "Fine. You can come with me. If I tell you to run, you'd better run."

"That won't be necessary. We both know he's already gone."

"Probably." Galen took the lead into the ditch. He spent a few minutes sniffing the air. He crouched and ran his hands over the trunks of a few trees. When he finished, he held his hands out and shook his head. "There's no one here now. I can see a few footprints but they're not good enough to identify the tread. Did he say anything?"

"No. He just came out of nowhere and started hacking."

He closed the distance between us and gently slipped a strand of hair behind my ear. "You're okay? Other than flipping out a bit, I mean? That's pretty normal."

I wanted to smack him around. "I'm fine. What happened was not normal. It was pretty far from normal."

"Well, all that matters is you're okay. Let's get you home and we'll talk about it some more there. I bought Chinese. We'll probably have to heat it up, but we can eat it in bed. What's better than that?"

He had a point. "I have pie."

"You have pie?"

"Wesley sent me home with blueberry pie. We could eat that in bed."

"Now you're thinking." He grinned at me, although danger lurked in the depths of his eyes. I understood he was putting on a brave front for my benefit. He was furious someone would dare attack me. He would redouble his efforts the following day. This was personal to him.

"How are we going to get the cart home?" I asked. "Do you want me to drive in front of you?"

He looked amused at the prospect. "While that might be fun, I thought we would just tow it. I have some boards in the back. You can drive it right into the bed of the truck."

"Oh, that's a much better idea."

# TEN

*I* was confused when I woke. I remembered falling asleep, tucked in tight at Galen's side. I was full from the Chinese food and the terror of being trapped on the road alone had faded. I wasn't sure I'd be able to sleep, but I drifted off quickly. That's why waking in an odd manner, standing in front of an open window and peering out, was so jarring.

"What the ... ?"

In my haste to escape from my surprise I smacked into something behind me. Thankfully it was Galen. He was shirtless and sleepy, but he also appeared concerned.

"What happened?" I asked, confused.

"I don't know." He brushed my hair out of my face. I often braid it before bed so it doesn't get out of hand, but I'd forgotten this evening. "I didn't even realize you were up until I felt the wind on me."

"I ... ." I flicked my eyes to the window, confused. I had no idea what to say.

"It's okay." He pulled me to him and wrapped his arms around my back. His heart was a steady thud against my cheek as I tried to make sense of what was happening. "You were just sleepwalking again."

"Just?" My voice went unnaturally shrill. "*Just?* I've never done this before."

"Calm down." He rubbed soothing circles on my back as he swayed. "It's okay."

"It's not okay."

"I'll make sure it's okay." He sounded so sure of himself there was no argument to be had. "Tell me what you were dreaming about right before you woke up."

"I ... huh." I searched my memory. "I was walking down a long corridor again. There were a lot of windows. It wasn't here, I know that. I don't know where I was. It was the same corridor from the first dream."

He pressed a kiss to my forehead. "Were you afraid in the dream?"

"No. I was curious. I could hear ... something."

"What could you hear?"

"I don't know. It sounded like whispers. I wanted to check it out."

"And that's why you were walking to the window in your dream?"

"Yeah."

"Well, that's interesting." He studied the open window for a long time before closing it and latching the lock. "I think we should sleep with the window closed for a bit, just until you're over your dream marathons." He adopted a bright smile that didn't make it all the way to his eyes. "Let's get you back in bed."

He was trying to be upbeat, but I could read what he didn't say. He was worried.

"Do you think the sleepwalking has something to do with what's going on?"

He opened his mouth and then shut it, his mind clearly busy. "I don't know. I need to think about it. Right now, you need sleep."

"What if I sleepwalk again?"

"I have it all under control." He was calm as he pulled me back into bed, settling in the middle with his head on the pillows. He pulled me so I was practically on top of him and wrapped his arms around my back. My head nestled in the hollow between his neck and chest and his heart beat against my ear in a steady rhythm. "You'll be safe here," he whispered.

I wanted to believe him. I was still confused by the turn of events. "Galen, I think maybe something bad is going to happen, or at least try to happen."

He exhaled heavily. "I do, too. I've got you covered, though. We'll talk about everything in the morning."

He didn't sound happy at the prospect. "Okay. I just ... don't let me wander around. I don't want to fly out the window."

He gripped me tighter. "You're not going to fly anywhere. I promise you that. You're going to stay right here, with me."

There was no place I would rather be, so I did my part and focused on sleep. I managed to succumb twenty minutes later.


**GALEN WAS STILL HOLDING** me when I opened my eyes. I was happy to see the sunlight filtering through the window and I stretched long and hard — a few joints popping thanks to the awkward position I slept in — and when I raised my face I found Galen studying me with impassioned eyes.

"What?" Instinctively, I reached for my hair. I figured it was standing on end or something.

"Stop." He pushed my hand back. "I like it when your hair is one big bird's nest. It makes me laugh."

That made one of us. "I'm not a big fan of bird nest hair," I argued. "I prefer looking like a model when I wake."

"A model, huh?" His lips quirked. "Who's to say that models don't have bedhead, too?"

He had a point. Still ... . "I didn't try to sleepwalk again, did I?"

"Nope. You were quiet and down for the count. The thing is ... I was up for a bit after you fell asleep and I've been doing some thinking."

Oh, I so didn't like the sound of that. "Thinking?"

"I don't think you're having these dreams in a vacuum. I think someone is causing them."

I furrowed my brow. "Oh, wow. I never would've guessed that myself." The sarcasm slipped off my tongue before I thought better of it.

He poked my side to show his amusement. "Stop being a pain," he chided. "I'm serious. I watched for a long time to see if I could see someone outside the window. I didn't, but that doesn't mean no one was out there."

I was confused. "Who do you think was out there?"

"Well, I've given it some thought ... and I think it's probably a cupid."

"Why would a cupid be hanging outside my bedroom window?"

"Remember what I told you about cupids. They can make people do things if the individual is already predisposed to certain things."

I didn't like what he was getting at. "And you think I'm predisposed to certain things? Like what? I have no interest in flying out the window and killing myself."

"I didn't say you did." He was calm as he rubbed at the knots forming in my shoulders. "I don't think that whoever is doing this is whispering that you should kill yourself. Maybe that's not what happened with David or Mark at all. Maybe they were compelled to do something dangerous because the voice made them think they were doing something else."

That sounded ludicrous. "Like what?"

"Maybe they were telling you to come outside, and because you were asleep you didn't register what that would entail. The window would be the easiest way outside. You have no compulsion to stay away from the outdoors, so it was easy to sway you to do that."

What he said made sense. I remained uncomfortable with the entire scenario, though. "I don't understand why anyone would fixate on me. I mean ... I don't have anything to do with the cupids. Well, other than Booker. We're just friends, and I've barely seen him since this all started."

"I know. Calm down." His hands were on my back as he steadfastly rubbed. "I don't know why anyone would fixate on you either, but I have a few ideas."

"What ideas?"

"Well, for starters, I think that Darlene already told you in a roundabout way that the cupids have pegged you as powerful. She said she hired a private investigator — when I find out who that is, by the way, they're going to be sorry — and you were listed as one of the most powerful beings on the island. Perhaps someone has a plan and thinks you'll be a detriment because of your status."

"But ... I'm not powerful. Why would this cupid — and we're not even sure it's a cupid — believe something Darlene spouted? No one has proof that I'm powerful. It's all just a hunch at this point."

"It's not exactly a hunch."

"No? How do you figure?"

"Honey, when I found you last night you'd managed to erect a magical protection bubble. I've never seen that before. I've never even heard of something like that. I'm thrilled you can do that because I won't worry about you quite as much thanks to that handy contraption. I'm still amazed that you managed to pull it off. You've done no training whatsoever and you pulled off advanced magic. I would say you're a natural."

"And what if it was just a fluke?"

"I don't think it was."

"It could've been."

"Maybe," he conceded. "But I don't think it was. We can't test it right now anyway. We have to focus on the current problem, which is you sleepwalking. I can't watch you every second of the day. I didn't even feel you get out of bed last night. It's lucky I woke up at all."

"Wait ... ." Something occurred to me. "Did you wake me?"

He bobbed his head. "I did. I grabbed your arm right before it happened. I let it go because I remembered at the last second that it might not be safe to wake you that way. Thankfully you were only crabby when you woke and your brain didn't implode."

I shot him a dirty look. "Oh, you're so funny."

"I try." He flicked the end of my nose and leaned down to kiss me. "You're okay. That's the most important thing."

"You can't just assume it's a cupid without any proof," I argued. "I mean ... I agree that it's likely to be a cupid. Nothing like this has happened to me before and everyone on the island was acting fine until the cupids showed up. Still, we would be remiss to rule out everybody else without proof."

"And we don't want to be remiss."

"Exactly."

He scrubbed his scruffy chin. He was one of those men who grew half a beard overnight. Thankfully the stubble made him look even more attractive ... if that was even possible.

"I have an idea," he said after a beat, beaming. "I think I know how we can prove if it's a cupid."

I was dying to hear this. "And how is that?"

"Just ... trust me. I know exactly what I'm doing."

That was easier said than done because I was the one wandering around unprotected in my sleep. Still, he'd never let me down. I very much doubted he was going to start now. "Sure. I trust you. Let's see what you've got."


**WHAT HE HAD** was a crabby siren with an attitude. Aurora King, her long auburn hair damp from the water, stalked around the lighthouse making ridiculous sniffing noises as she proceeded. Galen had called her while I was in the shower. I could hear them arguing — loud and long — until she finally acquiesced and agreed to stop in at the lighthouse. It had been days since I'd seen her. In fact, now that I thought about it, she'd been scarce since the cupid convention came to the island.

"You definitely had something here," Aurora announced once we'd circled back to the window beneath my bedroom. "My guess is a cupid, but I can't be sure because they all smell different. Whoever it was spent a lot of time right here."

"Can you tell who it was?" Galen asked. He was somber as he watched the siren work.

"I'm not a drug-sniffing dog or anything," she reminded him. "I have no idea who it was. I don't think it was Booker. He has a distinctive smell and he's careful about reining in his pheromones."

I was utterly confused. "Nobody thinks it's Booker." I turned to Galen for confirmation. "Right? We don't think it's Booker."

"I'm doubtful it's Booker," he clarified, his expression telling me he was choosing his words carefully. "I just want to rule him out. It will be easier for everybody once I do."

He was lying ... and I didn't like it. "Booker would never hurt me." I was sure of it. "He had plenty of chances before this. I can't believe you think it's him."

Galen extended a warning finger. "I didn't say I believe it's him. Don't put words in my mouth. I trust Booker ... as much as I trust anybody other than you. I trust you implicitly."

I shot him a dirty look. That wouldn't placate me. "Booker would not hurt me."

Galen threw up his hands in defeat. "I don't think it's Booker. I've told you that multiple times now. It's not Booker. That doesn't change the fact that I have to rule him out. It'll be worse for us if I don't."

"He's telling the truth," Aurora interjected, hunkering down to study a patch of ground behind some sea grass. "Cupids are a funky bunch. Why do you think I've been laying low? I want nothing to do with them."

"You've been laying low because if you catch a whiff of one of them you'll want everything to do with him," Galen shot back. "Don't confuse her with half-truths. She's still trying to learn about all the intricacies of paranormal relationships."

Aurora pinned him with a withering look. "Thank you for spreading my private business all over the beach. I'm not the only one who has a bad cupid experience in her past. I don't suppose you remember Garnet Redfern?"

Galen's cheeks turned a fiery shade of red. "And thank you for bringing that up," he muttered under his breath.

"I don't understand." I was intrigued, but confused. "Who is Garnet Redfern?"

"It doesn't matter." Galen offered up a dismissive wave. "Aurora is just trying to cause trouble. She's good at it."

"I *am* good at it," Aurora agreed, amusement sparking in the depths of her eyes. "But that's neither here nor there. Galen and I both have experience with cupids and we're very careful around them."

I needed a translation. "Meaning?"

"Sirens are especially susceptible to cupids if they turn on the charm," Galen volunteered. "The magic — or whatever you want to call it — wears off fast, though. Once the insta-lust is gone, all that's left is two people who want to rip each other's hair out. There's a reason we are warned against siren-cupid relationships."

"Because they turn volatile?"

"Exactly."

I folded my arms over my chest. "What about you? You're not a siren. It sounds like this Garnet person was a cupid. What happened between you and her?"

Galen lowered his gaze. "It doesn't really matter. We should focus on the problem at hand."

"Oh, let it go." Aurora delivered a sharp elbow to his stomach and then focused on me. "Galen met Garnet when he first started as sheriff. She was here visiting and caught his attention on the beach.

"They had a torrid affair," she continued, relishing the story. "They were all over each other for a week straight. That's usually how long a cupid can infatuate a person before holes start showing in the relationship. That's exactly what happened to Galen and Garnet ... and when the holes showed, they were big enough to drive a Mack truck through."

"She's not wrong," Galen grumbled. "We shouldn't be talking about this. It's rude. Hadley doesn't want to hear about a former girlfriend."

"Are you crazy?" I was incredulous. "That was long before I was part of your life. I'm not jealous. If you dated her while you were dating me I would have something to complain about. It's not as if you were betraying me or anything."

Galen scowled. "I still don't think you need to hear the story."

"And I think you should stuff it." I pressed a finger against his lips and focused on Aurora. "Tell me what happened with Garnet."

"She used to make Galen wait on her, deliver her drinks and rub her feet." Aurora's eyes lit with mischief. "It didn't last long. Once Galen woke from the pheromones, he realized what was happening and completely melted down. He called her out in front of hundreds of people on the beach and she tore off, completely humiliated and furious."

I felt a bit let down. "That's it? Nothing else happened?"

"That's it," Galen confirmed. "I told you it wasn't a very good story."

"It was simply anticlimactic." I flicked my eyes to where Aurora was studying the ground. "What about the cupid coming here? Can you tell me anything about him? Heck, I guess I don't even know if it is a him."

"It's a male." Aurora wrinkled her nose and went back to sniffing. "He spent a long time under your window. If you think someone was trying to lure her out, Galen, that sounds about right to me."

"Is there any way to track him down?" Galen asked. "I can't pick up a scent at all."

"No, although ... whoever this cupid is, he has an odd scent. It's not like a normal cupid. It smells different."

"Different how?"

"I don't know how to describe it. Sweet, but also sour. It's weird."

I rubbed my forehead, frustrated. "So, what do we do?"

"We make sure all the windows are locked and that you're safe while sleeping," Galen replied without hesitation. "I won't let anything happen to you. I promised and I meant it. You'll be kept safe first and foremost. We'll figure out what to do after that."

"Okay, but I won't handle it well if you try to put me under house arrest. You know that, right?"

"Oh, definitely. We'll have to come up with a compromise."

That sounded like an interesting possibility. "Which one of us is going to compromise?"

"I don't know. Let's find out."

## ELEVEN

"*G*ive me a kiss."

Galen grabbed the front of my shirt and planted a long kiss on my lips when I walked him to the door to say goodbye. He'd lingered over breakfast to the point he was making us both uncomfortable — his intense stare was much more fun when he wasn't watching me like a bomb about to go off.

My eyebrows flew up my forehead and I was considering putting up a token fight until his talented mouth got to work. Before I realized what was happening I was breathless and a bit flustered. He looked proud of himself when he pulled back.

"What was that for?" I asked.

"I happen to be fond of you."

"Why really?" Something occurred to me. "You think this is the last time you're going to see me."

His smile fell. "No ... and don't say things like that."

"It's true. You're afraid I'm going to walk into the surf the second you leave and that will be it."

"If I thought that was a possibility I wouldn't leave you. Exactly what kind of sheriff do you think I am? More importantly, what kind of boyfriend do you think I am?"

He had a point. "You're a great boyfriend." I meant it. He was everything I could've ever dreamed. Sure, he snored sometimes, but nobody was perfect. He said I snored, too. I was pretty sure he was making that up. "It's just ... you're worried. I see it whenever you think I'm not looking."

"You shouldn't be looking when I'm not ready for you to look." He kissed the tip of my nose. There was trouble in his eyes. "You'll be okay. I won't let anything happen to you. More importantly, you won't let anything happen to you. You're strong ... and powerful ... and now you can make weird bubble shields. If someone comes around, I expect you to do that again."

The worry I felt rolling through him was painful. "I'll be careful. I plan to stick close to the lighthouse today."

"Okay." He forced a smile and leaned over to give me another kiss, his fingers gentle as they moved over the back of my head. "Why don't you stay on the first floor and sit on the couch the entire day, just to be on the safe side?"

That sounded like a surefire way to drive me insane. "Do you want me to go crazy?"

"It's preferable to the alternative."

That was true. "I promise to be careful." I wrapped my fingers around his wrists and gave them a squeeze. "You have a job to do. You're the one who should be careful. You'll be more of a threat to whoever is doing this."

"Obviously whoever did this doesn't feel the same. Either way, I do have to go. I'll figure this out one way or another. I'll be available by phone all day if you need me. If something happens and you feel as if you hear things or feel weird, I want you to promise you'll call me."

If he were being bossy I would've argued. His fear was obvious, though, and I couldn't torture him. "I'll call you if I so much as stub my toe."

He looked amused. "Do that." He graced me with another kiss, this one somehow sweeter. "Okay, I have to get going. I'll bring dinner home. What do you want?"

"Lobster and steak." I was being funny, but he nodded without hesitation.

"I'll grab it from the hotel by the office. They won't give me grief about packing lobster in a plastic bag."

"I was kidding. That's way too expensive."

"It's fine." He rubbed his hands up and down my arms. The gesture was meant to be soothing, but it only served to put me on edge. "I'll bring back extra rolls and dessert, too." Another kiss. He was really packing on the affection. "I'll text you throughout the day to make sure you're okay. Make sure you text me back."

I nodded. "Okay. Now ... go to work."

"I'm going." He cast a worried look over his shoulder as he reached his truck. "Be careful, Hadley. Be alert."

"I will. You have absolutely nothing to worry about."


**TEN MINUTES AFTER HE LEFT,** I was antsy. Now that I knew I couldn't leave the lighthouse all I wanted to do was hit the town. Galen would have a meltdown if he heard reports about me speeding around the beach in my cart — and that seemed somehow torturous for no good reason — but I was already beginning to chafe under his rules.

That's when things got worse.

"Hey." Booker let himself into the lighthouse without knocking. He scanned the room until his eyes fell on me ... and then he broke into a wide grin. "How's it going, super witch?"

I frowned. "You can't just let yourself into someone's home. You're supposed to knock."

"I'm sorry. Do you want me to go back outside and knock?"

"It's kind of ridiculous now."

"It is," he agreed, moving around the coffee table and throwing himself on the couch next to me. "How are you feeling? I heard there was an incident last night. Actually ... I heard there were multiple incidents."

That's when things slipped into place for me. "Galen called and asked you to serve as my babysitter."

"I think that's a huge exaggeration."

"Am I wrong?"

"Nope." He smirked. "He's a little worked up. He called this morning when you were in the shower. I told him it wouldn't be a problem because I was looking for a reason to escape from my mother. Then he called again five minutes ago to make sure I planned to stick close. He's a little ... whiny."

"He's on edge," I corrected, lightly slapping Booker's knee. "He's worried about me."

"He's a big, gooey marshmallow where you're concerned," he agreed. "It's kind of funny. It's the sort of thing we would've teased each other about back in high school. I understand why he's worried — and I happen to agree this isn't a good thing — so I'm kind of turning into a whiner, too."

"He's not a whiner. He just ... he was afraid last night. I saw it on his face when I woke up. There was real fear there. This is something he can't fight."

Booker pursed his lips, thoughtful. "How much has he told you about cupids?"

Now we were getting somewhere. "Not much. I asked him about this mind control thing you guys can supposedly do, but he didn't have many answers."

"He wouldn't. He'd only be up on the rumors. He's not part of the inner circle."

"Are you?" I had my doubts. "The way people have been talking, you're not considered part of the 'in crowd' of the cupid circle."

"I don't want to be part of the 'in crowd.'" He made a face that would've been comical under different circumstances. "If Aurora says that a cupid was outside the lighthouse last night, I have to believe her. She knows what she's doing when it comes to tracking."

"You look as worried as Galen." That only made my stomach flip harder. "What aren't you guys telling me?"

"We're not keeping anything from you." He was firm. "It's just ...

cupids are supposed to live by certain rules. We're supposed to be above the follies of men." His smile was snide. "That's what cupids say, by the way. They pat themselves on the back and place themselves higher than all other species of paranormals. As for humans, they're considered pets."

I felt sick to my stomach at the admission. "Pets?"

"Like cats." His eyes fired with unhappiness as he held my gaze. "Cupids like playing with their pets, but they're still just animals."

I swallowed hard. I couldn't remember ever seeing him this upset ... or cynical. He was generally a pretty "go with the flow" guy. "I think you should probably start at the beginning," I said. "I need to catch up."

"There isn't a beginning. Not really. Cupids held themselves separate from other paranormals for centuries. They played with emotions, enjoyed setting factions against each other for war, and essentially played games while others suffered."

"Wow. Tell me how you really feel."

"I really wish I wasn't a cupid and could completely sever ties with my kind."

He wasn't kidding. "I don't think that's a possibility, so why don't you finish with the rest of the story?" I suggested.

"Some paranormals are immune to cupids and eventually figured out what was going on."

"What sort of paranormals are immune? Shark shifters?"

His lips quirked. "You need to let it go with the shark shifters."

"I can't. I need to see one. I hear they're like unicorns."

"Perhaps one day you'll luck out." He absently patted my hand and stared at the ceiling as he rested his feet on the coffee table. He appeared lost in thought. "Vampires are immune to cupids. Apparently they think cupids stink, too. That makes it easy for them to stay away. It's actually kind of funny. That's why I can't attend funerals."

I thought about the ghoulish — and altogether creepy — funeral home director, who also happened to be a vampire. I'd met him only once, but he'd left a lasting impression. "That's probably a good thing."

"Yeah. Pixies are immune to cupids, too. They're from a different plane, though. It only makes sense that they wouldn't fall in line and follow the rules our cupids set."

"I've never met a pixie."

"You will one day. They're more common than you think."

"Anyone else?"

He flicked his eyes to me, his expression unreadable. "Certain witches."

I frowned. "I'm obviously not immune to cupids," I argued. "Galen found me in front of the window last night. He's still messed up over it. That's the only reason I agreed to stay close to the lighthouse and not get in trouble today. I don't think his poor heart can take much more strife."

"Oh, you're a big, gooey marshmallow, too." He poked my side, hoping for a laugh. When he didn't get one, he sighed. "You're immune to me," he pointed out. "We already tested that. You remember your friend Aisling? She was a reaper and fell all over herself even though she was with her husband. You're at least partially immune to cupids."

"Then how do you explain last night?"

"I have a few ideas."

"Oh, well, good. I love ideas."

He laughed at my exaggerated expression. "The first revolves around the cupid himself. He might not be a full-bred cupid. That would mean he only has partial powers. Cupids are influencers. It could be our cupid is focusing on one thing to influence and that he's not very good at it."

"David Fox is dead. Your buddy Mark the cupid almost joined him. He has to be better than you're giving him credit for."

"Or maybe he managed to make it work because the individuals he approached were weak of spirit. Mark is definitely a douche canoe. He's always been a mealy-mouthed little ferret. I didn't know David very well, but I never heard anything good about him."

"That doesn't explain what happened to me last night."

"It doesn't," he agreed. "Except ... you were asleep."

I waited for him to expound. When he didn't, I let my irritation out to play. "What does that have to do with anything?"

"The others were clearly approached when they were awake," he responded. "That means they were hypnotized."

I hadn't considered that. "Do cupids hypnotize people?"

"Definitely. That's how we operate. You, however, were only approached while you were sleeping. I think that's on purpose. Someone is trying to invade your mind when your guard is down. The only time you might be open to suggestion is when you're under."

I didn't like the sound of that. "Why go after me at all?"

"Oh, come on." His eyebrows drew together. "You can't be serious. You're one of the most powerful beings on this island. We knew that before you surrounded yourself in magical bubble wrap last night. Your powers are growing exponentially. I can't wait to see what you'll do next. It's exciting."

It wasn't all that exciting to me. "How could someone else know that? Only a few people in our inner circle know."

"People talk. Gossip spreads. News of what happened with the cult was too big to contain. I've heard whispers, Hadley. Your grand-mother was a powerful witch. You might be more than that ... which brings me to another option on what's going on. You could be a super bruja."

He said the words as if I should understand them. "Excuse me?"

He chuckled. "In olden times, powerful witches who were more than normal witches were called beldams. Over the years, that term has been corrupted and people picture old, craggy women who can barely stand, cursing people with eye of newt. That is not a good description."

He had my attention now. "I guess I don't understand what you're saying."

"No, you wouldn't. You were raised outside this world. Still ... you've manifested some interesting abilities. It makes me wonder what you would be able to do if you were raised on this island."

"May mentioned it before — and Galen, for that matter. She said that the island can amplify magic. Do you think that's true?"

"Do I think the island itself is magic? Not necessarily. This isn't *Lost*. Do I think the convergence of paranormals on this island is a coincidence? No. Something calls to us here. There's an underlying current of ... something. I think the island is a part of all of us, including you."

I debated how far I wanted to press the issue. "What does being a super bruja mean?"

"Most witches have one or two powers they can call to regularly. You seem to have no limit to the number of powers you can call."

"I've only done a few things," I argued.

"True, but you've done those things under duress. That seems to indicate you haven't tried to control your magic. You've just let it take over when you were in need and required help.

"If you were to truly explore your abilities, I think you'd find you can do almost anything," he continued. "It would take practice and hard work, but I have no doubt you could be the stuff of legends if you put your mind to it."

I wasn't sure that was a compliment. "Are you saying I'm not the stuff of legends now?"

He chuckled. "I'm saying that you haven't been here that long and you've got plenty of time to figure things out. There's no reason to get worked up. We'll figure it out."

"You still haven't explained how being a super bruja — and I'm not sure I like that term — explains what happened last night."

"See, that's the thing." He turned serious. "I talked to Aurora before she disappeared back into the ocean. Apparently she doesn't like all the cupids hanging around."

"She told me."

"She said that whoever was outside the lighthouse was definitely a cupid. The smell is rather obvious. She also said the scent was off. I'm wondering if whoever is after you is more than a cupid."

I finally caught up to what he was trying to say. "Like ... half cupid and half something else that can control people?"

He smiled. "Now you're thinking. That's exactly what I was considering."

"What other creature can control people's minds and make them kill themselves?"

"I don't know. I've been giving it a lot of thought and have come up empty so far. We might need to do some research."

"I'm confused. I thought only full cupids were allowed to play in your conference games. If this creature is only half-cupid, how did he or she manage to get this far up the cupid ladder?"

"That's a very good question. I don't have an answer. I don't even know we're dealing with a hybrid. We could simply be dealing with a mutant cupid whose magic is somehow malfunctioning."

"How do we find out?"

"I don't know." Booker turned thoughtful. "Galen asked me to look around the lighthouse grounds to see if I had any ideas about setting traps. I'm not sure what we can do, but I'm not going to leave you vulnerable."

"You sound like him."

"We don't always fight. Some things we agree on. Keeping you safe is one of them."

"He's afraid." The words hurt coming out. "I don't like it when he's afraid."

"Caring about someone makes you vulnerable. Galen has never been the vulnerable sort ... until now. He wants to control everything, but realizes there's very little he can truly control where you're concerned. He won't feel better until we figure out who's doing this."

"Then I guess we should probably get on it."

"Definitely. Between May's books and scouring the yard, I figure we can keep ourselves busy for most of the day."

Oddly enough, his gung-ho attitude made me feel better. Being proactive was always better than sitting back and waiting for something terrible to happen. At least if we were moving forward we wouldn't constantly be looking over our shoulders.

# TWELVE

*G*alen texted twice after he left and then stopped in at mid-morning. He had a box of doughnuts in his hand, which he immediately handed off to Booker. It looked like a peace offering of sorts. I was convinced I would never understand the strange bonding rituals of men.

"What are those for?" I asked, peering around Booker for a better look. There were three cake doughnuts with chocolate frosting and sprinkles — my favorite — which meant he had me in mind when he selected them. "Can I have one?"

Booker slid me a sidelong look. "Seriously? He's bribing me, but he filled the box with your favorites. I'm pretty sure they're for you."

"They're for both of you." Galen made a face as I selected a dough-nut. "I just wanted to stop by and make sure there were no noses out of joint because I asked you to come over."

"Basically, you're saying that you want to make up now rather than later if we're going to fight." I bit into my doughnut and moaned softly. "Oh, wow. They're still warm."

He grinned at me when I spoke with my mouth full. "Is it any wonder I'm desperate to keep you safe? I mean ... you're pretty, witty and oh, so classy."

I ignored the dig and allowed him to kiss me. I was more interested in the doughnut, but if he felt the need to stop by the lighthouse hours after he left, the fear had to be threatening to take him over. I didn't want that. "I am classy," I agreed as I pulled off part of the doughnut and shoved it toward his mouth. "I'm so classy I'm not going to jump all over you for calling a babysitter when I don't need one."

He accepted the doughnut bite but kept his eyes on me. He waited until he finished chewing to speak. "I'll keep you safe through any means necessary. I'm not going to apologize for it."

"I didn't say you needed to apologize. Besides, Booker and I have been doing some talking and we've come up with a few hunches."

"Oh, really?" Galen cocked an eyebrow and then reached into the doughnut box to grab a cinnamon twist. "Do you want to share them?"

"Sure." We sat at the kitchen table and talked over coffee and doughnuts. Galen nestled his knee against mine and listened intently. When we were done he looked more thoughtful than blown away. "It's an interesting idea."

"Which one?" Booker asked. He was busy dunking a plain doughnut in his coffee. I happened to find that habit disgusting. He was helping me, though, so I decided to keep my opinion to myself.

"All of them." His eyes flicked to me. "I'm especially interested in the one about Hadley being a super bruja."

"I think we should come up with a different term," I argued. "That one sounds a little too *Justice League*."

Galen bobbed his head. "Sure. What term would you like?"

"Wonder Witch."

He smiled. "Will you wear a skimpy outfit and tie me up with a lasso if I call you that?"

"Oh, don't get all gross in front of me," Booker complained. "I'm already at my limit with all the cupids here. I can't take you two verbally copulating in front of me, too."

Galen snickered as I shot Booker a sympathetic look.

"We're sorry," I offered.

"I'm not," Galen countered. "I had to listen to you verbally copulating with Marie Lincoln in high school. Oh, and Susie Barton ... and Michelle Graves ... oh, and Lemon Langford."

I wrinkled my nose. "Who names their kid lemon?"

"Stupid people," Booker answered automatically. "She was stupid, too. The stupidity was rampant in that family." He sighed as he pinched the bridge of his nose. "What do you suggest we do for the day? I think we should work to verify your hunches — especially if that leads us to our killer cupid — but I get the feeling you don't want Hadley to leave the lighthouse."

Galen's gaze was filled with trepidation when it landed on me. "I would prefer she stay here," he said. "But she's an adult. If she wants to head out, there's nothing I can do to stop her."

I could read between the lines. He was basically saying, "I shall not be held responsible if you two idiots get yourselves in trouble." I felt for him, but there was no way I could stay at the lighthouse now that I thought there was a possibility that there was some mutant cupid out there. "I think we should go down to the festival."

Galen narrowed his eyes. "Why? You've been to the festivals before. They're nothing special."

"Hey, elephant ears are always special." I jabbed my finger at him. "As for this particular festival, I think it's likely that our culprit will be there. I was reading the brochure at Lilac's bar yesterday and I happen to know they're having a 'meet your representative' function in the main tent at noon."

Galen's face remained blank. "So?"

"So, I'm betting whoever we're dealing with has ties to the bigwigs and will be there. Maybe we'll be able to witness someone acting squirrelly."

"And maybe someone will go after you and hurt you." Galen immediately started shaking his head. "I don't like that idea. Can't you do something else?"

Ugh. He was starting to wear on me. The cuteness factor comes and goes at a fantastic rate sometimes. "I'll be with Booker," I reminded him. "Someone would have to be an idiot to go after me when I have another cupid as my sidekick."

Booker cleared his throat. "Um ... if we're going to play that game, you're going to be my sidekick. I'm Batman, not Robin."

I shot him a withering look. "And I'm Wonder Witch. You're more like Cyborg than Batman."

"Oh, whatever."

Galen snickered as he glanced between us. He didn't look happy at the prospect, but I knew he wouldn't put his foot down and demand I stay at the lighthouse. We were constantly learning about one another ... and compromise. He knew I balked when someone tried to tell me how to live my life. Even though he was bossy, he reined in those urges all the time because he didn't want to risk a blowup that would fundamentally change our relationship.

"Do you promise to be careful?" he asked finally. It was obvious he was already resigned to the fact that I was going to do it. He was only pretending to go through the motions.

"We'll be careful," I promised.

"We will," Booker agreed. "Besides, I think there's a reason whoever is doing this approaches Hadley at night, when she's sleeping. He or she — and I'm leaning toward a he — believes that she's only approachable when her defenses are down. Our guy isn't gutsy enough to do this in daylight."

"I hope so."

"Even so, I'm coming back this afternoon and adding some locks to the windows. The downstairs windows are already secure. The upstairs ones — well — let's just say that someone on the inside trying to get out and hurting themselves was never a fear. I'll have it fixed before I leave for the day."

Galen looked profoundly grateful. "Thank you."

"Don't mention it. I'll keep you informed if we find anything of interest at the festival."

"That would be great." Galen dragged a hand through his hair and grabbed another doughnut. Like me, he was a stress eater. During times of strife we could each put away our own pizza. "Watch your back while you're there. More importantly, watch her back."

"I'll keep her close." Booker leaned back in his chair, a smug smile playing at the corners of his lips. "Not so close you'll be jealous, though. I know how you get when I steal your women."

Galen growled. "I wouldn't go there if I were you."

"You're, like, zero fun now that you're an adult."

"I can still take you."

"Promises, promises."


**THE FESTIVAL WAS THE SAME** as the two other Moonstone Bay festivals I'd attended. The same rides seemed to be permanently planted in the downtown park. The same game booths were spread from one end of the park to the other. The only difference was everything at this festival was accented in pink and red. It reminded me of Valentine's Day ... if the holiday had exploded and thrown up all over everything.

"I don't mind the pink, but when you pair it with the red, it's really garish," I complained.

Booker, who was keenly watching the crowd, snorted. "My mother hates a cliché ... unless it's one she can use to her advantage. Darlene is trying to get the official cupid colors changed to blue and silver. My mother has suddenly embraced red and pink — even though she used to believe much the same as you — and now they're locked in a fight to the death."

I was understandably confused. "Cupids have official colors?"

"They do. The pink and red motif isn't just a greeting card thing."

"Well ... that is odd."

"Tell me about it."

Booker took his job as my protector seriously. His eyes continuously roamed the crowd and he made sure to keep me close as we cut through the fairgrounds. I was certain no one would be able to approach without setting off his danger alarm. That conviction allowed me to relax enough to truly watch the participants.

"Is everyone here a cupid?" I asked.

"Pretty much. I see a few locals, but I'm guessing they're here because of the cupid pheromones."

That was a freaky thought. "Aurora mentioned that she was careful around cupids because she was especially susceptible. Is that a siren thing?"

"Pretty much. Sirens and cupids don't mix. Air and water. You know how that goes."

I'd never really thought about it. "She also said sirens and cupids burn out on each other and end up fighting all the time. What's that about?"

Booker chuckled, seemingly amused. "It's a byproduct of the pheromones. Sirens can entice people, too, don't forget. Those stories of sirens luring sailors to their deaths? Those are true."

"And why did they kill sailors?"

"For sport. The thing is, sirens and cupids aren't that different. They have a lot of the same abilities. Cupids can control sirens, though, and the sirens don't like that. Sirens eventually fight off the lure of cupids. When that happens, all that lust is burned away and the only thing that's left is fury."

I was intrigued by the premise. "I've always thought of cupids affecting the mood of people in a positive way. Even after I found out you guys were real, I never stopped thinking along those lines. Now, with people dying, I'm starting to think there's a lot more than that lurking under the surface."

"There is. You should be glad you're immune."

"We don't know I'm immune to everything," I hedged. "Galen did find me by the window two nights in a row."

"And I guarantee Galen will make sure that doesn't happen again." Booker was firm. "I might not always agree with the man — and messing with him is something of a favorite hobby of mine — but he's good at his job. He'll die before he lets something happen to you."

There was fire in his eyes when he uttered the declaration.

"I don't want him to die. Not even to save me."

AMANDA M. LEE

"I don't think you have a choice in the matter. Are you saying you wouldn't die for him?"

The question made me uncomfortable. "I've never really thought about it."

Booker let loose a dismissive snort that got under my skin and rankled. "You almost died yesterday because you refused to let a stranger drown. Are you really going to argue this point with me?"

I wanted to on pure principle. He was right, though. "No." I pinched the bridge of my nose and furrowed my brow when the sound of two voices — both female and both shrill — assailed my ears.

"I saw it first!"

"No, I saw it first!"

I tracked my eyes to one of the flea market booths on the east side of the fairgrounds. There, two women I didn't recognize appeared to be arguing over a piece of jewelry.

"You can't have it!" The first woman, a brunette, practically shrieked as she grappled with the smaller blonde and tried to dislodge her from the front of the case. "I saw it first."

"Your fingers are too fat for it," the blonde shot back.

I slid my eyes to Booker and found him watching the scene with equal parts curiosity and wariness. "Do you know them?"

"Yeah. They're locals, not cupids."

That didn't make me feel any better. "Should we go over there?"

Booker took a moment to look around, as if debating the answer to my question. Finally, he nodded and pressed his hand to my back. "Stick close. I don't want anything to happen to you because I was distracted."

"Yes, that would suck."

He smiled but remained focused on the women as we crossed to them. They were sweating and red-faced when we closed the distance. The fight for the ring continued.

"It's mine." The blonde dug her fingernails into the brunette's wrist, causing the other woman to shriek with rage.

Booker made up his mind on the spot. "Knock that off." He put his hand over the ring and used his hips to box out the two women as he

108

took possession. "You're acting like children. Is a ring really worth acting like this?"

"It's my ring." The brunette's nostrils flared. "I saw it first."

Booker pinned each woman with a warning look before lifting the ring for a better look. His expression was incredulous when he handed it to me.

"That's mine!" The blonde looked as if she was about to jump me.

"Shut up," Booker ordered. "Hadley, tell me if there's something special about that ring that I'm missing."

I dutifully stared at the item in question, frowning when I realized how cheap it was. "Um ... I don't even think this is real silver."

Booker agreed. "That's, like, a ten-dollar ring. Why are you fighting over it?"

"Because it's mine!" The blonde practically dripped venom as she took a threatening step closer toward the brunette. "She tried to steal it."

Something sizzled in the back of my mind as the women locked gazes. "They're going to throw down," I warned Booker, wrinkling my nose when a familiar scent wafted past. It was sickly sweet, so sweet that I felt I would vomit. "I ... ." I broke off and turned around, frantically searching the crowd. As far as I could tell, no one was watching the show. The attending cupids appeared to be bored more than anything else.

"What's wrong?" Booker took a step in my direction and then slowed when the two women made as if they were going to jump on each other and start clawing out eyes. "I said to stop that!" His voice boomed, but the women paid him little heed.

"I'll make you wish you were never born," the brunette hissed.

"I already wish you were never born," the blonde tossed back. "Isn't that enough?"

Booker instinctively shot out his hands to keep the women at bay. "Enough is enough." His eyes landed on me. "Call Galen. I think these ladies need to cool off in a cell for a bit."

I had other things on my mind. "Do you smell that?"

"What?"

"That ... rancid honey smell. It's the same thing I smelled the day David Fox jumped to his death."

Booker immediately dropped his hands and stepped in my direction. "Do you sense something? Do you feel danger? Do that force field thing right now. Protect yourself."

His tone told me he meant business. I couldn't focus on him, though, because the women stormed toward each other like rampaging bulls.

"Hey!" I tried to draw their attention to me but it was already too late.

They collided with snarls and flailing fists. Neither looked to be much of a fighter, but they grabbed hair and tugged for all they were worth, all the time screaming profanities at each other.

Booker appeared confused as I ran past him. Something inside was ticking ... and I had a feeling it was my temper.

"Knock it off!" I commanded, planting myself directly next to the women and putting a hand on each of their shoulders. "I'm not kidding. You need to stop this right now!"

With the last word a bit of magic escaped. I had no control over it. The sparkling burst of energy smacked directly into the nearest woman. After rushing through her, it rammed itself down the blonde's open mouth.

The two women stopped fighting and sagged to the ground. They looked utterly defeated ... and completely bewildered.

The burst of magic zipped back to me and disappeared into my chest, causing me to gape in shock.

"What was that?"

Booker rapidly moved his gaze from the subdued women to me. "I have no idea, but it was cool."

I wasn't quite as thrilled as him at the outcome. "I think I need to sit down."

He grabbed my elbow before I could sink to the ground next to the women. "Good idea. There's a table over here. We have a few things to talk about."

# THIRTEEN

*I*f Booker expected me to be able to explain what had happened, he was in for a rude awakening. Instead of peppering me with questions, though, he positioned me at a table that was cut off on two sides and then sat across from me as he curiously watched the women rouse themselves.

They appeared confused more than anything else but shame colored their features as they slowly came back to reality.

"Beth?" The blonde fixed her gaze on the brunette and frowned. "I ... um ... were we just fighting?"

Beth looked equally sheepish. "I think so, Brenda. I just don't know why."

"It was over this ring," I offered helpfully, holding up the item in question. "Do either of you want it now?"

Brenda furrowed her brow. "Um ... I think I'll pass. In fact, I'm not feeling so well — a little queasy really — and want to get home."

"Me, too." Beth avoided the other woman's gaze. "I don't know what just happened, but ... um ... I didn't mean any of it."

"Me either."

The women acted as if they were strangers, which I found interesting. The man running the flea market booth finally poked his head from behind the table and inclined his chin in my direction. "I'll be needing that ring back."

Booker collected it from me and tossed it to him. "Way to step in there, Doug. You really helped the situation."

Doug was having none of it. "My mother taught me at a young age that the last thing I wanted to do was step between two squabbling hens. That's one lesson of hers I'll take to the grave."

Booker rolled his eyes. "Yeah. You're a real prince, buddy." He was more sympathetic when he focused on Brenda and Beth. They appeared to be lost ... and yet they were in no hurry to scurry away despite their words. "I don't suppose you two could answer a few questions before you go?"

Beth was the first to raise her eyes. They were akin to brown death rays when they locked with Booker's more curious look. "And what questions would you like us to answer?" she spat.

"Look, you're obviously embarrassed." He had a pragmatic way about him and refused to back down. "I get it. If it's any consolation, I don't think you ladies were acting out because you had a deep desire for a cheap ring."

"This ring is an heirloom," Doug shot back.

"That ring will turn someone's finger green," Booker argued. "That's not the point, though. The point is that Beth and Brenda are friends. I know because I see them walking the beach together several times a week. They're always laughing and having a good time. What happened today was out of character."

"And you think something was done to us?" Brenda straightened her shoulders and then, to my surprise, glared at me. "I wonder who could've done it."

I was taken aback. "I didn't do it. In case you didn't notice, I'm the one who stopped you."

"Maybe you knew how to stop us because you're the one who caused it," Beth suggested. She was obviously warming to the idea, because she lobbed a threatening look in my direction as she dusted off the seat of her pants. "We were perfectly fine until you guys showed up."

"And how do you know when we showed up?" Booker challenged. He seemed to be taking umbrage with the insinuations. "You were already arguing when we saw you. Hadley didn't do this."

"How do you know?" Brenda folded her arms over her chest and glared at Moonstone Bay's resident jack-of-all-trades. "You don't know her any better than we do. The grapevine is thick with gossip about her. People say she's more than just a normal witch. How else do you think she got Galen?"

"By being cute," Galen announced, joining the cluster. He looked out of breath, as if he'd run the entire way to the festival. It was obvious someone had contacted him. I'd forgotten about making the call two seconds after Booker suggested it. "What's going on?"

Brenda and Beth had the grace to look abashed, but that didn't stop them from casting hateful glares at me. Booker answered the question. He kept the story short, was careful to keep talk of my magical intervention to a minimum, and when he was finished Galen merely shook his head.

"So ... more people acting out of sorts?" He rubbed his chin as he shifted his eyes to me. Something heavy passed between us, but he made sure to keep his distance. I had a feeling that was because he didn't want the two women later claiming he'd played favorites. "May I see the ring?"

Doug held it out for Galen's inspection. "It's a valuable piece."

"It's tin and a glass stone," Galen shot back, returning the ring to Doug's open palm. "I don't think the ring is bewitched."

"No," Booker agreed. "Someone managed to make them act like middle-schoolers fighting over the last boy at the homecoming dance, though."

Beth's cheeks flooded with color. "It was her." She pointed directly at me. "There's no other explanation. She was at the beach yesterday when that cupid walked into the surf. She's been present for both instances."

My heart dropped. I should've seen this coming. "I didn't do anything."

"Of course you didn't." Galen cast me a silencing look. He clearly didn't want me wallowing in the mud with my accuser. "Beth is just embarrassed because she made a fool of herself in public. Three different people called to tell me what was going on. And guess what? Not one of them mentioned Hadley's involvement."

"That doesn't mean she's not to blame," Beth sputtered. "Everything was fine on this island until she showed up. Now weird things happen all the time."

"Yes, everything was normal on the island that has zombies wandering the cemetery every night. I'm the one who made things weird."

Booker snorted. "She has a point, Beth. Besides, I was with her the entire time. She didn't do anything. We were talking about how garish the red and pink decorations were before we heard you guys arguing."

"Do you hear that, sheriff?" Beth's tone had teeth. "Booker spent the afternoon with your girlfriend and now he's serving as her alibi. How does that make you feel?"

"As if you're trying to make yourself feel better at Hadley's expense," Galen replied without hesitation. "She didn't do this and I'm not going to sit around and listen to you spout nonsense. For now, I want you to head home and cool off. I'll be around tomorrow to talk to you again. You might want to change your attitude."

"Oh, so basically you're saying that as long as someone is sleeping with you she can hex the entire town to do whatever amuses her and nothing will happen?" Beth jerked her head in a manner that reminded me of an angry chicken. "Well, that's just great. Where can I sign up for that treatment? I don't know if I'm looking forward to the sex or special treatment more."

Galen's eyes narrowed to dangerous slits and I recognized the fury rolling off him. "How far do you want to push me, Beth? I could arrest you right now for disturbing the peace. You're also throwing around false accusations. I'd be very careful how far you take this."

"Come on." Brenda tentatively reached over and grabbed her friend's wrist. "We should get out of here. We're just making things worse by hanging around this long."

"You've got that right," Galen muttered, dragging a hand through his inky black hair. "Just ... go. I'll talk to you again tomorrow."

"We're going, sheriff." Brenda appeared nervous. "She didn't mean any disrespect."

"I know what she meant." Galen wet his lips as he waited for them to leave and then focused his full attention on me. Most of the festival guests had already gone back to their normal activities, so no one was paying attention to us. "I see your bag of tricks keeps growing."

I didn't know what to say. "It just happened."

"Whatever it was, she did a good job," Booker offered. "It was as if she managed to un-curse both of them with one shot. It was pretty interesting."

"And I'm dying to hear about it." He extended his hand. "Come on. Let's get some lunch — somewhere else — and we'll talk about it."

That was a nice offer and I was all for it. I remained worried, though. "I swear I didn't make them act that way," I offered as I took his hand.

"Of course you didn't." He gave me a reassuring squeeze as he looked to his left to make sure Booker was sticking with us. "Let's head to Lilac's. They have her famous shrimp boil on special today."

Booker brightened considerably. "That sounds right up my alley."

"Then we'll talk." His smile was thin-lipped when he aimed it at me. "I know you didn't curse anyone, Hadley. You don't have to keep reassuring me. I know you and what you're capable of. That's not in your wheelhouse."

"You seem to be the only one who thinks so," I muttered.

Galen and Booker exchanged unreadable looks. "Not the only one," he said after a beat. "People who know you are on your side. As for the rest ... it doesn't matter. I don't care about their opinions. I only care about figuring out the truth. On that front, I have some information to share."

My interest was officially piqued. "What? Do you know what's happening?"

"Not here. Wait until we're at the restaurant."

I sighed. "Okay. But I want a big bucket of shrimp."

He smiled. "You've worked up quite the appetite, huh? You've had two big showings of magic in less than sixteen hours. That has to be a new record."

I hadn't considered that. "I want cheesecake, too."

"I think you've earned it."

**GALEN PICKED THE QUIETEST CORNER** of Lilac's bar to settle in. He sat on one side of the booth with me, our backs to the wall, and Booker sat across from us.

"You guys look like you're in plotting mode," Lilac announced as she delivered glasses of water. "Do I even want to know what's going on? Check that. If it's anything like the gossip I'm hearing, I think I'll take a pass."

"What gossip are you hearing?" Galen asked. "And how did the gossip beat us here? It just happened."

"Yes, well, Brenda and Beth have big mouths and they were apparently stopping anyone they could find on the street to tell them Hadley is doling out curses."

My stomach sank. "This is the worst."

Galen patted my knee under the table. "It's going to be okay. I promise. You don't need to get worked up or anything. This will die down ... and fast."

I wasn't so sure. "People are afraid of me." The realization hit like two trains colliding. "Ever since I found out what I was, I thought it would be cool to learn certain things, magical stuff and the like. But I don't want people to be afraid of me."

Galen slid me a sidelong look. "People aren't afraid of you."

"I don't know what festival you were just at, but people are definitely afraid of me."

"Fear isn't necessarily a bad thing," Booker pointed out. "Once word of what she did today spreads, that might stop whoever is trying to go after her. Would you mess with the woman who magically managed to bring two women to their knees in three seconds flat?"

"Wait ... I think I'm missing part of the story." Lilac's nose wrinkled. "Catch me up."

Booker and Galen did, with zest, while I stared at the table and contemplated my lot in life. Fear was a funny thing. I always wanted to be the woman in control, the sort of person who awed everyone she came in contact with, but I never wanted people to feel fear simply because of my presence.

Once the men were finished with the story, Lilac took our orders and then disappeared into the kitchen without saying another word. I figured she wanted to put as much distance between us as possible – until she returned with a slice of cheesecake and slid it in front of me.

"I think you need that." Her gaze was kind as I flashed a sheepish smile. "I can already tell you've had a long day."

"And that's on top of the protective bubble she conjured last night to protect herself from whoever was following her on the highway," Galen added. "She's definitely had a full few hours."

"Don't forget the sleepwalking," Booker added. "That's actually our biggest concern right now. We know she's not cursing people to drown themselves or fight. But the sleepwalking, that's something we should definitely be worried about."

"You have been busy." Lilac slid into the booth next to Booker and rested her hands on the table as she considered the conundrum. "It has to be the cupids," she said finally. "A lot of paranormals can influence humans and other paranormals, make them do things, but the timing seems to suggest we're looking at a cupid."

"That's what I think," Booker agreed. "But I'm wondering if it's not a full cupid. Perhaps someone is overcompensating for something."

"He picked a funny way to do it ... if it's a him," Lilac mused.

"I think it's probably a man."

"Except the victims are men and women," Lilac pointed out. "David and that cupid Hadley pulled out of the water were male. Hadley, Beth and Brenda are all female."

"She has a point," Galen said. "We can't be sure it's a man. It could just as easily be a woman."

"Fair enough." Booker held up his hands in defeat. "We need to figure out who it is no matter what. I don't think the guilty party will stop unless we stop him or her. So far, only David has died. There have been no other instances besides the ones we've already heard about."

"That we know of," Galen cautioned. "I've had my men looking for people trying to kill themselves. What happened today between Beth and Brenda suggests that's not all I should be looking for. Maybe I should be pulling assault reports, too."

"How many assaults happen on the island on any given day?" I asked.

"A few," Galen replied. "I've been caught up with this and haven't checked to see what else is going on. I will once I get back to the station."

"It can't hurt," Booker agreed. "You said you had other information for us. Spill."

"I have the autopsy results for David Fox." Galen turned grim. "There are a few interesting things to note. First, he died from the fall. He had no other injuries that weren't consistent with that fall."

"Were you expecting other injuries?" I asked. "I didn't realize we thought that was a possibility."

"I wasn't expecting anything. I was open to all manner of things. It turns out, other than the head injury and broken bones, he was fine. There were no marks on his wrists ... or scars ... or anything that would suggest he'd previously tried to harm himself."

"Oh." Realization dawned. "If he was really suicidal, you think he would've had a few failed attempts under his belt before he managed to pull it off. That's pretty normal, right?"

"Pretty much."

"Men usually use a gun or rope to kill themselves," Lilac noted. "Women use pills or contain it to the bathtub. I read a study once. It said that women are more worried about who has to clean up the mess."

Her matter-of-fact tone put me off. "That's a lovely thing to have in my head."

"I'm just saying." Lilac smirked at my discomfort. "If he really was suicidal, we might not know it. He could've put a gun to his head ten times and we wouldn't be able to tell."

"Fair enough," Galen acquiesced. "I can't do anything about that. I'm still waiting for full toxicology reports, but the medical examiner did find something odd in his blood."

Booker leaned forward. "Don't leave us in suspense, man!"

"I don't know."

"You don't know?"

"I don't know." Galen held his hands palms out and shrugged. "The medical examiner is stumped. He's calling for more tests and trying to see if he can find a lab on the mainland that can help."

"Do you think the compound is responsible for what's happening?" I couldn't help getting excited. "If you figure out what it is, can we make an antidote?"

"We have to figure out what it is first."

"I know that."

"I'm not a scientist," he reminded me. "That's above my pay grade. Unless you have a scientist you can tap, we have to wait for the lab to come through."

Actually, I had an idea on that front. "What about Aisling's brother?"

"The mouthy reaper who just left two weeks ago? You want to contact her brother?" Galen looked horrified. "Why?"

"Because she said her brother Cillian could find out anything, that he was the brain of the family and a full-on genius. I think that it might be worth a shot. I've been meaning to Skype her anyway. I don't see why we can't at least ask for help."

Galen looked caught. "Do we have to call her?" he whined after a moment's contemplation. "She's mean."

"You just don't like that she bosses you around."

"She's like a tiny drill sergeant," he complained. "Still, you have a point. The reapers have extensive resources. I might be able to get them a sample and see what they say."

"Thank you." I blessed him with an impulsive hug. "If we can find out what this compound is, I just know we can combat it."

"And if it's some sort of poison you'll be off the hook," Booker deduced. "You don't want it to be a curse."

I was embarrassed to admit he was right. "Let's just focus on one thing at a time," I suggested, digging into my cheesecake. "Let's identify the compound and go from there."

Galen rubbed the tense muscles at the nape of my neck. "That sounds like a plan."

## FOURTEEN

*J* wanted to call Aisling on the computer as soon as I got back to the lighthouse. Galen politely asked if I would wait ... and then gave me "the look" when I started whining. Ultimately I gave in when he pointed out that I wouldn't be able to explain about the compound until he had a breakdown from the medical examiner. He had a point, so I spent the afternoon with Booker going through books and peppering him with questions about cupids.

After two hours, he stopped answering and pretended he was deaf. I might as well have been alone. By the time Galen showed up with dinner after his shift, Booker couldn't get out the door fast enough.

"Is something on fire?" Galen asked lazily as Booker slid into his shoes.

"I don't know how you put up with her." Booker's dark hair was wild from running his hands through it at regular intervals. "All she does is talk."

"You didn't want her to do anything else, did you?" Galen pinned Booker with a pointed look. There was no doubt about his reference.

"Oh, get over yourself." Booker made a hilarious face. "She might have that added something that has cupids from all over sniffing around — and don't kid yourself, they're definitely looking — but most people couldn't put up with the nonstop chatter."

Galen's expression was fond as he handed me a bag of Chinese food. "Did you drive Booker up the wall?"

"I was just asking him questions." I jutted out my lower lip. "They weren't invasive or anything."

"You asked me if the first girl I ever had sex with thought I smelled like chocolate chip cookies, and whether my mother explained about the birds and the bees. How much more invasive can you get?"

Well, that was a loaded question. "Do you really want me to try?"

"No." He moved toward the door in a huff. "I need some air. You swallow all the oxygen in a room."

Galen chuckled as he smoothed my hair. "You'll be available if I need you tomorrow?"

I expected a resounding "No." Instead, Booker just nodded. "Call me in the morning. I might have stuff going on. If we have to, we can drag Hadley along with us. Although ... you could just drop her in Lilac's bar. She's looking for a job. She can fill in there for the day. No one would dare take on Lilac. People are talking about her nonstop again since the cult thing."

"I know, and she's not happy about it." Galen absently moved his hand to my arm. He was obviously in a touchy-feely mood, which I found interesting. "I'll consider it. I'll let you know what's going on in the morning."

"I can't wait." Booker slammed the door so hard on his way out it rattled some of the photos May had left hanging. I hadn't gotten around to changing any of the decorations, though I was seriously considering it ... once I talked to my dead grandmother and okayed it with her, that is. It's hell being roommates with a ghost.

"He didn't even say goodbye," I noted.

Galen tipped up my chin and planted a long kiss on my lips. "That's okay," he said when we separated. I was a little breathless and giddy thanks to the effort he put in. "I'm here to say hello."

I smiled. "Hello."

"Hello." He kissed me again. "Now come on. We'll set up dinner in the living room at the table and then call your buddy."

I'd almost forgotten I was going to get to see Aisling again. I'd texted her, explaining what was going on, and she said she would be available at her father's house when I was ready to Skype. I was kind of excited ... which made me feel a bit foolish.

As if reading my mind, Galen tilted his head to the side. "You're feeling girlie and happy, aren't you?"

"Is that a bad thing?"

"Nope. It's better than how you were feeling this afternoon when you kept telling me you weren't to blame. Just for the record, I don't blame you for this. I won't pretend there won't be times when you do something wrong — or that agitates me — but this is not on you. I don't want you thinking that."

Emotion was naked in his eyes and it warmed me all over. "I won't blame myself again. It's just ... I don't want people to fear me."

"Yes, you do. On this island, that's a benefit."

"Fine. I don't want the people I care about to fear me."

"All Booker is afraid of is your mouth. Lilac isn't afraid of anything, because she doesn't have to be. As for me, I'm afraid for you, not of you."

"That's kind of sweet."

"I'm a sweet guy." He gave me one more kiss and then gestured toward the table. "Let's get set up. I'm starving, and I'm betting you and your little buddy will chat half the night away once you get going. I'd like to get the important stuff out of the way and then turn on a game while you ... talk about whatever it is you two talk about."

"Mostly we talk about the men in our lives."

"I pity that poor fool she married." He shook his head. His relationship with Aisling was tempestuous. She got what she wanted in life — no matter what — and she didn't care who she ran over in the process. He liked rules and boundaries. They didn't mix ... and yet they had a grudging respect for one another. It was interesting to watch. "Let's get this show on the road, shall we? I got crab rangoon and spring rolls."

"Yum."

**I'M NOT TECHNOLOGICALLY CHALLENGED** or anything, but Galen is better with computers. He had the call up and running within five minutes, and I was impressed when Aisling answered and I got a gander at the room behind her. There were marble statues, expensive settees and a bar cart that looked as if it cost more than my first car.

"Wow. You weren't lying about your father living in a castle."

Aisling's long dark hair, which was shot through with white streaks, was pulled back in a loose bun. She sat on one of the settees and fanned herself. She looked as if she was putting on a show ... and then I realized her face was red and she was sweating.

"Is something wrong?" I asked, instantly worried. She was pregnant and the thought of her losing the baby was horrifying.

"Something is definitely wrong. It's a hundred degrees in this house and my devil baby doesn't like it. Open a window or something!" she ordered someone off screen.

Behind her, I saw multiple dark-haired men scrambling into the background to do her bidding. Aisling's family genes were the sort that you apparently couldn't escape. She and her four brothers looked exactly like their father, who I had also had the good fortune to meet. He was the reason Aisling was so spoiled, but he was a dedicated father and smart man, especially when it came to paranormal issues.

"Is everyone there?" I asked when bodies started to settle.

"Everyone is here," she said, briefly smiling when a dark-haired man who looked nothing like her handed her a glass of a clear liquid. "Thank you."

Griffin Taylor, her husband, sat on the couch next to her and instantly positioned himself so her feet were resting in his lap. He started rubbing without complaint.

"Hi, guys." He grinned at Galen and me. "How's life on the island?"

"Busy," Galen replied. He looked as impressed with the house as I felt. "Maybe we'll have to arrange a visit to Michigan one day. I would love to see that place."

"It keeps the rain off," Aisling said dryly, causing me to laugh. "What's going on with you guys?"

I opened my mouth to answer, but Galen held up his hand to quiet me. "How about I start? Once we get done with the part of the conversation I need to be present for, you two can talk about whatever you desire. How does that sound?"

"Like you're just as bossy as I remember," Aisling replied darkly.

"Look who's talking." Galen pinned her with a dark look through the computer screen, but he couldn't hide his smile. "You look pretty good. Obviously pregnancy agrees with you."

"Not really. I have heartburn every morning ... and at night. My back hurts. My ankles are swollen. And my boobs are already bigger. Griffin likes it, but I need new bras."

"Aisling! That is not the sort of thing one says on the internet," a male — and grouchy — voice barked from the background. I couldn't see the speaker but recognized the voice.

"Tell your father I said hi."

Aisling snickered. "He's camera shy. Seriously, though, what's going on?"

Galen launched into the tale. When he finished, the Grimlock brothers who had been buzzing about before were grouped around the computer and listening. They were obviously fascinated.

"Well, that sounds stupid," Aisling announced. "I can't believe someone has been trying to lure you out of the lighthouse. You should get on that, Galen."

Galen growled softly. "Thanks for the tip," he snarked. "I never would've thought of that. I'm so glad we called."

Griffin very deliberately squeezed Aisling's feet to get her attention and shook his head before speaking. "I'm not familiar with cupids. I don't think we've run into any ... other than that guy we met while we were there. The one my lovely wife sniffed constantly."

"That scent is quite the aphrodisiac," Aisling agreed, smiling sweetly at her husband. "I guess it's good that I was already knocked up by you, huh?"

"Yes, we're all thrilled about that," Cormack Grimlock, Aisling's father, said as he appeared on screen. "This compound, can you get a sample to us? We can have our lab techs look it over."

"I can send one out in the morning," Galen replied. "I'm guessing you've never heard anything like this before."

"We've heard weird things, but Griffin is correct. We haven't crossed paths with cupids much. We probably wouldn't notice even if we did ... other than Aisling rubbing herself against strangers because she thinks they have cookies."

"Ha, ha." Aisling rolled her eyes and made me laugh. "Cillian can conduct some research, right?" She looked to her long-haired brother. They all looked alike but he stood out in a fashion model sort of way.

"I can see what information we have at the reaper library," he offered. He didn't appear put out about his sister volunteering his time. "It doesn't strike a chord with me, but I'm more than willing to look."

"Thank you. We're in your debt."

Aisling opened her mouth again but Galen cut her off.

"We're not that far in debt," he said. "Whatever you're thinking, mouth, think again. We'll visit when we have time."

"Oh, you're such a joy," Aisling drawled. "Is that all the business stuff then? Hadley and I want to talk in private for a bit. That means all the men have to leave."

"Gladly." Galen kissed the top of my head. "Come find me and we'll go for a walk before bed. I'll be watching the game in the other room."

I waved him off. "Sure." I smiled brightly at Aisling. "So, can you take me on a tour of the house with the laptop?"

"Absolutely. I'll show you the basement where the snakes live."

"There are no snakes in the basement, Aisling," Cormack barked. "For crying out loud, why must you be such a pain?"

"I think I inherited it from you."


**AISLING AND I SPENT TWO HOURS** on the call. I felt better when we were finished. I told her some of the things I'd been worried about — including what the warring women accused me of earlier in the afternoon — and her rebuttal of their words was much more colorful than Galen's. By the time I collected him for our walk, I was almost chipper.

"I know you don't like her, but she makes me laugh."

We held hands as we walked the beach, the moonlight glinting off the placid waves. The wind was much lighter today.

"I didn't say I didn't like her," he countered. "I said she's a pain in the behind."

"I think she's fun."

"I think she's a hellion, and if karma is real she'll get a kid exactly like her."

Funnily enough, Aisling thought that, too. "Are you still worried about me?" I lifted my eyes to study his strong profile. "I'll be okay. You know that, right?"

"I do know that," he confirmed, squeezing my hand. "You'll be okay because we'll both make sure of it."

"I smelled the smell again today. The one that reminds me of rancid honey. I've been thinking about it. Do you think it's possible that I smell it because it's a bad cupid? I mean ... normal people are supposed to smell good things when they're around cupids because it attracts them. What if I smell something bad because something inside of me recognizes I'm up against a monster?"

He exhaled heavily and skirted to the side as two men, neither of whom I recognized, passed us. They both jerked their heads in my direction as they crossed beyond us, and Galen met their gazes with a challenging one of his own.

"Can I help you?" he asked pointedly.

"What?" One of the men, the blonder of the two, looked momentarily dazed as he dragged his eyes from me. "We're not doing anything. We're just walking."

"I know what you were doing." Galen tugged me closer and continued to glare. "Keep going."

"Okay. Chill out, dude."

Galen rolled his eyes until they landed on me. "What were you saying?"

I opened my mouth to answer but giggling a few feet away caught my attention. This time it was two women walking past, and they were clearly fixated on the men we'd just seen. I watched them go, my lips curving down.

"It's busy out here tonight," I said finally. "We usually have the whole place to ourselves."

"I noticed." Galen stiffened, his head whipping around as if he sensed someone following us. He growled — no, he actually growled — when he realized the men were circling back. "You've got to be kidding me."

I followed his gaze. "They're probably just heading back to where they came," I offered, although I had my doubts. Those doubts were reinforced when I realized they were both staring at me, and walking with a purpose. "Or they're idiots."

"They clearly want me to beat them," Galen groused. "Seriously, I thought we would have a nice walk. You know, a little light romance out here before I romance you the proper way in the lighthouse. They're ruining it."

The night definitely wasn't going as planned, but I very much doubted it was ruined. "Just ignore them." I tugged on his arm. "Focus on me."

Nothing could force him to stop glaring at the men. They slowed their pace as they approached, but they didn't turn away this time. "What do you want?" Galen demanded, his voice dropping an octave.

"We're just curious." The blond man spoke. He appeared to be the designated speaker of the group. "What are you?"

The question was directed to me. "I'm an Aquarius," I replied. "What about you?"

"That's not what I meant." He shook his head and ignored the giggling behind him. The women had returned, too. They seemed engrossed in the men, though, and paid us little heed. "Why aren't you attracted to us?"

That's when I put it all together. "You're cupids and you're playing games. That's why those girls are acting like morons."

If the women heard me they didn't show it. They remained solely focused on the men.

"We're just having a little fun," the blonde replied. "You didn't even bother to look at us. I find that ... fascinating."

"Oh, yeah?" Galen had had enough. "You know what I find fascinating? Tying cinder blocks to cupids' ankles and dumping them in the ocean to see if they can swim."

"That was a little over-the-top," I noted.

He ignored me. "Keep going," he gritted out.

"We're not after your woman," blondie argued. "We're simply curious about what she is. This is a paranormal island, right? She must be something special."

"She is," Galen agreed, tugging me so I was directly in front of him. "But she's with me, so I think you should take your game someplace else."

"And if we don't, will you call the police?" The man played it coy. "I mean ... would you take it that far?"

"I'm the sheriff," Galen countered. "I don't have to call the police."

That was enough to have the man take a step back and swallow hard. "I'm sorry. We were just playing around."

"Well, knock it off." Galen prodded me in the direction of the lighthouse. "I know you see it as a challenge because she's not susceptible to your charms, but she's off limits. Spread the word."

"Consider it done."

Galen let loose a smile more grim than welcoming. "Great. Then we shouldn't have a problem."

## FIFTEEN

G alen was alert the entire way back to the lighthouse. He kept one arm around my back and both eyes open for any signs of movement. He pushed me through the door before locking it and then proceeded to prowl to each and every window to make sure it was locked before following me to the bedroom.

"You're kind of taking this to a weird level," I offered finally. "There's no reason to get as upset as you are."

He pinned me with a furious look. "Oh, really?" He shook his head so hard I thought he might fall over as he stripped off his shirt. His naked chest, I'm ashamed to admit, was enough to distract me. He looked like one of those men in a beefcake calendar he was so defined.

I lost my train of thought. "Um ... what was I saying?"

Despite the fact that we were on the verge of a fight, he smirked. "Come over here and I'll remind you what we were talking about."

His flirty tone snapped me back to reality. "Oh, right. We were talking about you acting like a Neanderthal with those guys we saw on the beach tonight. Don't you think your reaction was a bit much?"

"No." He answered without hesitation. "Didn't you see the way those guys were looking at you?"

"Um ... yeah. They were looking at me as if they were guys. That's fairly normal."

"No, they were looking at you harder than that. Word is spreading that you're seemingly immune to the cupids. That will make you a challenge for them."

He looked legitimately worried. "Are you afraid I'm going to run off with some guy I just met? I can promise you that won't happen."

"I know. It's just ... I don't like it." He looked so petulant I couldn't swallow my laughter.

"Well, you have to let it go." I was serious. "Believe it or not, despite your show of testosterone, I only have eyes for you."

He smiled. "That's a very nice thing to say. I wish you would come over here and show me."

"In a second. I want to talk about what happened tonight first."

"Oh, man." He rolled his eyes. "You aren't going to let this go, are you?"

"Not until I better understand what you're so afraid of. Don't you trust me?"

He balked. "I wouldn't be with you if I didn't trust you."

"So, what's the problem? If you trust me and we have free will in all this, what did you think was going to happen with those guys?"

"Well, it was a long shot, but I thought it was possible one of them — or maybe both of them — were the guys we were looking for. They were extremely intent on you and their location made me suspicious. I wanted to make sure they didn't try to hit you from behind and take you or anything."

"Oh." Well, crap. I hadn't even considered that. "I'm glad that didn't happen."

He lifted an eyebrow, amused. "I'm definitely glad that didn't happen. The thing is, I'm worried things will get worse. As word spreads that you're immune to the cupids, they'll turn it into a game."

"What sort of game?"

"The sort where they all compete to see which of them can seduce you."

"And, again, you have nothing to worry about."

"I'm not worried about you cheating on me." He was matter-of-fact. "The thing is, with that many cupids trying to invade your mind, you might not be able to hold them all off."

I was intrigued. "I thought you said free will always won out."

"With individual cupids, that's true. I'm betting you could even hold off three or four of them because you're you. What happens if seven of them try invading your mind at the same time? I would like to believe you'd have the fortitude to stand up, but we obviously don't know the answer to that.

"I want you safe, Hadley, and if that makes me a testosterone-fueled maniac, I'm not all that sorry," he continued. "The more attention you draw from the cupids, the more worried I get. If they see you as a challenge, they'll want to win that challenge."

I hadn't even considered that, but it made sense. "Huh." I tugged a tank top over my head and grabbed a pair of tiny sleep shorts as I shuffled toward the bed. Galen waited until I was under the covers to hit the light and join me. He wore a pair of boxer shorts and nothing else.

"Come here," he murmured when I was quiet for a long time, his arm slipping around my waist as he tugged me to him. His fingers were gentle as he brushed them over my face. "I trust you. If I've been making you feel otherwise, that's on me. It certainly wasn't my intention."

"I just don't want you thinking you can make all my decisions for me."

"When do I think that?"

"Occasionally, like when you order me to stay in the lighthouse and stuff."

"I always have your best interests at heart when I do things like that. You have a point, though. I'll try to request you do the smart thing for your safety instead of ordering it going forward."

That sounded too good to be true. "Can I ask you something?" I rested my head on his chest as he stroked his hand down my back. He was trying to lull me into sleep so I wouldn't keep him up all night with inane questions. I knew him.

"Sure."

"Have cupids ever banded together before to overwhelm certain individuals?"

He hesitated for far too long. Finally, he heaved a sigh and nodded. "Cupids aren't exactly respected in a lot of circles. They're considered tricksters of the highest order. Very few paranormals trust them."

"Why didn't you mention that?"

"Because you're very fond of Booker," he replied after a moment's contemplation. "At first, I didn't want to color your opinion of him. He and I don't always see eye to eye, but we respect each other. I doubt we'll ever be the best of friends because of everything that's gone down between us, but we're not enemies. We could've easily grown up to hate each other."

I could see that. "I think you're both too good to let personal grievances get in the way of the greater good."

"And I think you're giving us too much credit." He tweaked my nose. "We both love the island. We have a lot of the same friends. We respect one another. I think that's as good as it will ever get. Still, I trust him, and I didn't want you to be suspicious of him without reason.

"After you were already fond of him, well, there didn't seem to be a need to tell you," he continued. "This has only come up because so many other cupids are on the island. If he was the only one, you probably would've been saved this entire ordeal."

It was a lot to think about. I pressed my ear to the spot above his heart and closed my eyes. "You don't think whoever has been outside will come back, do you?"

"Not if he wants to live." He tightened his arms around me. "I'll be right here, Hadley. Don't be afraid to sleep. I won't let anything happen to you. I promise."

I could tell he meant it. "Okay. We never did get the romance, huh?" I was sliding into sleep faster than I'd imagined possible.

He rubbed his hands over my back and kissed my forehead. "There's always the morning to look forward to."

. . .

133

**I SLIPPED UNDER QUICKLY.** I didn't immediately dream, which was probably a good thing. When my mind grew animated hours later, though, I recognized right away that something was going on.

"What the ... ?" I woke in a circular room. The design had me believing it was a castle of some sort, although I had no idea if it was medieval or Disney. "Hello?" I called out even though I was certain no one was near. "Galen?"

I didn't expect him to answer. A rush of warmth washed over me as I remembered exactly where I really was. I was asleep, in bed, and Galen was still wrapped around me. This was the dream I had every night since the cupids showed up. I was well aware of my surroundings at this point.

"It's a castle with nothing fun," I muttered, tossing off the covers and frowning when I realized I was dressed in an ornate gown. This detail was different from the previous dreams. "Oh, well ... this is weird."

The dress was an ethereal blue, so pale it was almost white. It was luminescent, which caused me to flick my eyes toward the mirror on the wall. I looked like a Cinderella wannabe, which was interesting on a variety of different levels. Matching gloves sat on the dresser and there were glass slippers waiting for me to slide my feet into them. I wisely sidestepped both and headed for the door.

"I don't like this," I muttered. I was talking to myself as I tested the handle. I didn't expect anyone to answer. Still, there was a whisper ... and it sent chills down my spine.

*Come to me.*

I frowned at the voice, jerking my head to the left and the right. I was alone in the room. Still, I didn't feel isolated. Someone — or more likely, some thing — was close and ready to make itself known.

"You know, I don't appreciate games," I called out. "This whole seduction bit you've got going with the Cinderella gown is nice and all, but you missed your mark with me. I never fancied myself a Disney princess."

As if on cue, the dress I wore swirled and was replaced with something that looked authentic and straight from medieval times. "Also off the mark."

*Tell me what you desire and I will make it happen.*

"Aren't you supposed to know what I desire?" I grabbed the bedroom door handle and turned it. Unlike previous dreams, it didn't open so I could discover another room to explore. That was even more distressing than the strange voice. "If you try to keep me locked in this room, it'll only tick me off. That's not much of an aphrodisiac, for the record."

*Tell me what your heart yearns for.*

"You're supposed to already know," I shot back, frustration getting the better of me. "I don't understand why you're doing this. If it's to prove that you're the mightiest cupid on the block, you might as well stop now. This isn't going to work. I already have a favorite cupid, and you're not him."

*I can give you everything you've ever wanted.*

I thought of Galen, cuddled next to me in bed. "I already have that. There's nothing you can offer that's better than the life I'm already leading."

*I could make you forget him.*

"You can't. He's part of me already. He owns the largest spot in my heart. You can't remove him from that place because he belongs there."

*Whatever lies he's been telling you, I can make you forget him.*

"No, you can't."

*I can.*

"It's not possible." I was firm on that. I believed it with my whole heart. Galen said I had free will and I believed him. There was a reason he wanted me to know that. It was so I could stand up to the dream monster ... whoever he was. "How about you stop hiding behind fancy smoke-and-mirror tricks and show yourself? Don't you think you've been playing it coy for far too long?"

Silence, for a long time. Then, the slow hiss of annoyance. *I could end him,* the voice whispered. *Not in this dream either. I could end him in the real world. Who would protect you then?*

My blood ran cold. "I don't need protection," I snapped. "I can protect myself ... and him. Don't even bother trying to go after him. He'll rip you from limb to limb. I'll be with him when it happens. I'll hurt you, too."

*Ah, there it is.* The voice sounded smug. *Your fear is for him, not yourself. That's interesting. It means you're a giving person.*

"I don't care what it means." My voice was laced with venom as I struggled with the door handle. "Let me out of here right now!"

*I thought you could protect yourself. More importantly, I thought you could protect him.*

For the first time since I woke in the dream, fear threatened to take over. I couldn't help wondering if the creature was keeping me busy in the dream so he could kill Galen in the real world. The mere thought was enough to send my heart rate skyrocketing as I redoubled my efforts on the door.

"Let me out!" Magic burst forth in conjunction with my temper and the door blew off its hinges. I was through it before I could think about which direction I should head. And when I plunged through the door I landed in reality.


**"WHAT'S GOING ON?"**

My eyes went wide when I escaped from the dream and realized I was sitting on the floor next to my bedroom window. Galen, in his wolf form, was battling with a man. Growls filled the room as the wolf grabbed the man's arm and bit hard.

I scrambled away from the fight and took stock of my surroundings. The window was open, which meant I had probably opened it ... or somehow the man fighting Galen was stronger than we realized. I didn't recognize him. He had dirty blond hair and what looked like strange talons for fingers. He was moving too fast for me to get a good look at him.

Galen, his dark fur gleaming under the muted moonlight, fought furiously. His jaws continuously snapped and he grabbed the man by his forearm at some point and viciously ripped at his skin.

For the first time since I woke, the man made a sound ... and it wasn't happiness speaking. He shrieked in pain, which allowed me to remember that I wasn't some helpless waif who could do nothing but cringe in a corner while her boyfriend fought to the death. No, I had a few tricks in my arsenal, too.

"Enough." I bellowed as I got to my feet. Galen slowed his attack, as if surprised by my reaction, but the man was another story. He took advantage of Galen's confusion to reach into his pocket and draw out a dagger of some sort. I recognized his plan a split second before he could slam the weapon into Galen's chest.

In an instant I used the pooling magic to blow Galen clear of the man. At the same time, I wrapped my magic around the man's throat and slammed him against the wall. "Don't touch him," I ordered, furious.

Galen shifted into human form and hurried to my side. "Don't kill him," he warned. "We need him."

"You cannot contain me," the man rasped, fighting against my magic. "I am more powerful than you can imagine."

"Yeah, yeah, yeah." I wasn't impressed. "That's why you have to go into dreams to get girls. You're powerful."

"You have no idea." The man pushed back with his own magic, something I wasn't expecting, and managed to loosen my grip. I reared back as something cold knifed into my head and forced me to drop him. "You've still got a lot to learn, witch," he hissed before diving out the window.

I reared back, surprised at the cold clap trying to encompass my brain. Galen caught me rather than giving chase and slowly lowered me to the ground.

"I've got you," he whispered as I pooled my magic to push out the invader. "You're okay. Just stay with me."

There was no place I would rather be than with him. Still, the outside magic was threatening to take over.

"Hold on," I gritted out as I pressed my eyes shut. "He left me with a parting gift."

Worry clouded Galen's eyes. "Do I even want to know what that means?"

"Probably not. I ... hold on." The magic I was still getting a handle on listened as I commanded it to seek out the invader and destroy it. My blood rioted as the unseen forces collided. My magic was much stronger and eradicated the threat quickly. I was still breathless when I finished.

"That wasn't so bad, huh?"

Galen's gaze was dubious. "Speak for yourself. Don't ever do that again, by the way."

I was confused. "What? Save you? I'm allowed to save you as often as you're allowed to save me. Those are the rules of feminism."

He chuckled as he pulled me in for a hug. "Not that. You scared the life out of me. You were almost out the window this time. He managed to keep me away from you until the last second when you woke up. He was going to take you out of the room and there was nothing I could do about it." He rested his cheek against my forehead. "We need to figure this out because he's going to come back."

He was right. I knew that deep down. "Did you recognize him? He's a cupid, right?"

"I didn't recognize him and he is most definitely not a cupid."

I furrowed my brow and shifted so I could stare into his eyes. "If he's not a cupid, what is he?"

"An incubus."

I wasn't sure that was an answer. "Is that a different sort of paranormal creature?"

"Yes."

"Well, great. That's exactly what we need." I threw my hands up in frustration. "Why can't things ever be simple?"

He snorted as he held me tight and rocked. "The most important thing is that we're together and you're safe. The rest of it ... well ... we'll figure it out. I promise I won't stop until we have all the answers and you're safe."

I believed him completely.

## SIXTEEN

$\mathcal{W}$e stood like that for a long time before Galen pulled back to study my face.

"What happened with you? Why did you open the window?"

I frowned. "I didn't open the window. I mean ... did I?" I was confused. "I don't remember opening the window. He had me trapped in a castle room and was trying to ply me with Cinderella stuff."

He cocked his head. "I ... don't understand."

"Welcome to the club. It was different from the other dreams. He kept me in a room and there was this weird dress ... and shoes ... and he whispered for me to find him."

Galen calmly ordered my hair. "Did you want to find him?"

He asked the question calmly, but I knew what he was really worried about. "No, I most certainly did not. I told him Cinderella wasn't the way to my heart, and then I tried to get out of the bedroom."

His eyebrows drew together. "Did you say anything in the dream when you tried to unlock the door?"

"Does it matter?"

"It might. You were muttering when you unlocked the window."

I understood what he was getting at. "Oh, um ... let me think." I rubbed my forehead. A tension headache was brewing and I wanted nothing more than to lie down. I didn't think that was a good idea, though. That's how we got in this mess in the first place. "I think I was just complaining about being locked in."

"Could you have said 'I don't like this' before trying to get out? That's what I thought I heard you say."

"Probably."

He cupped my face. "He didn't hurt you in the dream, did he?"

His gaze was earnest, but I was fixated on the marks I found on his arm. I didn't initially see them. "What happened here?" I gently grabbed his forearm and looked closer. He'd been cut ... by something extremely sharp. "How did this happen?"

"The incubus did it. That's how I knew he was an incubus instead of a cupid. His hands shifted."

"Huh. Does it hurt?"

He offered me a small smile. "You can kiss it and make it better if you want."

He was joking but I did just that. "I'll get some antiseptic."

He protested, said it wasn't necessary, that he would heal overnight, but I went anyway. My mind was muddled. Then, out of nowhere, I remembered something from weeks before. I had peroxide and bandages when I returned ... and a huge problem.

"Um ... I just remembered something."

The window was shut and locked tight again, and he'd used a hair scrunchie to wrap the handles tight to add another layer of safety. It didn't matter. I was certain sleep was out of reach for me.

"Please tell me it's not your birth control." He was going for levity but the joke fell flat.

"It's not my birth control. I have an implant." I held up my arm by way of proof, although he couldn't see the implant, so it was completely unnecessary. "Do you remember the day right after I landed on the island when Ned Baxter took me out on his boat to kill me?"

"Do you really think I would forget that day?" His eyes darkened.

"I only wish I would've killed him instead of letting Wesley have the honors."

I preferred not thinking about that part so I herded him toward the bed instead. "There was a moment with Booker when I thought I saw his hand shift. It happened really fast and there was too much going on for me to focus on it, but ... if the incubus shifted and hurt you, does that mean Booker is an incubus, too? I don't even know what an incubus is."

"Come here."

He tried to pull me onto his lap but I fought the effort. "I have to fix you. It's important."

He let loose a dramatic sigh but held out his arm. "This would be more fun if you were dressed in a skimpy nurse's costume."

"Maybe you'll get your wish for Halloween ... although I'm thinking I want to be Wonder Woman this year."

"Aren't you Wonder Woman every day?"

He was charming when he wanted to be. "I'm being serious. I swear I saw something that day."

"I'm sure you did." He licked his lips and I got the distinct impression he was choosing his words carefully. "The thing is, cupids can shift. Not all of them. Heck, not even most of them. Only a rare few can do it. Booker is one of them. It runs in his family."

Huh. You learn something new every day. "Why can he shift?"

"At one time all cupids could shift."

"And they can't now?"

"No. The lines got diluted. That's why there are seven powerful families now. They had the most undiluted lines. They tried for years to breed out the weak lines but it was already too late."

I didn't feel as if I was catching up, merely falling further behind. "Galen, I need to understand. You can't just tell me what you think I need to know. I want to hear all of it."

He blew out a sigh and pinched the bridge of his nose. "I told Booker this was going to happen. He doesn't want me to tell you. He thinks it will frighten you."

"I don't care. I need to know. This involves me as much as him now. There's a strange man trying to entice me to jump from a two-story window."

"Actually, I think he's trying to do something else." Galen looked grim. "I'll get to that part. Will you do me a favor and get comfortable in bed for this? I think you need to relax."

"That's not going to happen."

"The getting in bed part or the relaxing?"

"Both."

"But ... I'm in pain and need to lie down." He held up his bandaged arm and caused me to roll my eyes.

"Fine. I'll lie down. But I refuse to sleep."

He held up the covers so I could crawl underneath. He wisely left the lamp on the nightstand lit when he snuggled down with me. "If only there were something else we could do in a bed besides sleep," he lamented.

"If you think I'm going to fall for that, you're a crackhead. Spill."

"Okay." He tugged so I was pressed to his side and then stared at the ceiling, perhaps gathering his thoughts. "Cupids are old. They're so old they date back to the early Greeks. We're talking before Jesus Christ. They were something else then, though."

"What?"

"Elementals."

"I don't know what that is."

"To break it down to its barest form, elementals can control powers that derive from the elements. That would include earth elements, fire, water and air."

"So ... they're magical fire starters?"

He laughed despite the serious nature of the conversation. "They're more than that. They were powerful beings. They were only supposed to breed with each other, but as you know, the heart can't be contained that way. Over time, they started breeding with others ... including humans and other paranormals.

"Air elementals turned into our modern cupids today," he continued. "They're nowhere near as powerful as they used to be. In their natural form, they looked like magical hyenas. I guess that's the best way to describe them."

"Are you saying Booker is a hyena? I don't think he's going to like that."

"I guarantee he's not going to like that. It's the truth, though. Elementals waged a war long before this continent was even conquered. They wiped out most of their own beings. After the war, the four contingencies broke apart and became separate entities."

"So ... air elementals became cupids. What about the others?"

He shifted a bit, uncomfortable. "It doesn't really matter for the purposes of this conversation."

"Galen." My voice was low and full of warning. "I mean it. I need to know."

"Ugh." He rubbed his forehead. Perhaps my incoming headache was catchy. "Water elementals became the merrow, or merfolk."

Something clicked in my head. "Sirens are merfolk, right?"

"Yup."

"So ... Aurora."

He didn't confirm my suspicion. Of course, he didn't need to. I already knew. "Fire elementals became demons."

"Oh, geez." I had already figured out where he was going. "And earth elementals?"

"They became witches."

I wanted to crawl under the covers and never come out again. "So, you're saying that these elementals were mortal enemies and now my closest friends on this island are supposedly my mortal enemies? Lilac is half-demon. Booker is a cupid. Aurora is a siren. That's weird, right?"

"It's not the same," he soothed, brushing his hand over my hair. "You weren't part of the wars. You're descendants. You can be with whoever you want to be with, spend time with whoever you want to spend time with. There's nothing guiding your life."

That sounded convenient from his point of view. He wasn't one of the warring factions. "I still don't like it."

"Do you suddenly hate Booker, Lilac and Aurora?"

"Of course not."

"Then it doesn't affect your life." He was firm. "You have free will. That's always the most important thing to remember."

"Fine." I threw up my hand, which he proceeded to catch and press a kiss to. The simple gesture made my heart stutter. "What about what I saw with Booker that day? The hand thing."

"Like I said, he can shift. He doesn't do it, almost never. I've only seen it once, and that was when he completely lost his cool. By the way, when I said he looked like a mutant hyena when he shifted, that's true. That hyena also has wings."

I bolted to a sitting position. "No way! He said he couldn't fly."

Galen chuckled. "I don't know that he can."

"He has wings."

"Ostriches have wings and they can't fly."

I hated that he had a point. "Keep going. What does the incubus have to do with all this?"

"Incubi are fallen cupids."

"Fallen? Like ... if they're shunned from the cupid council they become an incubus?"

"No. If they use their powers for bad, they morph into an incubus. The cupid council watches new entries carefully. If a youngster can't control his or her powers, well, they're destroyed."

"Destroyed?" I felt sick to my stomach. "That's harsh."

"Incubi and succubi are extremely dangerous. They can wipe out entire towns. That was more prevalent before television and the internet, but it's still possible. An incubus is soulless. It preys on women. It kills ... with intimacy."

It took me a moment to realize what he was saying. "Wait ... are you saying that an incubus has sex with his victim and that's how she dies?"

"Pretty much. He sucks her soul through sex."

"And I thought it was bad when orgasms were missing."

He poked my side. "You better be talking about someone else."

I smirked. "I was just joking. I ... don't know what to think about any of this."

"That makes two of us." His hands moved to my back so he could rub. "Whenever an incubus lands here — it's very rare — we take it out right away. I'm not sure how this one flew under the radar the way it did."

I had an idea about that. "Maybe it's passing as a cupid."

"I don't see how that's possible. It shifted enough to attack me. Keeping that hidden can't be easy."

"Booker can keep it hidden. Although ... does the incubus shift like Booker shifts?"

He shook his head. "They're different creatures. The incubus looks like a serpent with feathers."

"Why couldn't it just look like a bunny? I wouldn't be afraid of a bunny. I'm terrified of serpents."

He poked me again, a wide grin swallowing his handsome features. "Not all serpents."

"Don't be a pervert." I wagged a finger in front of his face. "I'm trying to understand. This might be important if this thing comes after me again."

"Oh, I definitely think it's coming back. It wants you for a specific reason."

"What reason?"

"Probably because he believes he can absorb your powers if he ingests your soul."

I stilled, surprised. "Is that possible?"

"Anything is possible. Is it probable? I can't say. You won't be hanging around here tomorrow to find out."

That was news to me. "Are you putting Booker on duty again?"

"No. He'll melt down when he realizes I've told you all this. We agreed he would be the one to tell you should it ever become necessary."

"Well, you didn't have time to wait. It's not your fault."

"It's not anybody's fault," he corrected. "It's just an unfortunate circumstance. I'll make sure he knows tomorrow. I'll probably need him – and Aurora – when it comes time to start searching."

"So, what? You want me to sit here alone all day tomorrow? That doesn't sound like any fun at all."

He kissed my pouty bottom lip. "I don't really care if you have fun. I already told you, you can't stay here."

"Why not? This is my home."

"And the incubus has linked you to this place. He'll come back. Now that you've wounded him, he'll want revenge. He'll torture you in ways you can't possibly imagine."

I swallowed hard. "I'm strong," I said finally. "I can fight him off."

"You are strong. You're my strong girl." He hugged me tight. "But I need to find this thing. There's no way for it to get off the island. We don't have a ship leaving for several more days. No commercial planes are due. He's stuck here until I can find him ... and then I'm going to rip his head off."

"While I do what? Do you think I'm just going to sit around and knit while you go all caveman?" If he believed that, he didn't know me at all. "That's not going to happen."

"I don't expect you to do nothing."

"Good. At least we agree on something."

"But you can't be here tomorrow. I need to make sure you're someplace safe until I start figuring this out. I can't take off from work. There's too much going on. That means you're going to have to go to the safest place I can think of."

"Disney World?"

"Wesley's place."

"No." I immediately started whining, not caring in the least how I sounded. "I don't want to go to Wesley's house. I want to be part of this."

"You will be, once I get more of the finer details in place."

"I want to be part of it now."

"No. You're going to Wesley's house."

"I can take care of myself. I think I proved that tonight."

For the first time since we'd started talking, Galen's temper made an appearance. "The only reason you didn't disappear out that window with him is because I was here. He can control you when you're asleep."

"Then I won't sleep."

"Oh, you're going to stay awake for the rest of your life? That sounds healthy. You're already half nutty. If you go without sleep, Booker will smother you to keep you from talking."

"I want to be part of this." I was adamant and refused to back down. "My life is on the line."

"Don't you understand that's why I'm so frightened? I want you safe above all else. I can take a lot, but losing you … that just isn't part of the equation. The incubus won't be able to get near you at Wesley's house. It's just until I can figure things out."

I folded my arms across my chest. "I'm not going."

"You're going."

"I'm not." I tried to roll away from him but he snagged me before I could. "You need to stay close to me. I don't care how angry you are. If the incubus comes back, I need to know if you get up again."

"How did you know last time? I'm sure I'll make enough noise to wake you." I kept my body stiff. "I'm mad at you right now."

He ignored my tone and wrapped his arms around me, nestling his chin on my shoulder. "I know. You can be mad. I think you've earned it. But I can't willingly put you in danger. Besides, Wesley has a lot of books out there. You might be able to find something to help us track down the incubus."

"You're just trying to placate me."

"Is it working?"

"No."

"Can we finish fighting about it in the morning? My arm is sore and I need some sleep."

How could he possibly sleep at a time like this? "What about me? I won't be able to sleep. Am I just supposed to sit here and listen to you snore?"

"That would be great." He kissed my cheek and snuggled even closer. His body was wrapped entirely around mine. Even though I was annoyed with him, I had to admit I felt safe.

"Hadley?" He whispered against my ear, causing me to wiggle as excitement shot down my spine.

I worked overtime to keep my voice petulant. "I'm not in the mood for that."

"I know. You don't have to be. That's not what I was going to ask."

"Oh. What were you going to ask?"

"I need you to give me just a little bit of room on this," he pleaded. "I don't want to cut you out, but I'm afraid. I'm doing the best I can here."

I wanted to argue, put up more of a fight. Instead, I exhaled heavily. "Fine. I'll go to Wesley's tomorrow. You only get one day, though. I'm not some child you can just shove off to play at Grandpa's house when something like this happens. I'm supposed to be part of the team."

"You are the most important member of my team."

"It doesn't feel like it."

"I'm sorry." He kissed my cheek again. "You are. That's why I need to keep you safe. We'll figure things out. We always do."

"I certainly hope so."

"I *know* so. We can't fail as long as we're together."

It was a nice sentiment, but I was still annoyed. "You'd better not drool on me."

"Oh, if that's the rule then you're retroactively in trouble."

I was scandalized. "I don't drool."

"It's like being caught in the rapids."

"And we're done talking."

"And you thought we couldn't agree on anything tonight."

# SEVENTEEN

*J* was still pouting when Galen dropped me off the next morning. The fact that he made me pack an overnight bag – just in case, he repeatedly told me, before giving up the ghost and admitting he had other plans – caused the anger to return to with a vengeance.

"You didn't say anything about staying the night," I complained as he carried the bag to Wesley's front porch. My grandfather sat at his favorite table, a book open, and looked amused more than worried when he saw us.

"I hadn't worked everything out in my head last night," Galen admitted. He dropped the bag on the porch next to Wesley. "Thanks for doing this."

"She's my granddaughter. It's my job to keep her safe, too."

"Yeah, well ... ." Galen dragged a hand through his hair. He was freshly showered, but it already looked as if he'd spent twelve hours in a wind tunnel. "She's not happy."

"I heard the kvetching from the driveway." He pinned me with a serious look. "You're not going to be trouble, are you?"

"Oh, I'm going to be so much trouble you'll wish Galen had kept me with him rather than you." I was deadly serious. "You can't just leave me here."

Galen rested his hands on my shoulders. "The thing is ... I can." He smirked when I swatted his flank. "Get over it, Hadley." He turned serious when I started stomping my feet. "You're staying here whether you like it or not."

"You're not the boss of me."

"I'm not," he agreed. "But you don't have a way back to town. That's why I insisted on dropping you off instead of you driving your cart."

My mouth dropped open. "I knew you were up to something sneaky."

"Yes, I'm sneakily keeping my girlfriend safe. I should be publicly flogged." He flicked his eyes back to Wesley. "I'm sorry about this, but it's important. You still have that security system on all your windows?"

"I do." Wesley nodded. "I'll make sure it's engaged tonight."

"I should be back in time for dinner. We'll spend the night here. Maybe then I'll get more than a few hours' sleep."

"That's fine. I have plenty of rooms, so you can each have your own."

"Why can't I just sleep in Hadley's room with her?"

"Because you're not married." Wesley looked a little too pleased with himself.

Even though I thought he was being antiquated with his beliefs, I couldn't help but laugh. "It's not so funny now, is it?"

"We'll work it out." Galen was firm. "Your safety is more important than sleeping arrangements. Although ... I'm still hopeful that your grandfather will see fit to change his mind about us having separate rooms when I return tonight."

Wesley snorted. "Not likely."

"Yes, well, we'll talk about it when I get back. I'll bring dinner."

"That won't butter me up enough to let you fornicate with my granddaughter under my own roof."

"I don't want to take his side or anything, but you and May weren't married and you were fornicating everywhere," I reminded him. "You two got divorced and still kept fornicating. I bet that's frowned upon in the eyes of ... whoever you're trying to appease."

"I'm only trying to appease myself," Wesley shot back. "And, what do you know? I'm fine with being a hypocrite."

Galen growled. "Well, great. I think we're all going to have a lovely night together. I can't wait to see how it all turns out." He leaned over and gave me a hard kiss. "Just remember, it's because I care that I'm leaving you here. I'll be back as soon as I can."

"Whatever." I wasn't in the mood for his apologies. "Just so you know, I'm going to walk back to town as soon as you leave. Your plan didn't work. You didn't win."

"I won the day I met you." His grin was sly as I rolled my eyes. "Also, there's no way you're walking back. The heat index will be over a hundred degrees today. You hate the heat."

"I don't hate it. I just don't like it."

"Yeah, well, suck it up." He lowered his voice and rested his forehead against mine. "I have to do what I think is right. I know you're capable of ... whatever it is you put your mind to. This is a terrifying situation. I'm doing what's best for you, even if you don't want to believe it."

"You've said that a million times."

"I'm hoping that if it's the last thing you hear from me you'll take pity on me when I get back."

"Doubtful."

"Well, I had to try." He planted another kiss on me and then turned on his heel. "I'll text if I find anything."

"I still think you suck," I yelled to his back.

He merely waved as Wesley chuckled. That forced me to turn my attention to my grandfather.

"It's not funny," I announced. "It's ridiculous. I'm a grown-up."

"You're not acting like one."

"Oh, no? How do you figure?"

"A grown-up knows when a loved one is struggling and tries to make things easier. You're making things harder on Galen ... and that boy is clearly struggling."

I faltered. "But ... I want to help."

"I'm sure you will help when it's time. Incubi are rare. They're also dangerous. He did the right thing bringing you here. Finding this thing won't be easy. He's got his hands full."

"I can't believe you're taking his side."

"And I can't believe you're not. Suck it up. We'll be in another battle together soon. It would help if we had all the facts first. Galen is trying to get the facts."

I squinted until my eyes were nothing more than slits. "I don't like that you're taking his side."

"I didn't think the day would start this way either. It just goes to show that life can change with the wind. You need to remember that and not hold this against the boy. He's doing his best."

"I'll consider it." I grabbed my bag and stomped into the house. "Is it okay if I use your library today? I want to research incubi."

"That's a fabulous way to spend your day. I'll be in the barn. One of my mares is about to give birth."

"Really?" I was intrigued. "I want to see a baby horse."

"When it gets close I'll call you outside. How does that sound?"

It sounded as if my day was looking up.


**I WAS DETERMINED TO** keep feeling sorry for myself, but it didn't last when May showed up to help with the research. She was chipper, and because I was still getting to know her I didn't want my mood to sour things.

"What do you know about incubi?" I asked as she floated around Wesley's extensive library. I'd pulled a few books but wanted to get a basic grasp of the creatures before I dove in.

"They're horrible." May wrinkled her nose. "They have sex with women until they kill them."

"I already know that much. What else do you know?"

"I only know stories." She sat on the couch next to me, and I couldn't help wondering how she managed to keep from falling through the furniture. It probably took practice. She had nothing better to do but argue with Wesley, so practice was most likely part of her daily regimen. "None of the stories are pretty."

"Life isn't pretty. Galen says the thing that's been trying to get into the lighthouse is an incubus. It clawed him last night. He can't turn into an incubus, can he? I mean ... I'll probably still date him, but that could put a crimp in our love life."

May chortled, the sound low and delightful. "Oh, you two are adorable. I'm so glad you found each other."

"Most of the time — when he's not making me stay out here against my will — I agree. Right now, he's on my list."

"Well, I'm sure you'll get over it." She shot me a sympathetic look. "As for your question, there's a lot of incubi lore, but I have no idea what's true and what isn't. For starters, I believe a lot of the stories were passed around by early Christians. That means they took on the life of the storytellers."

I had to read between the lines to puzzle out her true message. "You mean that the Christians wrapped the lore around their belief system."

"Pretty much," she confirmed. "For a long time, people believed an incubus mated with a human woman because he wanted to impregnate her and create a whole host of demon babies. The problem with that is no one ever managed to confirm that even one incubus baby was born. There's a question about whether it's possible."

"Galen said that incubi are fallen cupids. How does that work?"

"Cupids are mysteries themselves. They purposely try to keep the truth about what they're capable of quiet. They want to be revered — at least most of them — but they also enjoy being secretive."

"Did you know Booker's mother? She seemed to know you ... and Mom."

"Judy?" May's face twisted into a grimace. "I know Judy. I knew her mother better. She was a regular fixture in Moonstone Bay. She was a cranky woman, but I respected her. She believed cupids should keep their magic to themselves. Judy was a different story."

Now we were getting somewhere. "What does Judy believe?"

"I have no idea if she still feels this way, but the last conversation we had included an argument about how cupids were superior to all other supernaturals. She said that controlling the hearts and minds of humans was important because they were too stupid to figure things out on their own."

I didn't like the sound of that. "She believes that cupids should influence humans?"

"She believes cupids should control all humans. It's not just a bit of a push here or there to give a human courage. She thinks that cupids should be able to control everything."

"That sounds ... blech."

May chuckled. "I never had much use for Judy. I thought Booker was destined to follow in her footsteps. You'll never know the relief I felt when I realized he was his own man and didn't believe as his mother. That's a hardship for her."

"Because Booker is special, right? He can shift."

"How do you know about that?" May leaned forward, intrigued. "Did he tell you? I thought for sure that was a secret he would take to his grave."

"He didn't tell me. I saw his hand do a weird thing the day Ned attacked. I forgot about it — there was a lot going on that day — until Galen mentioned the incubus shifted and managed to claw him. I thought the two were linked."

"I guess, in some ways, they probably are," she admitted. "What else did Galen tell you? Do you know the story about the splitting of the elementals?"

I bobbed my head. "I do."

"Good. That simplifies things. As for Booker's ability to shift, my understanding is that it occurred because his mother and father were both from pure lines. It's rare now because the cupid lines have been diluted. The cupids of today aren't the same as the cupids of a millennia ago.

"An incubus occurs when a cupid doesn't rein in his talents, so to speak," she continued. "A succubus is the female version. The same thing happens to her. With practice, cupids can become extremely powerful. If they don't balance the power with a shot of humanity, that's when you get an incubus.

"Given how an incubus operates, the laws in the paranormal world are fairly straight forward. If you come across an incubus, you're expected to kill it. They're dangerous and no incubus has ever managed to overcome his inner wants and needs to turn back into a cupid ... or even exist without killing."

This was heavy stuff and it twisted my stomach. "Do incubi reproduce?"

"No. They're basically fallen cupids. Even if all of them are eradicated, more can be born through misdeeds and greed. They're dangerous creatures."

"But Galen won't turn into one because of the scratch, will he?"

"No. He's perfectly safe."

I rubbed my chin. "Does an incubus look like a cupid when shifted? I mean ... if Booker was to shift fully and the incubus was to do it at the same time, would I be able to tell them apart?"

"I believe an incubus looks like a deranged anaconda. That's what I was told anyway."

"Galen said they were serpentine with feathers. I thought maybe he was messing with me."

"Galen would probably know better than me."

"Do you think that an incubus can shift because, back when their lines were pure, cupids could shift, too?"

"I've never really thought about it, but that makes sense."

"Yeah. I guess it's time to conduct some research." I sighed as I opened the book. "I really am going to punish Galen for leaving me here all day. It's not that I don't like spending time with you and Wesley or anything, but this is about me. I should be involved."

May's eyes twinkled. "Something tells me you will be before it's all said and done."

Something told me she was right.

·   ·   ·

**AS PROMISED, WESLEY COLLECTED ME** when it was time for the foal to be born. He positioned me in a spot in the corner so I was out of his way, and then he stood with two men and waited for the chestnut mare, which was whinnying and neighing as if her life depended on it, pushed out a slimy baby ... hooves first.

I was in awe as Wesley and his men sprang into action, wiping down the colt and checking his airways before stepping back and allowing the mother to take over. She carefully licked her foal and nudged him with her head as he climbed on to wobbly feet.

"It's like *Bambi*," I offered, delighted. I wanted to touch the foal — I didn't care about the slime at all — but I didn't want to ruin the moment. "He's adorable."

"He'll be a nice-looking boy," Wesley agreed, running his hand over the colt's flank. "His father was one of my favorites before he had to be put down a few weeks ago. I hope this little one will grow up to be as strong as him."

"Why did you have to put him down?"

"Cancer. It took him quick. I'm glad he didn't linger, but I loved that old boy. I couldn't ride him once he got sick, but he still loved taking his walks. He and I would go down to the spring once a week just so he could enjoy the view."

This was a side of my grandfather I'd never seen. "You walked your horse?"

"Yup."

I smiled as the new foal focused on me for the first time. "Can I touch him?"

"Sure." Wesley watched with joy as I tentatively reached out and touched the horse's ear.

"He's kind of slimy," I said.

He chuckled. "He'll be cleaned up by morning. He'll also be walking much steadier."

"It's weird. Humans have to learn to walk over months. Horses are born knowing how to run."

"It will be a bit before he runs."

"You know what I mean."

"I do." Sincerity showed in his eyes as he pinned me with a look. "Is that why you're so worked up about Galen leaving you here? Do you want to run?"

"I want the option to run if I feel the need," I clarified. "I feel better on this island, freer than I've ever felt. I don't want to leave, not you or Galen. I still want the ability to make my own decisions."

"That's all well and good, but you decided to get involved with the sheriff. Saving people is in his nature. He's pretty fond of you. You don't want your nature infringed upon. Why do you assume he wants differently for himself?"

I worked my jaw. "I didn't realize I was laboring under a double standard like that. It doesn't seem fair to him, does it?"

"No. It doesn't seem fair to you either. You two have to learn to compromise. That's something May and I never did very well. You can learn from our mistakes. Being right isn't as important as being happy, and I'm pretty sure you and Galen are happy."

"When an incubus isn't trying to pull me out a window, we're very happy."

"Then learn to compromise."

"He has to compromise, too."

"That's a given."

We lapsed into amiable silence for a bit, watching the trembling colt. I was the first to break it.

"This was wonderful to see. Thank you for letting me be part of it."

"Part of it? You get to name him."

I was taken aback. "Really?"

"Yup. It's a big deal. He's going to be stuck with that name for his whole life. Make sure it's a good one."

"I need to think on it. Is that okay?"

"Absolutely. Thinking is good. For now, let's get out of here and leave the momma to tend to her baby. I think she'll be looking forward to visitors later."

"Okay." I cast one more look at the foal over my shoulders. "He's beautiful."

"He is. Life has a lot of twists and turns, Hadley. You have to remember that there's always good and bad no matter the day."

I understood. "You're still not going to let Galen sleep in the same room with me, are you?"

"I want a good day, so no."

"I figured."

"You're a smart cookie."

# EIGHTEEN

*I* couldn't get over the foal. He was small, adorable and perfect ... and I wanted to give him a good name. Even when I returned to researching incubi he was at the back of my brain. May lost interest in helping at some point and wandered out to spend the afternoon with Wesley. That left me to do my own thing.

I got so lost in what I was doing that I didn't hear the library door open. It was later than I realized – much later – and when Galen sat next to me on the couch I almost came out of my skin.

"What are you doing here?" Something occurred to me and I grabbed the front of his shirt so he couldn't flee. "Are you here to rescue me? Did you see the error of your ways? Are you springing me early?"

He arched an eyebrow. "It's almost five," he said finally. "You've been here all day."

I was taken aback. "Oh." That didn't sound right. How had the day passed so quickly? "I didn't realize."

"Obviously it wasn't as torturous as you thought it was going to be."

"It was mental torture." I skirted his lips when he tried to kiss me in greeting. "I'm still mad at you."

"Are you mad or just pretending to be mad? Your answer will dictate how I plan to woo you back to my side."

His grin was cheeky. Under normal circumstances I would melt in the face of his smile. These weren't normal circumstances, though. "I don't pretend to be mad."

"You do sometimes." He poked my side. "Tell me what you did today."

"I was stuck here. I didn't do anything."

"You must have done something."

"Well ... I researched incubi with May. Oh, and I saw a horse born." Despite my determination to remain cold and evasive, I couldn't keep the excitement from my voice. "You have to see him. He's so cool. Wesley says I can name him."

"That's a big responsibility." Galen's fingers went for the ends of my hair. "What are you leaning toward? Galen is a nice name."

The look I shot him was withering. "I'm mad at you. I'm not naming my horse after you when I'm ticked off."

"Your horse? What does Wesley have to say about you laying claim to him?"

"Wesley thinks I'm being a big baby. He hasn't come out and said those words, but it's written all over his face. I hate it."

"I always knew your grandfather was a smart man."

"He still won't let us sleep together."

"With a few issues," Galen quickly corrected, smirking when he caught me grinning. "I missed you today." He wrapped his arms around me and offered a lingering hug. "I missed not seeing you."

"Am I supposed to feel sorry for you? You exiled me."

"I most certainly did not." Galen's voice dropped and his eyes went dark. "I'm protecting you to the best of my ability. You may not like it, but I don't know what else to do." He pulled away from me and dropped his head in his hands. The misery etched across his handsome features was enough to tug on my heartstrings. "We searched every hotel ... and all the buildings on the beach. We asked everyone we came in contact with. No one has seen him."

I took pity on him and edged closer, my hand automatically landing on his knee. "You can only do what you can do."

"I know. But I don't like this. I don't like being afraid."

"You don't have to be afraid." I meant it. "The next time I'm in the dream I'll know not to try to get out of the room. I'll just sit there."

He was incredulous when he raised his eyes to mine. "And how do you think that's going to work? You only woke up because you got out of the room. If you don't try to escape you might be stuck there forever."

I hadn't thought of that. "Well ... um ... then I'll wake myself up right away. You don't have to sit around worrying about me. That's not what I want."

"I don't see where I have much choice." He leaned forward and pressed his forehead to mine. "I'm kind of fond of you, in case you haven't noticed."

"I'm fond of you." Even though I was angry, that remained true. "But I need to be part of this."

"I know. I need you to be part of it. I just thought that if I could find this guy right away, that if I could somehow luck out, I would be able to save you from a big battle. It's stupid but ... I guess I wanted to be the hero."

Oddly enough, I understood. "You are a hero. Sometimes you're even my hero. Right now I'm mad you planted me out here for the day, so you can't be my hero until you grovel and beg. Something tells me you'll be back on your throne relatively soon, though."

He barked out a laugh. "I really don't know how I managed to get through a day before you. I'm not joking about missing you. I kept looking up and down Main Street because I expected you to zip around the corner in your cart at any minute. You changed my life."

"And you changed my life." I tugged on his hair, probably harder than necessary. "But you can't be Mr. Bossypants all the time. I don't like it."

"I know." He kissed me softly. "I just don't want anything to happen to you."

"We need to work together. We're stronger when we're on the same team."

"Yeah." His fingers grazed my face as he brushed my hair back to make room next to my ear for his lips. "We'll stick together from here on out."

"Does that mean we can go home tonight?"

He didn't look happy at the prospect. "I guess. I'm still afraid to do that. What if the incubus figures out a way to get past my defenses?"

"He won't. Besides that, he would have to beat me, too. I don't want to toot my own horn, but I'm pretty strong. I don't think he can beat me."

Galen chuckled as he wrapped his arms around my waist and stretched us both out on the couch. He buried his face in the hollow between my neck and shoulder and inhaled deeply. "You're very strong. I'm not sure anyone can beat you. The problem is, you're also still learning. I have faith you'll learn everything you're supposed to. I just don't want you hurt in the process."

"I'm not sure you can guarantee that won't happen. Not everything is going to be easy."

"No." His stubbled cheek tickled my ear as he got comfortable. "It's too bad we couldn't talk Wesley into letting us share a bedroom. Then we might get a good night's sleep."

"I'm pretty sure that he'll shoot you before he gives you his blessing to fornicate."

"We don't have to fornicate. I just want some sleep."

That's when I realized how truly exhausted he sounded. The mental aspect of the case was starting to grate on him. "You can sleep tonight," I offered. "I have a plan to make sure nothing can entice me out of the windows."

"What's that?"

"We'll tie all the indoor shutters together and put empty soda cans in front of them. The cans will make a lot of noise if someone tries to open the shutters. You'll be able to relax. Besides that, now that I know what's happening in the dream, I don't think he'll be able to catch me again."

"That would be nice. I'm still not going to be able to sleep until I know he's not coming after you."

"Yeah, I've been thinking about that." I shifted to stare into his eyes. "Why do you think he keeps coming after me even though his plan failed several times? Why not simply move on to another target?"

"I don't know." He sighed as he wrapped his arms tightly around my back. "The whole thing doesn't make much sense, especially when you consider that two of the people affected have been men."

I lifted my head when reality hit me square in the face. "I kind of forgot about that, even though we talked about it. Do we think that more than one thing is going on? I mean ... maybe there's a killer cupid and an incubus on the loose."

"I can't rule it out, but I think there's more to it than that. I just can't wrap my head around it. There's something I'm missing."

I had faith in him. "Well, you'll figure it out. You're smarter than you look."

He smiled. "Oh, yeah? How smart do I look?"

"Like you've decided to get through life on your looks."

"Oh, well, thanks for that."

I laughed at his hangdog expression. "Thankfully, I happen to like the deceptively smart and overtly pretty." I grabbed his hair and gave him a kiss. "Did you bring dinner?"

The abrupt change in topic caused him to arch an eyebrow. "I did. Why? Are you suddenly starving to death or something?"

"I'm a little hungry," I admitted. "It's not just that. I think we should eat dinner with Wesley to be polite. Then I want to show you the foal. I can't believe Wesley is letting me name it. Then I want to go home. I don't like hiding out here. Besides, all that's doing is making Wesley a target. I don't want that."

"Fair enough." He graced me with another kiss. "I got Italian. I thought some pasta and pizza would be good."

"I love Italian."

"So do I." His eyes locked with mine and something unsaid passed between us. It was an understanding of sorts. "I love you, too." The

AMANDA M. LEE

words were out of his mouth before I had time to register what was happening.

I was suddenly breathless. "You do?"

He nodded, solemn. "I think I've loved you practically from the first moment I laid eyes on you. Sure, you irritated me to the point I wanted to shake you, but I still loved you. That's why I'm so afraid. I need you to know that I'm not trying to lock you up because I don't trust your instincts or think you're unnecessary to the process. You're necessary to my life, so I want you safe at all times. I can't help how I feel."

My cheeks warmed at the touching words. "And I love you." I meant it. He was impossible not to love. "You still can't boss me around. Wesley says relationships require compromise. That means both of us have to compromise."

"I'm willing to compromise."

"I am, too."

"We'll start with dinner here and then going back to the light-house," he suggested. "We'll work together to secure the place and then, hopefully, we'll get some sleep."

I was understandably dubious. "Just sleep?"

"Maybe a little more," he murmured, cupping my chin. He looked happy despite the dour circumstances. "This was a big step for us."

I nodded, solemn. "It was. I only wish it would've come on a day when I wasn't convinced you're a butthead."

He snickered. "Well, there are plenty of those days ahead of us."

"I certainly hope so."

"I know so. I feel it here." He tapped the spot above his heart. "Now, give me a kiss. I'm starving, and I want to talk to Wesley. I have a few ideas for places to search and he has a good head on his shoulders. He's a hunter. I want to hear what he thinks."

"I'm starving, too."

"Good. See. We're already compromising."

IF WESLEY NOTICED THE GOOEY looks Galen and I kept

164

shooting each other he didn't show it. He dug into the pasta Galen provided with gusto and paid very little attention to the way Galen split his breadsticks in two and gave me half so I could dip them in the sauce.

"What did you come up with today?" Wesley asked. He looked legitimately interested. "I suppose it's too much to ask that you caught the incubus."

"Not only didn't we catch him, no one seems to recognize the sketch I put together," Galen replied. "All the cupids deny recognizing his face."

"Do you believe them?"

"Some of them have to be telling the truth. Some of them ... ." His gaze darkened as he dipped his breadstick in marinara sauce. "The problem is that the cupids keep things close to the vest. The infighting in that group is tremendous. I mean ... it's off the charts. They don't turn on each other no matter what, though. They handle all their fights internally. We still don't know who killed who fifteen years ago."

"I remember that scene." Wesley took on a far-off expression. "I went to help at the hotel where it happened. I thought there was a need for first aid. But the cupids didn't trust us to help them. The ones who were dazed in the fight would rather sit there and bleed than let outsiders tend to them."

"They're a persnickety bunch," Galen agreed, leaning back in his chair. "I tried to talk to Judy and Darlene today. They both pride themselves on knowing everybody's business. They both claimed they don't know the man in the sketch."

Something occurred to me. "You don't think Booker's mother was involved, do you?" I was horrified at the thought. "That will be terrible for him."

"I don't know Judy all that well," Galen admitted. "Booker and I weren't exactly friendly as kids."

"That's because you were too busy competing," Wesley pointed out, earning a scowl.

"We weren't competing. We were just ... well ... we were kind of competing."

I shot him a look.

"Fine." He threw up his hands. "We wanted to beat the snot out of each other regularly. He always managed to steal my girlfriends, and it drove me crazy."

I snickered, genuinely amused. "I already know all this. I don't know why you try to save face the way you do."

"I don't either. It's just ... I'm a little old for middle school games. As for Judy, she was at the school all the time. She argued with the principal because she said that Booker's grades didn't reflect his intellect. She thought the teachers were somehow at fault. She argued with the coaches because he didn't show an aptitude for any sport."

I wrinkled my forehead, confused. "I thought you guys competed against each other ... at least in football."

"We didn't really have a football team," Galen reminded me. "There weren't any schools to play against. All our teams were essentially intramural. We competed against ourselves for the most part.

"I mean, we had a few flag football games here and there, but that's not a favorite sport of the island," he continued. "We surfed against each other from time to time ... and there was an incident during a rowing competition. For the most part, though, our competitions were usually carried out in a field of girls."

I scowled. "I don't want to hear this."

"I never loved any of them," he reassured me. "Your spot in my heart is safe."

"Oh, thanks." My cheeks burned. "You're kind of sweet when you want to be."

"Just you wait."

"Oh, geez." Wesley shook his head. "I see you two have taken yet another step in your little soap opera."

Galen snorted. "Tell me how you really feel."

"I really feel as if I want to smack you around because she's my granddaughter, and in my head I sometimes think of her as a child,"

Wesley supplied. "Unfortunately, she's an adult and nothing you guys are doing is forbidden. That doesn't mean I have to like it."

"You'll live." His hand moved to my back. "If you could get over yourself, we would spend the night out here. But because you won't budge on that separate bedrooms thing we're going back to the lighthouse."

"Oh, don't blame that on me." Wesley made a face that caused me to choke on my spaghetti. "You were always going back to the lighthouse. She wouldn't have it any other way. You might've been able to push her off on me for a few hours, but when it comes down to it you melt like a chocolate bar in the sun when she asks you to do anything."

"No." Galen vehemently shook his head. "We compromised."

"Right. You compromised and she won."

"We both won," I corrected, searing him with a dark look. "We agreed that we need to work on this together. That's what we're going to do. We're stronger as a team."

"Well, that's something I can get behind." Wesley wiped the corners of his mouth with his napkin. "Don't forget to see your horse on the way out. I expect you to give me a name for him by the end of the week."

I turned a set of expectant eyes on Galen. "See. I told you he was my horse."

"I stand corrected. I still think Galen is a fine name for a steed."

"I'm not done thinking about that yet."

"Just food for thought."

# NINETEEN

The foal was tucked in with his mother when we stopped in to say goodbye. He remained ridiculously cute.

"Isn't he awesome?"

Galen chuckled at my enthusiasm. "He seems a nice enough chap." He hunkered down and extended his hand so the mother horse could sniff him. When she didn't put up a fuss, he reached over and petted the colt. "You need to make sure he has an awesome name."

"That's the plan. I'm going to put together a list."

"A list?" His expression reflected amusement. "You're nothing if not diligent."

"I can hear the derision in your voice when you say stuff like that," I warned. "It doesn't make me feel warm and fuzzy inside."

"I'll handle that when we get home." He straightened and slipped his arm around my waist. "We should get going. I want to make it back before dark, just to be on the safe side."

"Do you really think the incubus will come back?" I had my doubts. "I think I might have hurt him."

"You definitely hurt him. Too bad we can't figure out what you did."

"I didn't consciously do anything," I admitted. "It just sort of happened. Sometimes ... ." I broke off and chewed my bottom lip, lost in thought.

"Sometimes what?" he prodded.

"Sometimes I wonder if the magic has a mind of its own." I felt foolish saying it. Magic wasn't a sentient entity, after all. I'd had the thought more than once, though. "Do you think that's possible?"

"I think that you're so strong that you inherently know how to protect yourself, even if you don't realize it yet. You might not understand about directing it or anything, but that doesn't mean you're not doing it."

"I'm not *consciously* doing it." I was firm on that. "I just react sometimes and it happens."

"As you become more sure of yourself you'll be able to be more proactive."

"I hope you're right. In fact, well, Booker had an idea of something I could do as a job." I felt stupid bringing it up now. But we were in a good place and I wanted to get it out of the way. "He thinks I should read tarot cards and tell fortunes. He suggested inviting people into the lighthouse, which I'm not comfortable with, or taking up a corner in Lilac's bar. I think that's sort of weird. I had a different idea ... but I want to know what you think."

"You want to tell fortunes?"

"I want to be good at something."

"And you think you're not?"

"I think ... I've never really taken pride in a job. That's on me. I realize that. You have a lot of pride in your job. You know you're good at it. Lilac is very proud of her bar even though she complains nonstop. Booker hops around but he has a good reputation and he seems to like when people clamor for his services. I want to be like that."

"I see you've given this some thought." He moved his hand to my back and tilted his head to the side, considering. "May could probably teach you to read fortunes. It might be a good bonding exercise."

"I thought that, too."

"I don't think you should invite people into the lighthouse.

That's your private sanctum, where you go when you need to get away and feel safe. I think you should find a different location. Maybe there's a building being vacated soon that you can rent or something."

"Oh, I have an idea for that, too," I admitted. "I was thinking I would use the cart."

His face was blank. "Use the cart for what?"

"To go to people's houses ... or set up sessions on the beach. I bet I could rent booths at the festivals if I get good enough. That's not for a while, though. I have to put work into studying before this comes to fruition."

"I actually think that sounds like a good idea, although I want you to run names by me before you visit houses. I don't want my girl-friend — the woman I love — going to some old pervert's house because she's not aware of his history."

I laughed. It was so like him to immediately jump to that conclu-sion. "I think we can work something out."

"Compromise?"

"Yeah."

He leaned over and gave me a kiss. "You seem excited about this. I think it's a good idea. You'll be able to set your own hours and still work with me on cases when you want."

"You're inviting me to work on cases with you?" I was understand-ably dubious.

"You said it yourself. We make a good team."

"We do." I squeezed his hand. "Let's go home. It's still early enough that we can stop at Lilac's bar and have a drink."

He balked. "I don't think we should get drunk when you have a late-night suitor possibly making a visit."

"I didn't say 'get drunk.' One drink won't hurt us. We'll still be a team at the bar. I don't want to hide for the duration of the cupid convention. I still want to live my life."

"Even if I can arrange it so we spend all our time hiding in bed?"

"Ha, ha." I poked his side. "I want to be able to live my life. That means going to the bar with you ... and seeing my friends ... and walking on the beach without fear. I'd also like to visit the cemetery again. I haven't seen my mother in a while."

He opened his mouth to say something. Apparently he thought better of it, because I recognized the moment he decided to switch gears. "We can stop at Lilac's place. I want to check in at the light-house and drop your bag off first. Can you live with that?"

"Sure. We can walk from the lighthouse. It's a nice night."

"This is more of that compromise you were talking about, right?"

"Yup."

"I think it's going to take a bit to get used to." He dropped a kiss on my upturned mouth. "For now, let's let little No Name here and his mother get some rest. I look forward to seeing your list of names tomorrow."

"Oh, you jest, but I'm totally making a list."

"I expect nothing less."


**THE INCUBUS WASN'T AT THE** lighthouse when we arrived — not that I expected him — but three female cupids I didn't recognize were waiting in the driveway when Galen parked. They didn't look happy.

"Now what?" He growled as he hopped out of the truck. "Can we help you?"

"We're looking for Hadley Hunter," one of the women replied. She was a short blonde with curly hair, stacked to the point I was surprised her shirt could contain her ample assets. "We have a bone to pick with her."

"Oh, well, good," I muttered, slamming shut the passenger-side door of Galen's truck. "Who doesn't love a picked bone?"

Galen shot me a quelling look, his message clear. He wanted to handle this one. I was fine with that. The last thing I wanted was to squabble with a bunch of women I didn't know.

"And what bone is that?" Galen feigned patience, but I could tell he wasn't in the mood for nonsense.

"She's stealing all our men."

"And how is she doing that?"

"I have no idea, but we're sick of it."

Galen slid his eyes to me, his expression unreadable. I couldn't tell if he was amused or annoyed, but it annoyed me because normally he could hide very little with his facial expressions. "Have you been stealing their men?"

Three heads snapped in my direction at the same time.

"Are you Hadley?" the blonde asked.

"I haven't decided yet," I said. "I think I might want to be someone else for the day."

"It doesn't matter who she is," Galen challenged. "This is her property and you're trespassing."

"And who are you to tell us what to do?" one of the other women asked. She was a willowy redhead, long hair hanging to her waist and a smattering of freckles broadcast across her nose. "We don't have to do what you say."

He reached into his pocket and retrieved his badge. "Actually, you do. I'm Sheriff Blackwood. If you have any questions, you can direct them to me."

The news that they were dealing with a law enforcement representative didn't slow the women down ... at all.

"Well, then that's timely," the redhead noted. "We want her arrested for illegally casting spells."

"She's a witch," the blonde added in a conspiratorial whisper. "Everyone is talking about it. She can make people do things."

Oh, well, I'd had just about enough of this. "That's rich coming from folks who can actually influence people's moods and make them fall in love or act out of character if they push hard enough," I shot back. "I don't know what you three are going on about, but I haven't done anything to your men. I don't even know who they are."

"Booker," the third girl piped up. She had short brown hair and a ski-slope nose that gave her an adventurous look. "You've been sucking up all his time. Someone said he spent the entire day with you yesterday ... and most of today."

That was news to me. "He wasn't with me today," I offered, full of faux sweetness. "I can't take credit for that. Sorry. I was with my grandfather."

"Booker was with me today," Galen offered. "Perhaps I cast a spell to get his attention."

The blonde's mouth dropped open. "Did you?"

"No." Galen made a face. "Hadley didn't either. If Booker isn't paying you the attention you feel you deserve, take it up with him. It's not Hadley's fault."

"What about the other men?" the redhead challenged. "All the other cupids are fixated on her, too. We're supposed to have a meet-and-greet tonight, just for cupids, but none of the men want to go because all they want to talk about is her." She pointed an accusatory finger in my direction. "She's practicing witchcraft on our people. You need to lock her up before she does irreparable damage."

"Oh, geez." Galen rolled his eyes. "Listen, Hadley hasn't been casting spells. If the guys you're interested in are chasing her, that's on them. Now ... get out of here." He made a sweeping gesture with his hand. "As I've already mentioned, this is private property and you're not welcome."

"And what will you do if we don't leave?" the brunette challenged. "I don't think you're strong enough to take all of us."

"Think again." Galen's voice dropped lower and was full of warning.

"Besides, he wouldn't be alone," I offered, moving to his side. "If I'm as strong as you seem to believe, taking out you guys should be easy."

The women exchanged looks, uneasiness permeating the air.

"Maybe you can only cast spells on men," the blonde said finally. "Maybe we have nothing to worry about."

"Do you want to find out?" I shot back. "If so, stick around."

The women looked from one to the other uneasily. Ultimately, they decided they didn't want to risk a fight and stomped off.

"I'm watching you," the redhead warned, extending two fingers and pointing them at her eyes before shifting their trajectory toward me. "Be afraid."

"Yeah, yeah, yeah." I slid my eyes to Galen and found his shoulders shaking with silent laughter. I couldn't hide my surprise. "Don't tell me you think this is funny."

"I think it's pretty funny," he admitted. "You're suddenly the wickedest witch on the island. Your reputation is growing."

"How is that a good thing?"

"If people are afraid of you they won't approach you. In fact ... ." He trailed off, the key to the front door in his hands. His gaze was on the back patio. Thanks to the setting sun, I had trouble figuring out what he was staring at.

"Is it the incubus?" I kept my voice low, preparing for battle.

"No. It's Aurora. I was just checking if she was naked." He must have read the dour look on my face because he quickly covered. "Because I would've sent you back there to talk to her alone if she was. Nobody wants to see that. I mean ... blech."

"You're not fooling anybody." I headed for the patio. "You're buying drinks at Lilac's to make up for that comment."

"I can live with that."

Aurora was stretched out on one of the loungers watching the sun set. She appeared lost in thought.

"Hey." I dropped into the chair next to her, barely paying Galen any mind when he slid into the spot next to me instead of grabbing his own seat. "What's up?"

"I wasn't sure if you guys would be back," she said, her eyes cloudy when they locked with mine. "I heard Galen forced you out to Wesley's place for the day."

"I did," Galen confirmed. "We had a long talk, and now we're back."

"In other words, you caved." Her lips curved. "I'm glad you're here. I've been giving it a lot of thought — the scent outside the window — and something has been bothering me about it. I can't get it out of my head. I think I recognize it."

"It's an incubus," Galen volunteered.

Aurora's eyebrows migrated up her forehead. "You figured it out. How?"

"He attacked again last night and we got in a fight. I got a good look at him. It's not hard to identify an incubus once you know what you're looking for."

"That's true." Aurora tugged on her lower lip. "How did you fight him off?"

"Hadley did something with her magic. I'm not even sure what it was. All I can say is that it was effective and he dove out of a second-story window to get away from us. When I find him again I'm going to rip his head off."

"He's a little upset about his sleeping pattern being interrupted," I said, patting his knee. "We're going to Lilac's bar to talk about it. Do you want to come?"

"I don't think so. On any other night I'd join you. That place will be thick with cupids. They give me the heebie-jeebies."

I thought about questioning her regarding the elementals mythology, but now didn't seem the time. I filed it away for later. "We won't be there long. Just long enough for one drink and to maybe get a look at the people who are there. We'd recognize the incubus if we saw it again."

"That's assuming he hasn't changed his looks," Aurora pointed out. "Incubi survive because they're malleable and change it up often. They would die out otherwise."

"I would recognize him regardless." Galen sounded certain of himself if the growl in his throat was to be believed. "Trust me. I'll never forget that face."

"I trust you. I only stopped by to tell you my idea. I should get going. I can't wait until these cupids are out of here."

"I'm just glad Hadley managed to protect herself last night," Galen noted. "Her magic is growing fast. I'm impressed ... and thankful."

"That's probably because her mother died giving birth."

I stilled, surprised. Aurora delivered the line bluntly, but she appeared not to realize what she'd said. "Why would that matter?" I asked finally.

"Blood magic," Aurora replied simply. "Your mother died giving birth to you. You took on some of her essence at the time. At least, that's the way it usually works. Her sacrifice fortifies your strength. It's a common belief in magical circles."

I looked to Galen for confirmation. "Is that true?"

He looked lost. "I don't know," he admitted after a beat. "It seems to make sense on the surface when you think about it."

"Can we find out?"

"You have a whole room full of books for research," he reminded me.

"Right. I guess I know what I'm doing tomorrow. Or maybe the day after, because finding the incubus is more important than skipping down memory lane. I'll make a mental note to research as soon as this is over."

"We definitely need to focus on the incubus. We'll leave the rest of the research for when this is behind us."

"Another compromise?"

"It's not a compromise if we already both agree."

"I guess you have a point." I heaved out a dramatic sigh. "I might be tapping you for information later, Aurora," I warned. "Be prepared."

"That's fine." She headed toward the water. "Just get rid of the cupids. I hate them."

"I'm starting to hate them, too," Galen admitted. "They'll be gone after the weekend."

"That's not soon enough."

That seemed to be the general consensus.

# TWENTY

$\mathcal{I}$ took a quick shower (pouting all day made me smell bad) and changed into a simple skirt and top. Galen spent the entire time I was getting ready jerry-rigging the windows and doors. By the time I tracked him down to leave, I found every window in the place tied shut. Tight. The concentration on his face made me laugh.

"You're determined to keep him out."

"Are you saying you don't want him to stay out?"

"No. But perhaps we should stop trying to keep him out and invite him inside."

The face Galen made was absolutely hilarious. "Do you want to serve him tea while you're at it?"

"No, I want to kill him ... or at least give him a stern talking to. I don't know how I feel about killing yet. I know it's necessary, but ... you know ... ick."

He belted out a gregarious guffaw that took me by surprise. "Ick, huh? I don't want him near you. If I could find him myself he'd already be dead. I don't have your qualms about killing."

I believed him. "Do you really think all incubi need to die? You don't believe in rehabilitation?"

"Not even a little." His tone was no-nonsense. "Even in the human

world, sexual predators are almost always the ones that can't be reha-
bilitated. Even murderers have a better shot of being reintroduced to
society. Incubi are simply rapists in a prettier package."

I frowned. "What do you mean?"

"I already told you about incubi."

"I mean the 'prettier package' thing."

"Oh, most incubi are ridiculously good looking. Didn't you get a
good look at the guy last night? He looked like a GQ model."

"Were you checking him out?"

"Hardy-har-har." He tweaked my nose. "It's a common fact. For
some reason, incubi are better looking than the general population.
No ugly incubi have ever been caught and killed ... at least that I
know of."

"I didn't look at the guy all that closely last night," I admitted. "I
was too busy trying to figure out what was going on."

"Well, he's not getting in tonight." He held out his hand and gave
me a long once-over. "You look pretty this evening."

"Are you saying I don't look pretty every evening?"

"You look beautiful every evening." His delivery was smooth, flaw-
less. "You look prettier than every other woman on this island
combined tonight."

"Oh, so sweet." I sidled up to him, rocked to the balls of my feet
and planted a kiss on the corner of his mouth. "That right there is
only one of the reasons I love you."

His smile broadened. "We could stay home," he suggested. "It
might be fun to celebrate our love in privacy."

"We can do that later. I want to see the cupids in action."

"I can tell you're serious about this. Okay. Ground rules first."

Ugh. There was nothing I hated more than ground rules. "What
did you have in mind?"

"You need to stick close to me, Booker or Lilac. Before you get up a
full head of steam, I'm not saying you can't take care of yourself. I'm
simply saying that there's safety in numbers."

"I believe I can agree to your terms." I stuck out my hand. "Let's
shake on it."

He grabbed my hand and pulled me forward so he could kiss me. "I prefer sealing my deals with a kiss."

My eyes rolled back in my head and I almost forgot I had a plan for the evening. By the time I remembered, Galen had me halfway down the stairs. "You're really good at that," I muttered as I smoothed the front of my shirt. "Did you have a lot of practice?"

"Who can remember?"

"You're not fooling anybody."

"I'm not trying to. I honestly can't remember. My life before you has turned into a dark blur of despair."

I snorted. "Are you going to keep saying stuff like that all night?"

"That depends. Do you like it?"

"Kind of."

"Then I'll keep doing it."


**LILAC'S BAR WAS PACKED. LUCKILY** a group was vacating a booth when we entered and she inclined her head in its direction to let us know where to sit.

"I've never seen this place so busy," I remarked as Galen led me to the booth. I slid in one side and expected him to slide in the other but he took me by surprise when he settled next to me.

"This looks weird," I announced, giving him serious side eye. "You can't sit next to me when the other side is empty. People will think we're mentally deranged ... or feeling each other up under the table."

"I don't care." He slid his arm over the back of the booth and smirked when Booker broke away from one of the clots of people and headed in our direction. "Besides, we won't be alone for long."

"I'm surprised you're here," Booker announced as he slid in across from us. "I thought you were spending the night at Wesley's place."

"He insisted on separate rooms, so Galen capitulated and we're back at the lighthouse," I replied, leaning forward to study his drink. "What is that?"

"It's a grasshopper, my mother's favorite drink."

I wrinkled my nose. "It's green. How does it taste?"

"Green." He took a sip as if to prove it. "It's the only way to keep her off my back. If I drink beer she won't stop complaining about how I'm reinforcing toxic male stereotypes."

Under different circumstances his hangdog expression might be funny. "Well ... let me try it." I took the drink from him and almost gagged at the taste. "You're a better son than she deserves." My eyes watered as I choked. Thankfully Lilac picked that moment to deliver water.

"Are you guys eating or just drinking?" she asked.

"Both," Galen replied pleasantly. "We'll have an appetizer plate with the fried pickles, wings with extra hot sauce and those mushrooms Hadley loves. Give us two servings of those, if you don't mind."

Lilac arched an eyebrow. "Sure. What do you want to drink?"

"I'll have whatever is on tap. I'm in the mood for a good beer." He cast a smirk toward Booker, who only rolled his eyes. "What do you want, Hadley?"

"I don't want that." I made a dismissive gesture toward the grasshopper. "Can I have a piña colada with extra cherries?"

"That sounds girlie and light." Lilac's gaze was shrewd as it bounced between Galen and me. "What's up with you two? You're acting extra ... what's the word I'm looking for?"

"Annoying," Booker volunteered.

"I was going to say glittery." Lilac shot the morose cupid a dirty look. "Don't rain on their parade just because your mother is the devil ... and make no mistake, your mother is the devil."

Booker nodded and took another swig. "You're preaching to the choir, sister."

Galen's hand moved to the back of my neck, where he started tracing light circles. The movement wasn't lost on Lilac. She was scatterbrained at times — a trait I loved about her — but she picked up on emotions better than most.

"Seriously, what's going on? If you hadn't just ordered a drink, Hadley, I would've assumed you were pregnant from the way you're looking at one another. I ... oh, I get it." Realization dawned on her pretty features. "You guys finally dropped the L-bomb on each other, didn't you?"

I ducked my head and focused on my water so as not to give it away. I didn't want her squealing and making a scene. Galen, on the other hand, merely smiled.

"We might have," he confirmed. "You can hear all about it when these cupids are out of town. Hadley can spend the entire afternoon in here reenacting the scene for you. Until then, it's nobody else's business."

"Oh, you guys are adorable."

Across from us, Booker's face twisted as he tried to figure out what was happening. "What's the L-bomb? Is that a sex game? I've never heard of it. It must be a Michigan thing ... but that wouldn't explain how Lilac knows about it."

Lilac flicked his ear hard enough to make him wince. "They told each other they loved each other, doofus. Don't give them grief about it." When she turned back to me she was beaming. "I'll put your order in and get your drinks. As for the gossip session, I'm looking forward to it ... just as soon as the devil and her minions leave." Her gaze was dark as she swept past Judy's table.

"Lilac doesn't seem to like your mother," I noted to Booker once she was gone. "Maybe you should ask your mother to be nicer to her. Oh, and tip better. Apparently cupids are cheap."

"Please. If my mother listened to me she never would've insisted on bringing the conference back to the island. I told her it was a bad idea, but would she listen? She just wanted to exert her power for the vote."

"What vote?"

"Yeah, what vote?" Galen suddenly looked interested in the conversation. "She never mentioned anything about a vote to me."

"You're not part of her inner circle." Now it was Booker's turn to look smug. "She's running for the presidency."

"Not of the United States?" I asked.

"No, of the cupid council. It's a big deal. The man who held the title for twenty-five years died a few months ago. All the other members of the council are jockeying for the position."

"Does that mean she would have a lot of power?" Galen asked.

"That's the most powerful position for a cupid. Once elected, you keep the job until you die. Back in the day, there was a lot of murder for gain when it came to becoming president. It doesn't happen quite as much now, but my mother still threw a party when Hank died."

"Nice." I happily sipped the drink Lilac delivered and considered the new information as she settled next to Booker. She looked worn out, which made me feel guilty. "Is Booker's mother running you ragged?"

Lilac shrugged. "They've been in here every day since they landed. It's beyond annoying. She's basically taken over. However, there was a bit of intrigue this afternoon when Darlene Metcalf — that would be the second devil on the other side of the bar — decided she was going to take up residence, too. Now I have two groups, and they're constantly going at each other."

I followed her gaze and frowned. I hadn't even noticed Darlene upon entry. So much for my well-honed observation skills. "Have they been throwing punches or just sniping at one another?"

"Just sniping so far. Once they get really drunk in two hours, I figure that's when the punches will start flying fast and furious."

"I hope not." Galen was grim. "I don't want to spend the night arresting cupids. I have other plans."

My cheeks burned at the gaze he leveled on me, and Booker mimed vomiting.

"I hope this phase doesn't last long," Booker complained. "You guys were barely tolerable before you dropped the L-bomb. That's a weird way to put it, by the way, but I like it better than my other options."

"I think they're cute." Lilac leaned back in her seat and briefly shut her eyes. "When is this conference over again?"

"Several more days," Booker replied. He looked equally exhausted. "The vote for council president isn't until the last day. These two are just getting wound up." He craned his neck so he could see Darlene better. "When did her son show up?"

I followed his gaze. "Which one is her son?"

"The guy in his thirties with the receding hairline."

I picked him out right away. "He looks ... kind of boring."

"Not everyone can be as exciting as me, honey," Galen teased.

"Don't verbally copulate in front of me," Booker complained. "I can take only so much, and I'm at my limit."

Galen ignored him. "You know, now that you mention it, the son wasn't with her the night she arrived. How else would he have gotten here?"

"He could've been on the plane that landed earlier today," Booker noted.

"What plane?" I was out of the loop. "I thought nothing was landing or taking off so the incubus couldn't get away."

"A plane landed." Galen was thoughtful. "It was unscheduled. It's not leaving again until after the conference. I checked to be sure. I should probably give it a good search, just to make sure nobody is hiding. That can wait until tomorrow."

"Is there something wrong with Darlene's son?" I asked. "Other than the obvious, I mean."

Booker made a derisive sound in the back of his throat. "Darlene has six sons. Byron over there is the youngest. We were pitted against each other quite often in competitions when we were growing up."

"Did you beat him?" Galen asked.

"Most of the time."

"You should've beat him all of the time. I mean ... look at that guy."

I swatted Galen's knee under the table. "Don't be mean to him. It's not his fault that his mother is the devil. Do you have any brothers, Booker? From the way it sounds, cupids have large families."

"I have no full brothers or sisters. My mother had two daughters with her second husband and another daughter with her third husband. She was bitterly disappointed I was the only boy."

I couldn't imagine anyone being disappointed to have Booker as a son. "Are you sure you're not exaggerating? Mothers are difficult. At least, that's what I've heard. Maybe she doesn't mean to drive you crazy the way she does."

"Oh, she knows exactly what she's doing." Booker grimaced as he downed the rest of the grasshopper. "As for Byron, he's a pain in the rear end but basically harmless. At least that's the way I remember him."

"I'm still checking that plane." Galen was determined. "I'm not letting that incubus off this island."

"I'll help you look again tomorrow," Booker offered. "He can't hide forever."


**TWO HOURS LATER I WAS** ready to call it a night. I had three drinks — instead of my promised one — and was having a good time. That didn't mean I wanted to get sloppy and stay out until morning.

I was exiting the bathroom, every intention of collecting Galen and returning home for some romance prodding me to move faster, when I careened into a man who was trying to skirt around me to enter the men's room.

"I'm so sorry." He stumbled over his words as he grabbed my arms to make sure I didn't go pinballing into the wall. "I didn't see you there. I apologize."

As I straightened I recognized the man who had managed to almost knock me to the floor. "You're Byron Metcalf." The words were out of my mouth before I could think better of them.

"I am." He straightened and smoothed his shirt as he looked me up and down. "I don't believe I've had the pleasure of making your acquaintance."

"Hadley Hunter." I stuck out my hand because it was the right thing to do.

He broke out in a wide smile as he took it. "Oh, I've heard about you. You're the witch who is immune to our powers. You're at the top of the gossip heap, my dear."

The declaration made me uncomfortable. "Oh, well ... ." I didn't know what to say.

"Don't be shy." His grin broadened. "You're much prettier than the women are reporting. The men pegged you right, though."

That was a weird thing to say "Um ... thanks?"

"You're quite lovely." His gaze lingered over my legs, which were bare thanks to the skirt. "I think it's fate that we've met this way. I was hoping to track you down tomorrow. I've only just arrived, but meeting you was at the top of my to-do list. I guess I can put a big check next to it."

Byron was hardly the first socially awkward person I'd ever met. I mostly felt sorry for these individuals and worked overtime to take up the conversational slack. Now I wanted to put as much distance between him and me as possible.

"I guess it's lucky for both of us." I attempted to edge around him. "I should get back to my party. It was nice meeting you."

He cut me off before I could escape. "Oh, now, don't be like that. We're just getting to know one another." He tried to slide his arm through mine, but I evaded the effort. "You should come with me to the other side of the bar. I'm sure my mother would love to meet you."

"I've already met your mother ... and she's not very fond of me." That was an understatement. "Besides, I'm here with someone. I should probably get back to him."

"I'm sure he can wait."

"Not really."

"Well, he'll survive." Byron was nothing if not persistent. "Now, come along. I insist we find a quiet table and get to know one another. What fun is destiny if you don't embrace it?"

"Listen, I'm here with someone." I was done being polite. "I don't want to get to know anyone else. If you'll excuse me, I must be going." This time I was more forceful when I broke away from him. That didn't stop him from giving chase.

"I'm not done with you yet." He grabbed my arm to whip me around, but his grip on me released in an instant when Galen intercepted him. "What the ... ?"

"I believe she told you she was with someone," Galen growled. "How would you like to talk over your destiny with me?"

Byron didn't look like the idea appealed to him. I couldn't blame him.

# TWENTY-ONE

ury was etched into the lines of Galen's face and, for a moment, I thought he might actually kill Byron Metcalf purely for the fun of it. An image of him twisting the man's head off his body and tossing it across the room invaded my mind. I was pretty sure I didn't come up with the image. That meant Galen did, and in an unguarded moment he let me see his imagination at play.

Worried, I took a step forward and placed my hand on his wrist. "We should go."

His eyes never left Byron's face. "I'm not ready to leave yet."

I pitched a terrified look in Booker's direction and noted he was already trying to muscle between the two men. "Let him go," he ordered, prying Galen's hands from the front of Byron's shirt. "He's not worth it. Trust me."

"I'm definitely not worth it." Byron visibly swallowed, allowing a breath to escape when Galen reluctantly released him and stepped back. After a few seconds, Byron recovered enough to remember he was a haughty jerkwad of the highest order. He puffed out his chest and glared at Galen imperiously. "I'll have you locked up for this. You can't just put your hands on another person. That's against the law."

Galen reached out to grab him a second time, but Booker muscled him back. I got the distinct impression that Galen allowed it to happen, that if he and Booker were really going to go at one another it wouldn't be this easy.

"He's a prat," Booker snapped. "He wants you to get worked up. Don't feed into his nonsense." He pinned Galen with a long look and then carefully released him to see what he would do.

For his part, Galen appeared calm. I felt the annoyance roiling under his skin, though, and it made me uneasy.

"I shouldn't have suggested we come here," I lamented. "It was a bad idea. I ruined everything tonight."

Galen flicked his eyes to me and the anger instantly dissipated. "You didn't ruin anything. This guy temporarily knocked us off track, but it's going to be fine." His fingers were gentle when they brushed my cheek. "It's fine," he repeated after a beat, probably more for himself than me. "Are you ready to get out of here?"

I was more than ready. I took a step in his direction, but the sound of Byron clearing his throat caused me to turn my eyes to him. "Don't make things worse. You have no idea how lucky you already are."

Apparently he was as dumb as he looked, because he didn't heed my warning ... and I felt something prodding my brain. It was like an annoying nudge, which made me realize he was trying to exert his cupid powers ... and failing miserably. "I believe you and I were about to get to know one another, privately." His eyes were heavy-lidded when they landed on Galen. "We don't need a chaperone, so you can go."

"Listen, you little pus bucket, I don't care what you thought," Galen hissed. "I know what you guys are doing. Everyone knows. More importantly, she knows." He jerked his thumb toward me. "You're playing games because you know she's immune and you've all convinced yourself that you'll be able to break her if you apply enough pressure. Well, I'm here to tell you that's not going to happen. She's stronger than you. All those plans you guys are making — the games you want to play — they're not going to work."

"They're not," Booker agreed, speaking for the first time in quite a while. "You can't push her. She's beyond us."

Byron's expression was smug. "No, *you* can't push her, Booker. You're not as strong as the rest of us. You chose to break from the confederation, so you're not in practice. We're beyond you."

"Is that what you think?" Booker shook his head. "The only thing you're beyond is help. I'm not telling you this to help her, though I would if I thought it mattered. I'm telling you this because she's stronger than you." He briefly flicked his eyes to an annoyed Galen. "He's definitely stronger than you. He'll rip your head off if you don't stay away from her."

"Gladly." Galen slid his arm around my waist. He'd regained control of himself, and he seemed prepared to escape from the bar and enjoy the rest of our night. "Let's get out of here, maybe go for a walk or something."

The offer took me by surprise. "I thought you would demand we return to the lighthouse and lock ourselves inside."

"I considered it. That was my first instinct." His expression turned rueful. "The thing is, it's not fair to you. This compromise thing only works if it benefits both of us."

His smile was enough to melt my heart. "Can we go by the cemetery?"

The question didn't surprise him. "Sure. I need to place a few calls anyway. You can have one hour to watch from your regular spot and I'll make my calls from the other side."

That sounded too good to be true. "Thank you."

"No, thank you." He leaned forward and kissed me, eliciting groans from Booker and Byron, although for completely different reasons. "Let's get out of here. I've had enough of this place for one night. I'm now on Team Lilac. The sooner these cupids get out of here, the better."

He wasn't the only one who believed that.


**THE CEMETERY WAS DARK AND** quiet. Even though I could tell he wasn't keen on allowing me to wander around by myself — Byron's testosterone display at the bar only bolstered Galen's argument that the cupids were crazy and I should stay away from them — he positioned himself on a bench at the front of the cemetery and offered up a wan smile.

"No more than one hour tonight," he prodded. "I know you haven't been here in a few weeks — that's honestly what's best for you — but I don't want to be out in the open later than necessary."

I stroked my hand over his arm. "An hour is plenty of time. They don't do anything but walk around."

"I know. Still ... it's your mother. You want to spend time with her because ... well, just because." He pressed a kiss to my forehead and hugged me. "I can't pretend to know what you feel when you visit her. It's obviously important to you, but I don't think sitting here every night is healthy."

"It settles me to see her. I don't know how to explain it. It's like ... I'm not completely cut off from her. And, yes, I know that's no longer her. But it still allows me to feel close." I felt ridiculous as his eyes locked with mine. "I don't think I'm explaining this well."

"You don't have to explain it." He was firm. "You just have to do what you want to do."

I pressed my head against his chest for a moment and squeezed him. "Thanks for this. I know it's not how you want to spend your time."

"It's not that. It's just ... I think there has to be a balance between watching the past and looking forward to the future. We need to look forward because constantly looking back is a good way to trip."

Leave it to a law enforcement official to be pragmatic at a time like this. "Good point." I kissed the corner of his mouth. "Come get me when you're tired of waiting."

"And you yell for me if a cupid shows up. I doubt they would be that stupid — and I'm guessing the cemetery isn't a place where they'd assume we'd hang — but I don't want to take any chances."

"Fair enough."

I wasn't nervous as I pressed to the wall of the cemetery. They were high and made of cement — probably because the zombies inside might be able to escape if they were wrought iron fences with open fretwork — and even though they were painted a pleasing color, it was still a fancy cage.

Galen told me once that the first time the zombies rose they killed three people. They didn't know it was going to happen. They had no idea who cursed the cemetery, or why, but they knew they had to round up the zombies and return them to their final resting places.

The initial inclination was to chop off their heads and be done with them. But because the bodies belonged to the loved ones of island natives, nobody had the stomach for that. Every day, the bodies crawled back into their graves, leaving an opening for maintenance of the grounds. At night, the zombies rose again.

Galen said the entire island worked together and erected the cemetery wall in three days. Nobody slept during that time. It was constant work. Because they were thinking ahead, they included a viewing window at the back of the property. This allowed residents to see their loved ones as often as possible without risk of limb or zomb-ification.

Galen had brought me to the cemetery not long after I moved to the island. He seemed nervous at the time. I initially thought he was trying to romance me in an awkward way. When I saw the truth – that my mother was one of the undead – I felt sick to my stomach. Over time, I stopped feeling that way and grew grateful. I hadn't known my mother in life. This little thing – seeing her walking around even though she was dead and gone – felt like a gift.

I sat on the bench and watched the beings inside shuffle around. Workers entered the cemetery during the day to make sure it stayed clean. During that time, solar lights were added to up the ambiance. That allowed me to see faces without direct light. Since some of those faces were decayed and falling apart, that wasn't always welcome.

It took me a bit to find my mother. She was shuffling along one of the inner aisles when I caught sight of her. She didn't look at me. She didn't look at anything really. She just walked ... and walked and walked. There was nothing going on in her head. Instinctively, I knew that. I was also glad for it. The idea of her being trapped in her own head with some semblance of time passing while her body was forced to endlessly walk at night was almost too much to bear.

After that initial revelation, I visited the cemetery almost every night for two weeks. It took a toll on Galen. That's when we were first dating, and he was fearful to push me too far. Once he got fed up, we sat down and had a long discussion. He laid out his concerns and I saw his point. I really was acting out of sorts. Sitting on a bench, wishing for things I could never have, definitely wasn't healthy. I stopped going every day after that and instead made my visits rare. Galen reminded me that the occasional daydream was okay and never once gave me grief about visiting the cemetery.

I admired him for that.

I rubbed my sweaty palms on my knees as I watched the zombies shuffle. They were mindless, soulless and sometimes eyeless. They were husks that used to be people. Still, I felt privileged to be part of the contingent that was allowed to see them.

I was lost in thought as I watched my mother. I'd seen photographs, of course. She was a beautiful woman. Even though she was dead and walking around, the beauty was still obvious ... although tainted.

I let my mind wander to what might have been if she'd lived. It involved a fantasy about her bringing me to the island to make up with Wesley and May. My grandfather spoiled me in the dream, which I made a mental note to tell him about later. He would get a kick out of it.

I was so lost in the reverie I almost didn't notice the telltale scent until it was right on top of me. The sickeningly sweet smell of danger was different than that of the crusty death on the other side of the wall. I hopped to my feet when the rancid honey smell threatened to make me sick to my stomach. It was already too late. A set of strong hands were on my back and I was being pitched forward.

"You shouldn't have done what you did," he hissed, his blackened fingernails digging into the soft skin of my shoulder. "You should've just played the game. The outcome would've been better than this."

I didn't get long to think about what he was saying. Almost before

I realized what was happening, I was floating upward — the incubus's arm still pinning me to the wall and causing the cement to scrape against my shoulder and cheek. I couldn't find my voice.

"Don't bother trying to call for your little boyfriend," he hissed, his voice oily and nasal. "I took care of him. He can't help you."

My heart thumped painfully. What did that mean? How did he take care of him? I didn't get a chance to think about the possibilities, because I was quickly dragged to the top of the wall and dumped over the side. It was only when I reached the top that I understood what he was going to do, but it was too late to stop him. I was twenty feet in the air when he let me fly ... and I landed so hard on the other side of the wall that it knocked the wind out of me.

I remained flat on the ground, wondering if I was in shock because I didn't immediately feel any broken bones. I did, however, hear moaning ... and that's what brought me back to reality.

"Oh, geez." Every muscle in my body screamed in agony when I rolled to a sitting position, my eyes going wide. The zombies, who had been following different walking patterns only seconds before, were fixated on me. They all shuffled in my direction.

"Oh, man!" I ignored the pain threatening to overwhelm me. Things would hurt a whole lot worse if I got eaten. I didn't know much, but it was obvious I had to get out of my current predicament. I couldn't let the zombies surround me. It would be all over then.

Because there was nothing else to do, I forced myself to hop on the nearest bench and then use the cement surface as leverage to haul myself to the top of one of the small mausoleums. I cringed when one of the taller zombies grabbed my foot, but he only managed to yank off my shoe before he lost his grip. I scrambled higher on the mausoleum, frowning when I couldn't see over the fence.

*Galen.* That's when my heart skipped a beat and I remembered what the incubus had said. Was he dead? I couldn't believe that. The thought was too much.

My fingers were shaking when I dug into my pocket and retrieved my phone. I could only hope that it wasn't broken. If it was, I would be stuck on the mausoleum with nothing to do but wait until dawn.

Even then, the cemetery was locked from the outside. I had no idea how I would get out ... or more importantly, call Galen.

To my relief, the phone appeared to be working. I found Galen on my contact list and my stomach twisted when I heard faint ringing on the other side of the wall. Could he answer? Was it already too late?

He picked up on the second ring.

"What are you doing?" He sounded amused. "If you're ready to leave, you can come back."

I almost collapsed at the sound of his voice. "You're okay." I was breathless, while the zombies groaned and fruitlessly reached for me when they heard my voice.

"Of course I'm okay." He chuckled. "Why wouldn't I be okay? You just saw me."

Hmm. How was I supposed to break the bad news without causing him to melt down? "So ... I need you to be calm."

He was instantly alert. "What did you do? Do I need to come back there?"

"Yeah. It couldn't hurt." I rubbed my forehead as I pictured him racing around the side of the cemetery to find me. I watched the observation window with trepidation until he appeared in front of the window. "Be careful," I warned through the phone. "The incubus was there a second ago."

"Where are you?" he gritted out, his eyes wide as he scanned the area where I usually sat. He didn't bother looking in the cemetery. I didn't blame him. It seemed impossible that I would've ended up where I was.

"I'm not that far away," I offered lamely. "Worry about the incubus, not me. He said he ... he said ... ." I fought off tears.

"Where are you?" Galen looked panicked as he looked behind the willow tree at the far side of the small clearing. "Does he have you?"

"No, but that doesn't mean I'm not in trouble."

"Hadley, I'm about to have a heart attack." Galen's tone told me he was at his limit. "Where are you?"

"Look through the window."

"What?" His brow creased with puzzlement as he swiveled. Then, as if by magic, his eyes immediately went to where I sat on top of the mausoleum and his mouth dropped open. "How ... who ... what ... um ... ?"

"All excellent questions," I muttered, rubbing my forehead. "I have an even better question: How am I going to get out of here?"

He didn't immediately answer, which told me he didn't know.

# TWENTY-TWO

"*I* don't want to say here all night."

That's all I could think to say as I scrubbed at my cheeks. It took everything I had to ignore the zombies reaching for me ... and not focus on the shoe they'd ripped off and thrown in the middle of the cemetery. It looked weird sitting there, alone and abandoned, as they tried to put their hands on something fresher. If I stayed in the center of the mausoleum roof they couldn't reach me. That was about my only stroke of luck.

"You're not staying there all night." Galen sounded breathless as he moved closer to the observation window and gaped. "Oh, geez. How did this happen?"

"I don't know." That was the truth. "Can an incubus fly? I guess that would make sense because he's been coming to my second-story window. I didn't think much about it before. He kind of floated me up the wall and dumped me over the top."

"Why didn't you yell for me?"

"Because ... because ... hey!" I went from feeling helpless to irritated. "It's not my fault. He took me by surprise. He insinuated he did something to you. It was over in a matter of seconds. Before I even realized what was happening he'd already dropped me. You need to watch your back."

"I'm not worried about my back. I'm worried about your back." He stared at the phone a minute and then pressed it to his ear again. "I am not abandoning you, but I need to disconnect this call so I can get help."

I didn't like the sound of that one bit. "I don't want to be alone."

He pressed his hand to the other side of the glass. He was close and yet so far away. "You're not alone. I'm right here. I need my phone to get help."

My eyes burned with unshed tears, but I nodded. "Okay." I moved to hang up but he stopped me.

"Wait. You weren't bitten, were you?"

I shook my head. "No. I acted fast ... but I hurt."

"Do you have any broken bones?"

"I don't think so. I can't really stretch out to test them right now."

"I guess not." He pressed the heel of his hand to his forehead. "You need to stay right there. Don't let them get hold of you."

"Oh, really?" I offered him a pronounced eye roll. "I never would've thought of that."

Instead of being offended, he chuckled. "There's my girl." He kept his hand pressed against the window. "I'll have you out of there as soon as possible. Don't panic."

"I'm not panicking." Yet. I wasn't panicking yet. I had no idea how long that would last.

"I love you, Hadley." He was earnest as he said the words and I knew, more than anything, he needed to hear them back.

"I love you, too." I meant it. "But I don't want to be eaten by zombies. Can you please get me out of here?"

"I'm working on it." He sounded sure of himself. "It won't be long. Trust me."

"I trust you. Just ... hurry."

"I'm on it."

·   ·   ·

**I WASN'T SURPRISED THAT** "the help" Galen called in took the form of Lilac and Booker. They arrived within minutes and seemed equally as stumped when they saw my predicament. What did surprise me is that the fire department arrived five minutes later. Galen had at least ten people milling on the other side of the window, but they didn't appear to be doing anything but talking.

Out of frustration, I called him again. He sounded tense when he answered.

"We're working on it," was all he said.

"Work faster. I'm starting to ache all over from the fall."

His gaze was grave when it locked with mine. "Do you think you have internal injuries?"

"How should I know?" I barked. "They would be inside, not somewhere I could see."

He remained calm, which I figured was due to his training. "Tell me what you feel."

"I feel ... achy. I don't think anything inside is broken. I just want to go home." I managed to swallow a sob, but just barely. "You're not going to leave me here all night, are you?"

He didn't immediately answer, which told me that he'd been considering just that.

"Give me the phone," Booker ordered. When Galen didn't immediately relinquish it, the cupid wrestled it from him and pressed it to his ear. "We have to be careful sending in a team."

"You must have a plan for this," I complained. "You can't tell me you didn't consider what would happen if someone got into the cemetery after dark."

"We didn't think anyone would be that stupid."

"Hey! It's not as if I walked in because I wanted to hang with the zombies. I was flown in ... or floated ... or something. Get me out of here."

"We're working on it." Like Galen, he remained calm. "The only plan we've come up with so far involves destroying the zombies."

My heart plummeted at the idea. "You can't do that. What about their loved ones?"

"The zombies are already dead. You're alive. You're our highest priority."

"You've got that right," Galen echoed. He was back to standing directly in front of the window, his nose practically pressed against the glass. "I don't see where we have another choice."

I couldn't deal with the idea of the zombies being eradicated. That would include my mother. I detested the notion I might never see her again. "Just ... don't." I was resigned to what had to be done. "I'll sit here all night and then you can just open the gate and I'll walk out in the morning ... or maybe you can do that manly thing and carry me because I'll probably be too stiff to walk out on my own by then. It's only — what? — eight hours. I can make it."

"I'm not leaving you in there," Galen snapped, grabbing the phone back from Booker when the cupid related my response. "It's not going to happen."

"You can't destroy them." My voice was weak. "Please don't do that on my account."

"There's nothing I wouldn't do for you." He was firm. "We're going to get you out no matter what. In fact ... ." He trailed off, his eyes going to his right, in the direction Lilac had disappeared seconds before. "What are you doing?"

I couldn't see what had him so worked up. All I heard was a weird scratching sound, and then, out of nowhere, Lilac appeared at the top of the wall. She looked grim as she surveyed her surroundings.

"I'm coming in," she announced.

Unlike me, who had a less-than-graceful landing, Lilac was on her feet when she hit the ground. The zombies remained focused on me, which I found interesting.

"What are you doing?" I was floored by her appearance. "Get out of here. They'll kill you."

"They're not interested in me." Lilac was blasé as she cut through the zombies. "I'm a demon. I don't smell like food to them."

"Oh." I didn't know that was a thing. "What are you going to do?"

"Help you." Lilac's answer was simple as she hopped onto the bench and then vaulted to the roof of the mausoleum, landing next to me. "I need to check you over first. Then I need to figure a way for us to get out of here without destroying the zombies."

"What is she saying?" Galen asked, irritation edging his words. "I can't hear her over the zombies."

"She says she's going to check me over."

"Oh, well, that's good." He impatiently waited as Lilac tested my legs and arms for broken bones. When she was done, she pressed her hands to my abdomen and asked me a series of questions. Then she grabbed the phone and pressed it to her ear.

"I think it's just bumps and bruises," she announced. "I can't detect any internal bleeding. She's persnickety and full of attitude, which is a good sign."

Lilac cocked her head as she listened to Galen's response. "I won't do that," she said after a beat. "Hadley doesn't want them destroyed. I think we should take her wishes into account."

More silence.

"That's all well and good, Galen, but I don't really care what you want right now. I'll handle this ... and I'll do it the way Hadley wants. I think she's been through enough tonight."

I couldn't agree more, and I shot her a warm smile in response.

"Oh, stuff it, Galen." Lilac looked fed up as she held the phone away from her ear. I heard Galen viciously swear on the other end. "Just give me a minute to think about this. I'm sure I'll come up with something. In the meantime, don't come running in here guns blazing. We'll figure this out. Just give us a minute."

She disconnected while he was still yelling, and handed the phone back to me. Her expression was thoughtful. There was no sign of the ditzy woman I'd first met upon landing on Moonstone Bay. I found her transformation fascinating.

"That's my mother," I noted, pointing toward one of the zombies congregated around the mausoleum.

"I know." Lilac gave me a sympathetic pat. "You know she's not in there, right?"

I nodded.

"You still want to be able to see her," she surmised. "I get it. The thing is, the zombies ignore me. I can't act as a distraction long enough for Galen and Booker to get you out through the gate. That means we're either stuck here or I've got to come up with a different solution. I don't happen to have one handy."

"Then you should go." I meant it. "I'll sit here until morning. It's better than watching them being mowed down like grass."

"Oh, so brave." Lilac rolled her eyes. "We can't do that. Galen will melt down and come in long before dawn. We need to think of a way to protect ourselves as we're walking toward the gate. If only we had ... ." She trailed off, her gaze sharpening when she focused on my face. "I heard that you created a shield the other night. Someone attacked and you held them off with a force field."

I realized what she was getting at. "I still don't know how I did it. My magic just ... reacted. I didn't put any thought into it."

"Perhaps it's time to put some thought into it."

"I don't know if I can. You don't have to wait here with me. You can go back over the wall."

"Friends don't abandon friends in zombie-laden cemeteries." Her smile was bright. "You either have to try the force field or I'm sitting here with you the entire night ... which won't be the entire night because Galen will bring the fire department through that door and hack the zombies to pieces to get to you long before dawn."

I felt sick to my stomach. "So ... it's the force field or nothing."

"Pretty much."

"Well, great." I briefly pressed my eyes shut. "This sucks."

"You're alive. Things could be worse."

Then why didn't it feel that way?


**IT TOOK ME TWENTY MINUTES** to work up the courage to try the force field. Lilac was in constant contact with Galen, and when we hung up for the last time she was gung-ho to get off the mausoleum and into a warm bath. The bath sounded good to me, too.

She held my hand, showed infinite patience and watched as I tried to engage the magic that came so easily the first go-around. I was a swearing and sputtering mess after an extended effort, and when I brought my fist down in complaint on the roof, teal magic spewed forward.

Lilac's eyes blazed with interest when she saw the phenomena. "That's interesting."

I managed to hold the magic in place as I slowly expanded the ball of light. I didn't risk a glance through the window because I didn't want to interrupt the spell. After a few seconds of feeding it power, the force field was big enough to accommodate Lilac and me.

"Great!" Lilac enthusiastically slapped my knee. "Let's get moving."

Getting off the roof was easier said than done. Lilac continuously shoved the zombies back when they tried to put their hands on me during the process. Eventually, though, we managed to slide away from the mausoleum and head toward the gate. An interesting side effect of the force field was that the zombies appeared to lose my scent and instead of following they went back to shuffling.

"This thing is neat," Lilac announced as we waited for the gate to open. "You should take it camping to see if it keeps the rain off. That would be awesome."

I was bone weary when the gate finally opened and we stepped outside the cemetery. The firefighters rushed to lock it tight in our wake, which allowed me to drop the force field and fall into Galen's arms. He didn't hesitate to scoop me up and cradle me against his chest as he pressed a series of kisses to my forehead.

I thought he might yell — or at least complain — but all he whispered were words of relief and comfort. "You're okay. I've got you. I'm taking you home."

"Good." I rested my head on his shoulder. "Every muscle in my body hurts."

"After we stop at the hospital," he added.

"Oh, come on. Haven't I been through enough?"

"Not yet. This is for your own good."


**IT WAS WELL AFTER MIDNIGHT** when Galen and I returned to

the lighthouse. He flexed some muscle to get us moved to the front of the line in the emergency room or it would've been even later.

"I need sleep," I muttered as he double-checked the locks.

"I think you'll be better with that bath you mentioned earlier. The hospital gave us Epsom salts. You might regret it in the morning if you don't take the time now."

I emitted a whine that I wasn't exactly proud of. "I'm so tired."

"I know." He led me to the stairs. "But the bath will be worth it."

I guess I would have to take his word on that.

He practically dragged me into the bathroom, turned on the bath and then stripped me out of my clothes. His fingers were gentle as they moved over my legs, hips and arms. "You're very lucky you didn't break a bone. You heard the doctor. He said that you could've died from that fall."

"I didn't die."

"No, but you could have."

To my surprise, he stripped out of his clothes and hopped in the tub. "What are you doing?"

"I don't want to be away from you right now. Besides, you're falling asleep. I'll keep your head above water."

I'd had worse offers. "Okay, but no hanky-panky. I don't think my poor body can take it."

"I'll see if I can refrain."

I moaned as I sank into the hot water, pure and unadulterated bliss washing over me. "Oh, I want to live in here. This is amazing."

He carefully drew me back against him. I shifted so I could rest my head on his chest as he sank lower and started sprinkling hot water on my back while rubbing my sore muscles.

"I thought he killed you," I admitted. "It almost broke me."

"Don't worry about me. Worry about you. What you went through tonight ... well, you did amazingly well. I'm proud of you."

"All I did was climb on a mausoleum and sit there."

"You kept your wits about you. Even though you were in pain, you made it to that roof and kept yourself safe. Then you managed to control your magic. What more did you expect of yourself?"

That was a good question. "Lilac still had to hop over the wall to keep me calm. How did she do that, by the way?"

"She's ... unique. I'm grateful to her. Still, you did the heavy lifting. I'm proud of you. You should be proud of yourself."

"I'm ... tired."

"I know." He kissed my forehead and continued rubbing. "You're going to be in pain tomorrow."

"You're not thinking of dumping me at Wesley's again, are you?"

"No. You more than proved yourself. I'm not sure how things will go down tomorrow. I need to think it over."

"Okay." I closed my eyes. "I'm sorry I ruined our romantic night. I know you had plans."

This time when he chuckled it was full of warmth. "We'll have endless nights together. The fact that you're alive and here to complain is more than enough for me."

"Still, it was supposed to be special."

"And you don't think tonight was special?"

"It was memorable."

"Life is never going to go exactly as you plan. You did amazingly well. In fact, you kicked righteous ass. I've never been prouder of anyone in my life. When your grandfather finds out, he'll be proud, too."

"Then he's going to want to join the fight to find the incubus."

"The more the merrier." His fingers were light on my back. "Now, close your eyes. You're exhausted and you need to rest. We'll come up with a plan tomorrow."

That sounded like a fine idea. "Okay. You'll have to cook breakfast, though. I'm warning you now."

"I will gladly cook you breakfast ... for the rest of our lives."

I smiled. "Goodnight."

"Goodnight, honey. Sweet dreams."

## TWENTY-THREE

Galen woke me with a kiss, clearing my muddled mind. I laughed when I opened my eyes and found him staring at me.

"Are you ready to romance me now or something?" My voice was gravelly, as if I'd been screaming at a rock concert all night, but it didn't hurt. I tried clearing my throat, but it didn't help. "I'm not sick, am I?"

He arched an eyebrow. "You tell me."

"I'm not sick." I was firm on that. "I guess I'm just ... tired."

"Yeah." He smoothed my hair and rested his chin against my forehead. "You didn't go wandering last night. I can't decide if that's because the incubus thinks he killed you or because he was too afraid to face me."

"It's probably better for your ego if it's the latter."

"I want him dead." His tone was so icy I shivered. "Are you cold?" He was gentle with me as he tucked the covers in tightly around my sore and battered body. "How do you feel? Nothing hurts inside, right?"

"I told you last night that I was okay. The doctor agreed with me."

"Doctors make mistakes."

"Yeah, well ... ." I rubbed my nose against his chin. "If you're angry with me now would be the time to get it out in the open. I don't want things to fester."

He was taken aback. "Why would I be angry with you?"

"Because ... I'm the reason our night was ruined."

"You didn't cause this. You haven't done anything to deserve this. Don't think that." His tone was scolding. "If you think I blame you for this, you're wrong. I don't blame you at all. I promise."

"I don't think blame is the right word," I said. "It's just ... you wanted to stay in last night. If we had I wouldn't have been tossed in the cemetery. I bet the firefighters were laughing at you because of what happened."

"They weren't laughing. They were confused."

"I might've laughed if it was someone else," I admitted. "Like Judy ... or Darlene ... or that Byron tool."

"That would've been funny," he agreed, his hands busy on my back as I moaned. "What happened to you was not funny. It was murderous ... and then some."

"Keep doing that."

"For as long as you want."

"Don't make promises you can't keep. If you keep that up, I'll want to stay in this bed for the rest of our lives."

"You might be able to persuade me to do that." He kissed my forehead and frowned when the doorbell rang. "You have got to be kidding me." He let loose a low growl. "Whoever that is better hope I don't get a chance to put my hands on them."

He gave me another kiss and rolled out from under me, leaving me alone in the bed ... and without my magic massage. "Stay here. I'll be right back."

He stormed out of the room wearing nothing but his boxer shorts — a look I found appealing — and I had every intention of following his orders. That changed when I pictured the various faces he might find on the other side of the door. The one I imagined had the best shot of being correct was Wesley's, and I wasn't sure my grandfather would find Galen in nothing but his underwear as attractive as I did.

I whimpered as I crawled out of bed — by back really hurt — and carefully slid into my robe. It took me longer than normal to reach the bottom of the stairs, and when I did I realized I should've stayed in bed after all. It wasn't Wesley hoping to check on me, but Darlene ... and she didn't look happy.

"I have a bone to pick with you," she announced, jabbing her finger in my direction when she caught sight of me.

Galen, hands on his hips, slid his eyes to me and frowned. "I thought I told you to stay in bed."

I held my hands out and weakly shrugged. "I thought it might be Wesley and I didn't want to leave you alone with him."

"I bet you wish you'd thought better of that now."

"You have no idea." I made a face as Darlene stomped into the living room. "Oh, won't you come in?" I drawled sarcastically.

"Actually, Darlene was just leaving." Galen's tone was firm as he reached for the huffy woman's shoulders. "You're not welcome here. Get out."

"I'm not here to talk to you, sheriff." The wrinkles at the corners of her mouth betrayed her disdain. "I'm here to talk to the mistress of the house, the woman who so rudely crushed my boy's spirits last night."

That so wasn't what I was expecting. "Byron?" I wrinkled my nose and aimed myself at the angled recliner located in the corner of the room. I started to lower myself into it with as much dignity as I could muster, but a piteous sound escaped.

"Hadley, you should go back to bed." Galen abandoned his position next to Darlene and hurried to my side. "Seriously, the doctor said you need to take it easy."

Darlene's expression was withering. "What's this? Are you faking illness to avoid me?"

"She isn't faking anything," Galen shot back. "Also, she doesn't have to come up with a reason to avoid you. This is her house. Get out!" He practically roared the last sentence. "I'm serious. I'll arrest you if you don't leave right now."

"You're not wearing your uniform." She tilted her chin in smug fashion. "You can't arrest anyone out of uniform."

"I don't know what crackpot television show taught you that, but it's not true. Besides, I don't wear a uniform unless I absolutely have no choice."

"I don't see a badge," she persisted. "You can't arrest me without a badge."

"Also not true. If you want me to get my badge, though, it's upstairs. I will happily get it and drag you out of this lighthouse by your hair if you're not careful. Is that what you want?"

Darlene's expression didn't waver. "I'm here to discuss a topic of great importance with Hadley. It has nothing to do to you."

"That did it." Galen moved as if he was going to physically attack the woman. I grabbed his wrist before he could.

"Don't. It's not worth it." My voice was still raspy and made me sound pathetic, but I didn't care. "Say what you have to say, Darlene, and then leave us to our morning. We had a long night and yours is the last face we wanted to see this morning."

"The last face," Galen echoed, his expression sour.

"Oh, get over yourselves," Darlene snapped. "Is this how you were with my son last night? I'll have you know you hurt his feelings. I mean ... leading him on the way you did was despicable. It's not as if I want him with a witch, but you should show some respect when dealing with a member of the upper echelon of cupid families."

"I didn't lead him on." I was horrified at the thought. "I barely said two words to him."

"That's not what he said."

"Then he's lying," Galen snapped. "I saw the whole thing. They almost ran into each other when Hadley was coming out of the bathroom and he was going in. He realized who she was and immediately started hitting on her. Hadley didn't encourage him."

Darlene narrowed her eyes until they were nothing more than slits. "Are you calling my son a liar?"

"Yes," Galen answered without hesitation. "He was persistent to the point I could've arrested him for harassing her. I was a witness. If you don't like that, I don't know what to tell you. Your son is hardly a victim, so get out."

"He wouldn't make up the fact that his feelings are hurt." Darlene was clearly determined to win a nonexistent argument. "Why would he?"

"I don't know. Why did you make up that story about Hadley cursing Mark Earle to go into the ocean the other day? Perhaps Byron learned it from you."

I had to bite the inside of my cheek to keep from laughing at the murderous glare Darlene managed to muster. She barely came up to Galen's chest, yet she stood toe-to-toe with him. I had to give her credit for her gumption. She was stupid, but she had guts.

"I didn't make that up," Darlene hissed. "I still maintain she was the one responsible for Mark's actions."

"And I maintain that you're full of it," Galen growled. "I want you out of here. Hadley is supposed to be taking it easy — doctor's orders — and I don't want you around bothering us. Do you understand?"

For the first time since she'd entered the lighthouse, Darlene actually spared me a lingering look. It was as if she was seeing me for the first time. "What's wrong with you?"

"Nothing." I didn't particularly want to share my woes with her. "Galen and I were up late being wild and crazy. I'm sure I'll be fine by lunch." That was a bit of an overstatement, but I didn't want to look weak in front of her.

"It's also none of your concern." Galen was firm this time as he grabbed her arm and directed her toward the door. "If you want to fight with someone, I suggest you track down your sister. You and Judy have been spoiling for a good fight for decades. I think now is the time to see which of you is the true master of your little cupid universe."

She rolled her eyes. "Judy is not my sister. She's an accident of birth."

"I thought she was older than you," I argued. "That makes her the true family heir, right? Wouldn't that mean you're the accident of birth?"

Her glare was so hot I had to check my face for scorch marks. "Judy was never the daughter she should've been. I was the better daughter. Me." She thumped her chest aggressively. "She only inherited the crown because she was born first. That's a stupid rule."

"I think most rules are stupid." I leaned back in the chair and enjoyed the view as Galen muscled her out of the lighthouse. "It was nice seeing you."

Galen fixed me with a dark look as he slammed the door and locked it. "Don't say things like that to her. Then she might come back."

"I'll keep that in mind." I held out my hands to him. "Help me up."

"Why? I thought you might just sit in that chair all day and pretend you're a queen."

"Oh, yeah? Are you going to hang around and be my servant?"

The look on his face told me that wasn't the case. He almost appeared guilty as he shifted from one foot to the other. "I'm going on a hunt this afternoon. I don't have much choice in the matter."

I understood what he wasn't saying. "You're not going to leave me here alone. There's no way after last night. Does that mean Booker is coming to babysit me?"

"No. I'm taking Booker with me."

"Did you call Wesley? Wait ... you couldn't have called Wesley. I've been with you all morning."

"I did not call Wesley. He has his hands full on the farm. Besides, I don't want him yelling at me because I allowed you to get hurt. I'm hoping to put off that argument until after the incubus is dead."

"Then who does that leave?" I was genuinely at a loss. "Lilac can't leave her bar. You better not have called her. That's not fair."

"I did not call Lilac. But she was my backup plan."

He was dragging it out. That meant it had to be good ... or bad, depending on which direction you were looking at it from. "Then who?"

"Let's just say I don't think you're going to be happy, but I'm convinced you'll be safe, so I'm happy."

"How is that a compromise?"

"I'm winning today. You can win tomorrow ... or next week if we don't find the incubus right away."

I glowered at him. "I don't think that's how compromises work."

"What if I make you blueberry pancakes and bacon?"

My stomach picked that moment to growl and betray me. "Fine," I said when it rumbled a second time. "Once my back is feeling better, you're going to be the one compromising all over the place."

He swooped down and planted a kiss on my lips before helping me stand. "I'm looking forward to it."


**IT TURNED OUT, GALEN'S IDEA** of a babysitter wasn't so bad. I pictured him parking one of his deputies in my living room and leaving me to entertain him all afternoon. Instead, two minutes before he left for the day, there was a knock at the back door.

"Who is that?"

He didn't immediately answer, instead leaving me at the table so he could usher in Aurora, who looked like she would rather be anywhere else.

"I'm here as ordered," she drawled, pinning Galen with a dark look. "Next time you want a favor from me it might help to ask. I don't respond well to texts that summon me to places at a specific time. Just saying."

His face expressed contrition. "I'm sorry. It's been a really long twelve hours."

"Yeah. I heard what happened at the cemetery last night." Her eyes traveled to me. "How are you feeling?"

"Sore," I admitted. "My back hurts like nobody's business."

"Oh, yeah?" She moved closer and ran her hands over my sore back without invitation. She didn't look impressed with anything she found. "You know what will probably help that?"

"Not getting thrown over a twenty-foot-high wall?"

She snickered. "I was going to suggest a leisurely swim. It will help stretch out those back muscles. Seawater is naturally buoyant and has healing properties. I think you'll feel ten times better after an hour in the water."

"I don't know," I hesitated, chewing my bottom lip as I glanced at Galen. "Are you going to put up a fight if we swim?"

He sipped his coffee, probably to give himself time to consider the question. Finally, he shook his head. "Actually, I think it's a good idea. An incubus won't be in the water during the day. You should be perfectly safe there. The saltwater really will help your back."

He turned to Aurora with expectant eyes. "She really is sore. It could've been a lot worse if she landed differently. Don't take her out too far ... and don't expect miracles from her on the swimming front. She knows she needs to work at that but now is not the time for a heavy workout."

"Don't worry. I'll take care of your precious witch." Aurora snagged an apple from the counter and shined it against her shirt. I was just glad she was dressed. She tended to swim everywhere she went, and she preferred doing it in the buff. "I'm assuming you'll be hunting for an incubus all day."

"I will," he confirmed, his eyes filling with malice. "I'm going to rip that thing's head off when I find it. Then I'm going to put his head on a spike and set it on fire."

I cringed at the visual. "I'm glad you've given this so much thought."

He winked at me. "Booker and I are hitting every spot we can think of today. We'll be back for lunch because I want to check on Hadley. Other than that, she's all yours."

Aurora rolled her eyes but she didn't look especially put out. "While you're checking places, you might want to stop in at that old shack by the hotel development. I haven't seen anyone hanging around, but that doesn't mean it's not in use. I thought I sniffed something weird when I was swimming the other day but it was gone fairly fast."

Galen furrowed his brow. "I thought that shack was gone. I was under the impression that the hotel construction folks were going to get rid of it."

"I'm sure they are ... eventually. They haven't done it yet. We've found more than one creature hiding in there over the years. I doubt the incubus would stoop that low, but it can't hurt to check."

"No, it can't," he agreed. "I'll add that to the list. Thanks for the tip."

"No problem."

"And thanks for this." He laid his hand on Aurora's shoulder to express sincerity. "You have no idea how much this means to me."

"You're not going to get schmaltzy, are you?"

"Maybe a little." He flashed Aurora a smile and then crossed to me. "As for you, take it easy. I'll be back for lunch. Do you have any requests?"

"Middle Eastern."

"I think I can make that happen." He leaned over and gave me a soft kiss. "I would take you with me if I could. You know that, right?"

I knew what he was getting at. He didn't want me to be upset in his absence. I couldn't blame him. In my current condition I would do nothing but slow him down. "I do. I'll be fine. Don't worry about me."

"I think that's part of the package now." He smoothed my hair and pressed another kiss to the top of my head. "I love you. Be safe."

I waved as he left, waiting until I heard the front door shut to turn to Aurora. She was watching me with expectant eyes. "What?"

"You guys are saying 'I love you' now, huh? That's kind of cute."

I shot her a dirty look. "Don't make fun of me. I don't know how much I can take today."

Sympathy replaced smugness. "Yeah. Let's get you in a swimsuit. I bet I can do something about that back."

"That would be great. Then Galen won't be able to leave me behind tomorrow."

"One thing at a time. We'll get you in the water and see how that goes."

# TWENTY-FOUR

Swimming with Aurora was hardly relaxing. She was something of a drill sergeant when she corrected my strokes. Apparently I'd been swimming the wrong way my entire life and she was determined to shake me until the bad technique fell out of my head.

"You're not rotating your shoulders the correct way," she complained after we'd been in the water for a full hour. The waves were calm today, which was good because I wasn't in the mood to be jostled.

"I can't fully rotate my shoulders because my back hurts," I complained. "It feels better than it did — so kudos on that because the saltwater and stretching helped — but I'm hardly up to swimming marathons."

Instead of plying me with sympathy, she rolled her eyes. "Stop whining."

"I'm not whining. It really does hurt."

She knit her eyebrows and stared hard, as if willing me to break. Finally, she let loose a sigh and pointed to the beach. "Fine. We can rest a few minutes. Then you're going right back in."

Aurora wore a swimsuit today — I swear it looked like she'd

purchased it in the eighties because it was gold and shiny — but anything was better than her normal choice of swimwear ... which was nothing.

"Have some water," she insisted as she cracked a bottle and handed it to me.

I greedily drank it before carefully lying on the blanket I'd laid out and stretching my back. "I don't know what it is about swimming in the ocean, but it always makes me thirsty."

"It's the salt." She sat next to me and corrected my stretching form. "Put your feet under you — yes, like that — and arch up. That will ease some of those aches and pains you're feeling."

I wanted to snap that I didn't need help stretching, that I'd been doing it my whole life without incident, but when I tried her method it actually felt better ... and I was floored.

"It feels like something has loosened up back there," I admitted as I tried the stretch again. "I honestly do feel better."

"See." Aurora looked smug as she sipped her own water and stared out at the ocean. "I notice things with you and Galen are progressing nicely. When did you start telling each other you love one another?"

I expected the question. I also expected it to feel invasive when she finally asked. Oddly enough, it didn't. "Yesterday. It sort of just happened."

"Just happened, eh?" She looked amused. That doesn't sound like something that usually just happens."

"Well, it did." I rolled my shoulders. "He said it first."

"Does that bother you?"

"No. I just didn't realize it was going to come so fast. It popped out of his mouth, and before I knew what was happening I was saying it back. It was kind of nice."

"It sounds nice. I'm happy for him ... and for you."

"Why? I mean ... why are you happy? I don't get the feeling that you always like me."

"It's not that I dislike you," she said quickly. "I just ... don't trust easily. You have to understand, sirens have been hunted by other paranormals for years. There have been wars. I'm the naturally suspicious sort."

I could see that. "I don't have any inclination to hurt you, Aurora. I like you, at least most of the time."

She snickered, seemingly amused. "I like you, too, at least most of the time."

We lapsed into silence and stared at the water. Aurora finally stood. "We should head back for another twenty-minute session. Galen and Booker will be back for lunch after that."

I would've preferred resting on the beach for those twenty minutes, but I reluctantly allowed her to pull me to my feet. I was feeling much better. "Okay, but I don't like it when you yell at me. How about asking instead?"

Her lips quirked. "Maybe. It depends on how much effort you give."

"I just need to finish my water." I swiveled with the bottle in my hand and halted when I turned in the direction of the lighthouse, the hair on the back of my neck hopping to attention.

"What are you looking at?" Aurora stepped next to me. "I ... what is that?" She pointed at the same shadow that had caught my attention.

"I'm not sure," I said, my frown deepening when the shadow detached from the wall and scurried into the bushes that led to the driveway. I couldn't see much of it, but there was no doubt it belonged to a human.

"That was a man." Aurora looked over her shoulder, probably to make sure we weren't about to be jumped from behind, and then focused on the lighthouse again. "Do you think he went inside?"

That was a good question. "I don't know. We locked the door."

"We did." She gnawed her bottom lip before bending over to grab her phone from the bag at the edge of her towel. "Hold on. I don't like this."

I wasn't a big fan of our predicament either. I didn't have to ask what she was doing because I already knew. She feigned patience until someone answered the call.

"It's Aurora," she announced. "No, she's fine. Didn't I say I would keep her safe? Do I ever break my promises? No, she's not driving me nuts with questions. She's been stretching her back and feels better."

She paused for a moment and rolled her eyes, using her free hand to flap her fingers to mimic someone talking. "Yes, I'm sure she's the center of your world and you don't like my attitude. That's not why I'm calling"

She laid out what we saw in a short, precise manner. When she was finished she had to pull the phone away from her ear so Galen didn't explode her eardrum with his curses.

"Yes, we're on the beach. We'll wait for you here," she drawled when he stopped yelling. "Please hurry. I don't like feeling as exposed as we are."

**IT TOOK GALEN AND BOOKER FOUR** minutes to get back to the lighthouse. That meant they were close. Booker carried bags of food and placed them on the picnic table outside the lighthouse as Galen stalked in our direction. He didn't look happy.

"Tell me exactly what you saw," he instructed as he pulled me in for a hug. He was so agitated I could feel the tension radiating off of him.

"We weren't even paying attention," Aurora admitted. "We were talking and getting ready to go back in for twenty minutes when something caught her attention by the lighthouse. I was curious, so I looked ... and that's when we saw the shadow. He disappeared into the bushes on the other side of the driveway from where you parked and we haven't seen him since."

"Well, I don't like that." Galen was grim as he kept me tight against him. "Did you check it out?"

"I considered it. Since my main job is keeping her safe, I decided to wait for you."

"That was the right thing to do." Galen released me and forced a smile. "You're okay?"

His overprotective nature was cute at times, but it was starting to grate. "I'm fine. It would be great if you didn't freak out. We don't know that it's anything. It could've been a delivery guy or something."

Galen shifted his eyes to a spot over his shoulder and met Booker's gaze. The cupid was already prowling the exterior of the lighthouse. "I guess we'll find out soon enough," he said. "Come on." He linked his fingers with mine. "Let's see what we've got, shall we?"

Galen made a big show of pinning me to his side and not shoving me behind him as a protective measure. Still, I couldn't shake the feeling that he was poised and ready should someone decide to strike. He kept me close as we circled the lighthouse, releasing me only when we were back at the front of the building and he and Booker were busy checking the ground for tread marks. For her part, Aurora offered up a series of bored expressions but held it together while eating warm bread dipped in garlic sauce.

After ten minutes, Booker gathered the food and Galen gestured for us to enter the lighthouse. The men had been quiet — except with each other — for a long period. They waited until we were inside to unleash what they were thinking.

"I didn't smell anything," Galen admitted. "That's normal for me on this one, though. This incubus manages to hide its scent from me."

"I smelled something faint," Booker said. "I think that's because it's not a normal incubus."

Oh, well, now we were finally getting somewhere. "What does that even mean? At first when the scent became an issue you guys said it was a cupid ... but not a normal cupid. Now it's an incubus, but not a normal incubus. How does that work?"

Booker licked his lips and planted his hands on his hips as Aurora went to the cupboards to get dishes for lunch. "I don't know how to explain it. I really don't."

"Maybe it's not an incubus," I offered. "Maybe it really is a cupid, but one who is different to the point of confusing you."

"It has to be an incubus." Galen sounded sure of himself as he grabbed a pitcher of iced tea from the refrigerator. "I've seen incubi before. I've destroyed them. This looked and acted just like an incubus."

"And I look and act just like a normal girl at times," I noted. "But I'm not a normal girl. I'm something special."

"Yes, you are." Galen's grin was flirty as he swooped in and smacked a kiss against my lips. "You're definitely something special."

"Oh, gag me." Booker shook his head. "Why am I being punished in this manner?"

"Leave them alone," Aurora advised. She was obviously more interested in the food than anything else. "They're giddy and goofy right now. It's annoying but it won't last forever. Besides, I think they're kind of cute."

I shot her a grateful look.

"But they turn my stomach, too," she added, smirking. "It doesn't matter. They're in their own little world. We wouldn't even see them if they weren't being hunted by a mutant incubus."

"Unless it's not an incubus," I added, my stomach growling when Aurora started pulling takeout containers from the bags. "That smells really good."

"I'm glad you have an appetite." Galen moved around me and grabbed a plate. "I got all of your favorites, including extra bread and Lebanese salads."

"Good plan."

"Who wants something to drink?" Booker asked, lifting the pitcher of iced tea. Everyone raised their hands and he began filling four glasses.

I filled a plate full of meat, rice and salad. I almost sat, but then remembered my drink and turned. That's when I noticed the liquid Booker was pouring looked slightly different.

"What is that?" I moved closer to him, confused.

"What?" Booker appeared bewildered as he looked around. "Do you see something out of place?"

"Yeah. That." I gestured toward the iced tea. "What did you do to it?"

"I didn't do anything to it. I was about to drink it."

"But ... it looks shimmery or something." I was adamant there was something different about the iced tea. "That's not how it normally looks."

Confused, Galen moved to the spot behind me and snagged the

pitcher from Booker so he could take a better look. He didn't seem concerned with what he saw. "It looks the same to me, Hadley. Are you sure there's something different about it?"

I was definitely sure. "It's shinier than usual."

"*Shinier?*" Galen's eyebrows hopped. "I don't understand what you mean."

"It's shimmery." I felt put upon. "It doesn't look like it normally does. I'm telling you, there's something off."

Galen didn't look convinced, but he lifted the pitcher again to study it and then shook his head. "Well, I guess we could have it tested."

"What for?" Booker asked. "What do you expect to find?"

"Someone was outside the lighthouse," he reminded Booker. "Maybe they made it inside and Hadley and Aurora simply didn't see it."

All traces of amusement fled from Booker's features. "You think someone poisoned the iced tea?"

"I think Hadley has a feeling ... and I've learned to trust her feelings."

"But I thought the incubus was trying to seduce her into going to him," Aurora argued. "This doesn't sound like the normal pattern for an incubus."

"It doesn't," Galen agreed. "Not even a little. The thing is, the incubus broke with pattern last night when he flew Hadley up a wall and tossed her into the cemetery. He was obviously trying to kill her."

"Yeah, how did he manage to fly?" I asked, thinking back to the incident. "I thought cupids couldn't fly. If an incubus is a tainted cupid, doesn't that mean he could fly as a cupid?"

"Let it go," Booker snapped. "I want to know more about this iced tea. How soon can we get it tested?"

"Sooner than you might think. I know a guy."

"Of course you do."


**THE GUY GALEN CLAIMED** to know was a local chemist. He

arrived at the lighthouse when we were still eating lunch — Booker insisted the food was fine because they brought it in from the outside — and he took the iced tea, removed several drops of liquid, plopped them in a beaker and then added liquid from a bag he carried before joining us at the table.

"It will take a few minutes," he announced, helping himself to the food without being invited.

Galen lifted an eyebrow as he made introductions. "Hadley, this is Morgan Porter. He went to school with Booker and me ... and now he handles a number of odd jobs around the island."

That was weird. What sort of odd jobs could a chemist do? I wanted to ask, but I figured it was rude so I swallowed the endless series of questions bubbling up. "It's nice to meet you." I flashed him a smile, which he returned even though he was intent on the shawarma.

"Is this from Mama Beale's place?" he asked.

Galen nodded, seemingly amused. "Help yourself."

I cast him a sidelong look, which he acknowledged by tweaking my nose and sliding his arm around my back. He sensed I was agitated waiting for the test results and this was his way of soothing me. "How long will it take?"

"Just a few minutes." If Morgan realized we were antsy, he didn't show it. "I'm starving. Your call came at the right time. I wanted to head to Lilac's place for a bucket broil, but it's full of cupids ... and you know how stupid cupids are." He flicked his eyes to Booker. "Present company excepted, of course."

"Oh, of course," Booker drawled. "I don't blame you. I hate them all, too."

"Speaking of that, what's the deal with your mother and Darlene?" I asked. I was stuffed from all the food and wanted to wash it down with something to drink. The iced tea was out of the question for now. "They're sisters and they hate each other. How does that work?"

"Oh, they make it work quite easily," Booker replied. "They've hated each other since long before I was born. I don't even remember interacting with my aunt in anything other than a cold manner. I was never to refer to her as 'Aunt Darlene.' My mother made that very clear. She also gave me a few colorful names to call her, but I managed to avoid those."

"I just don't get it," I said. "If I had a sibling, I would totally want to spend time with him or her. I would want to be close ... and do things that brothers and sisters do."

"What? Like give each other wedgies and rub their heads in your armpit?" Galen teased.

I pinned him with a dark look. "Not that ... and don't be gross. I just meant that I was sometimes lonely as an only child. It would've been nice to have a sibling."

"My mother says Darlene is dead to her. In fact, she's worse than dead. My mother would gladly kill her if she thought she could get away with it."

"That must make this election thing difficult," I mused. "Do you think, if one of them wins, the other will finally take a step back and try to make friends?"

"No. Things will only get worse and the loser will try to figure out a way to kill the winner."

That was a sobering thought. "You don't seem broken up about that. I'm guessing you want your mother to lose so she's not a target."

"Oh, I want my mother to lose, but only because it might actually kill her," he countered. "My mother would not be a good leader. She would be the worst possible leader. I mean ... if they had a line of terrible leaders, she would be right up there with the worst of the worst."

He seemed sure of himself so I didn't push him further. "Well, I guess we'll have to wait and see. We'll know if a few days, right?"

"Yup." Galen's hand was busy on the nape of my neck as he watched Morgan check his beaker. "What do you have?"

"Strychnine," Morgan replied grimly.

My heart rolled. "Are you sure?"

He nodded. "I'm guessing you didn't accidentally drop any pesticides in your tea?"

I felt sick to my stomach. "No." I turned to Galen. "What does that mean?"

"It means we're going to have to throw every item of food out to be sure." He petted my head. "It also means you stopped all of us from drinking that tea, so you saved our lives."

"Yeah. Good job." Booker offered up a haphazard salute as he kept eating.

"It also means that whoever did this managed to get in the lighthouse even though we thought we had it locked up tight." His expression reflected frustration. "I don't know how he did it, but there's a hole in our security ... and we need to find where it is."

"And fast," Booker added. "This guy is getting bolder. That can't be good."

On that we could readily agree.

## TWENTY-FIVE

*G*alen wasn't comfortable leaving me at the lighthouse alone given what had happened. He also wasn't thrilled with the idea of me spending the day in the ocean with Aurora, who was clearly getting antsy.

After lunch, he called two of his deputies and ordered them to dump every food item in the house — except for our Middle Eastern leftovers — and then took me with him and Booker to check several places they hadn't yet gotten to on their incubus search. They made me stay in Galen's truck but it was air-conditioned and I could stretch out in the back. He even stopped at the pharmacy long enough to buy trashy magazines so I wouldn't be bored. He didn't even give me crap about reading them.

Once they were finished, we headed to the grocery store. We needed everything new — that meant *everything* — and I was doing the math in my head for the groceries as the three of us moved through the store with two carts. I had money. I had a decent amount in savings. Since I hadn't been working, though, nothing had been added and I'd been slowly making steady withdrawals.

"What do you really think about my idea to read fortunes?" I asked

Galen as we stood in front of the dairy aisle and selected cheese. "I mean ... do you think I can make money at it?"

"Sure. There's going to be a learning curve, but you're good at everything you try as far as I can tell. I bet you'll catch on quick and start pulling in money in two months or so."

Two months seemed like a long time to me. "Maybe I should get a temporary job while I'm learning." I glanced around the store, thoughtful. "Maybe they need a cashier or something."

Slowly, very deliberately, he tracked his eyes to me. "You want to work here?"

"I don't want to, but I think I should be pulling in some money."

It was as if a lightbulb went off in his head. "You're worried about paying for all of this."

"No." I immediately started shaking my head. "I have more than enough to cover this."

"How much more?"

We'd never really talked about money, so it was an awkward question. "Plenty."

"Uh-huh." He grabbed several different types of cheese — sliced, string, shredded and block — and dumped them in the cart without looking at the prices. "You don't have to worry about paying for this. I'm going to pay for this."

I balked. "I don't think that's right. It's my lighthouse, which means it's my food."

"And there's no food at my place because I'm always at your place eating your stuff," he pointed out. "I'm paying. I don't want you worrying about this."

"You can't pay for my stuff."

"Says who?"

"Says ... every feminist I've ever met." I felt uncomfortable under his steady gaze. "I mean ... I love you, but it's not your job to make sure I'm fed."

"Actually, I believe that falls under the rules in the *How to be the Best Boyfriend in the World Guide Book*."

I pressed my lips together to keep from laughing. I didn't want to encourage him. "It's still my responsibility."

"I think it's our responsibility," he countered. "We spend every night together. We eat two meals a day — sometimes three — together. We spend every moment we can together. I want to help you."

"But I don't want to rely on you for everything."

"Why?"

"Because it's not right. We're not married or anything, so I should pay for my own groceries."

"Would you be more comfortable if we were married?"

I wasn't expecting the question and it threw me for a loop. "That wasn't a proposal, was it? If so, you need to work on your delivery."

He snorted. "That was not a proposal. I don't think we're there yet. That doesn't mean we won't get there."

The fact that he could say that without being embarrassed warmed me all over. A lot of men — even some I'd dated — withheld emotion as part of some annoying power play. He wasn't that way, and it was only one of the things I adored about him.

"That's ... wow!" I couldn't find the words to adequately describe what I was feeling. "That's a pretty cool thing you just said," I offered finally. "We're not ready, though. You were right about that. That means you can't buy all this stuff."

"No, it doesn't." Galen was having none of it. "I know we haven't talked much about money, but I'm well set."

My eyebrows drew together. "You're a sheriff. You pointed out at dinner the other night that you're a lowly civil servant."

"I shouldn't have done that." He was calm and I got the distinct impression he was choosing his words carefully because he was about to drop some big truth on me. "We actually don't go to that restaurant more often because it's so fancy and I don't always enjoy dressing up after a long shift. I have money, Hadley. A lot of money."

"You live in a regular apartment," I noted. He'd finally taken me there a week ago when I wouldn't stop squawking about it. The space was small, spartan and devoid of decorations for the most part. I figured that was the reason he always wanted to be at the lighthouse. "You don't even have art on your walls."

"I don't," he agreed. "That doesn't mean I don't have money. I'm just not much for decorating. I ... um ... well ... ." He trailed off, uncertainty dropping over his features like a dour curtain.

"What are you guys talking about?" Booker asked as he pushed his cart over to join us. "I got plenty of crackers and chips, by the way. You'll never run out of snacks."

"We're talking about why Galen can't buy all these groceries for me," I replied. "He doesn't have the money to foot the bill for everything."

Instead of nodding in understanding, Booker snorted. "Are you serious? The dude is a millionaire thanks to his trust fund. I think he can swing a couple hundred bucks' worth of groceries."

I couldn't have been more shocked if I'd been struck by lightning. "What?"

"That's what I was trying to tell you," Galen said hurriedly, murdering Booker with a dark look. "My money doesn't come from my job. It comes from a trust fund my father set up for me when I was born. I've had access to it since I was twenty-five ... and there's enough money in there that I'll never want for anything. That means you won't want for anything."

I was flabbergasted. "But ... I don't understand."

"My family is old money. My parents are well-to-do. They made sure that I wouldn't struggle even though I was determined to make my own way. I mostly live off my sheriff's stipend. There are times I dip into the trust, usually when I want to buy a new vehicle."

I had no idea what to make of this revelation. "You're saying you're rich."

"I'm independently wealthy."

I rubbed my cheek as I focused on the cheese case. "Shouldn't I have known that?"

"Most everyone who is a local is aware. I don't really volunteer it to people, because ... well, just because."

I understood. "You don't tell people because you want people to like you for who you are and not what you can give them."

"Basically," he confirmed. "With you, I just wanted you to love me as I am."

"Oh." Booker made an exaggerated face. "That's so sweet."

Galen punched him hard in the shoulder. "You're not helping matters."

"What's to help?" Booker turned his eyes to me. "You loved him when you thought he was poor, right?"

I slowly nodded. "Yes ... although I didn't think he was poor. I just assumed he was middle class."

"Well, that's poor on this island." Booker made a dubious face. "He's rich. He works because he enjoys protecting and serving. You should be happy about this. It means you don't have to buy all these groceries."

"I didn't say I wasn't happy." I was honestly at a loss. "I just kind of feel stupid for not realizing it. I mean ... you do wear really expensive boots."

"Those were a gift from my mother."

Something occurred to me. "Is that why you didn't want me to meet her?"

His sigh was long and pronounced. "My mother lives in a huge mansion on the other side of the island. She's been on me to meet you since she heard through the gossip vine that we were together. She's ... difficult."

"Like my mother is difficult," Booker offered.

"She kind of is," Galen agreed. "I just wanted you to have some time to settle before she started grilling you."

It was a lot to take in. "Well, I guess you can buy the groceries." I tugged the cart down to the meat case and started perusing. "In fact, how would you feel about having a barbecue with our friends this afternoon? You can pay for that, too."

"Is this a weird form of punishment or something?"

"Lilac needs a break from the bar. Booker needs a break from his mother. Aurora likes to eat. I thought it might be a fun way for us to entertain ourselves tonight without leaving the lighthouse and possibly getting thrown into the cemetery."

His expression darkened at the mention of last night's activities. "I would prefer sticking close to the lighthouse tonight. If you want a barbecue, we can make that happen."

Slowly, my lips spread into a smile. "Then I guess the money doesn't bother me. I'm still a little weirded out that I didn't realize the truth before but ... you're a well-to-do man. I guess that means I'll be getting good Christmas gifts?"

He slid his arm around my neck and gave me a kiss on the temple. "I'm the king of giving gifts."


THE BARBECUE ENDED UP bigger than I expected. Galen invited his deputies — who I was slowly getting to know — and Aurora brought a few of her siren friends. They were all laying low given the cupid invasion, but they were eager for conversation and shenanigans.

The one unexpected face belonged to Judy. She showed up about thirty minutes after Galen started grilling. She was alone ... and appeared to believe she'd been invited.

"Sorry I'm late," she called out gaily, causing Booker's head to swivel in her direction. He'd been busy holding court with the sirens and Lilac, telling stories that made them guffaw so loudly their voices echoed off the water. "I thought I would have trouble finding the place, but it turns out lighthouses are tall. It wasn't any trouble at all."

My mouth dropped open. "Oh, um ... ."

"I'm pretty sure you weren't invited, Mother," Booker snapped, hopping to his feet. "What are you doing here?"

"What do you mean I'm not invited?" She adopted an innocent expression. "If you're here, I'm certainly going to be here. We're supposed to be spending time together."

Booker looked mortified. "I can't even ... ."

"Don't worry about it," Galen offered, swigging from a beer. "It's fine. Everyone is welcome." He tilted his chin in Judy's direction. "Make yourself at home."

"Thank you." She plopped at the table where the deputies were telling tall tales, and smiled at each man in turn. "I feel so safe given everything that's going on. It's good to know that every deputy on the island is in one place and not spread out to monitor murderous behavior or something."

Galen scowled. "It's not every deputy on the island. These are off duty."

I sent him a warning look and shook my head when it appeared he was going to continue railing at her. It so wasn't worth it.

"Mother, can you come over here for a moment?" Booker didn't wait for her to answer. Instead, he gripped her arm and drew her away from the table, not stopping until he was under a stand of trees near the road. He was clearly about to unleash a tirade and didn't want anyone else to hear.

"What do you think?" I asked as I sidled up to Galen. He seemed to be having a good time playing master of the grill.

"I think you're the prettiest woman in the world," he replied, grinning. "Oh, you mean about Booker and Judy. I think that she is a busybody of the highest order and she expected Booker to spend time with her and her friends this evening. When he texted her to say he wasn't coming and had other plans, she took it upon herself to force his hand."

That was certainly part of it. I read that, too, but there was more. "She's worried he's interested in me," I explained. "She pretty much said that straight to my face that day at Lilac's bar. She has plans for his romantic life that I don't think he's going to like."

"I guarantee he won't like them." Galen handed me his beer so I could take a drink, his expression thoughtful. "If Booker is smart, he won't kowtow to her. She'll get bored of this place soon enough and leave on her own. He needs to put his foot down soon."

"I agree." I tilted my chin so I could study his profile. "Are you going to introduce me to your mother now that I know the big secret?"

He snorted at the topic shift. "Will you stop bugging me about it if

I promise to find a date that works for everyone after this incubus is captured and killed?"

"Yes. I just don't like feeling as if you're embarrassed and hiding me away."

He stilled. "Is that what you think? Honey, I'm not embarrassed by you. I'm embarrassed by her."

Now I was officially intrigued. "Why?"

"You'll understand when you meet her. She defies words. I don't want to cloud your opinion. I want you to come up with your own ideas where she's concerned."

"Okay. Fair enough." I rolled to the balls of my feet and pressed a kiss to the corner of his mouth. "Thanks for all this, by the way. I really appreciate it, but I did have the money. I'm not going to starve if you don't feed me."

His cheeks tinged with pleasure. "Maybe I want to take care of you. Have you ever considered that?"

"It's kind of nice."

"It's going to get better," he promised. "Once you meet my mother, you're going to want to curl up in a ball and hide in bed for a week. I'll take care of you then, too."

"I'm looking forward to it."

"Oddly enough, so am I."

**THE BARBECUE WAS A SMASHING** success. Booker opted to stay, sitting at the far end of the table from his mother and glowering at her as she told stories about his misspent youth. I lost track of Judy eventually as Lilac and I moved to the loungers on the back patio to gossip about Galen and everything that had happened. She was a good friend and she was excited for me. It was nice to have someone to share my feelings with.

After several drinks, I had to excuse myself to go inside and use the restroom. I thought I was the only one in the lighthouse until I heard a noise upstairs. It threw me, so I headed up the stairs. The first stop was my bedroom, but it looked the same as when I'd left it this morning. That is to say it was just as messy as always.

When I climbed to the top floor, the room May used as a laboratory and library of sorts, I found Judy with her back to me. She was riffling through the books and obviously hadn't heard me enter the room.

I cleared my throat. "Can I help you?"

She jumped and turned toward me. Fear momentarily clouded her eyes, and then she regained control of her emotions and plastered a wide smile on her face. "I was just looking at your lovely library."

"Uh-huh." I didn't believe her for a second. "I don't remember saying this room was open for visitors."

"Oh, don't mind me." She gave me a dismissive hand wave. "I got turned around when I came to use the restroom and ended up here."

"The bathroom is on the first floor."

"Yes, but somebody was inside and I really had to go. I thought maybe you had another bathroom upstairs — which you do — and I used that."

"This room is still upstairs from that," I argued. "Wouldn't you have naturally gone down when you were finished?"

"I just wanted to see the view." She gestured toward the window. "It's magnificent. I can't see myself living in a lighthouse, but the view from this one is so amazing it might change my mind."

She was lying. A quick study of the library, though, told me that everything looked to be in place. It was possible she was simply obnoxious enough to go through my things because she was looking for proof that Booker and I had a relationship she wasn't privy to.

It was also possible she was up to something else.

"Well, everybody else is outside," I prodded, gesturing toward the stairs. "We should probably join them."

"Absolutely." She perfunctorily bobbed her head. "I really do love this room. But you should spend some time decorating. It's a little drab."

"I'll take that into consideration." I waited until she descended the stairs to search the books she'd been going through when I found her. They all appeared to be accounted for, although I'd never done a proper inventory, so I couldn't be certain.

What had she been looking for ... and why?

# TWENTY-SIX

*I* was bothered enough by Judy's lie that I couldn't take my eyes off her once we returned to the barbecue. Galen's men left before dark. They were eager to hit up a few bars and pick up women. The rest of the party — including Judy — remained to sit around a bonfire and chat. I had a feeling Judy stayed only to make a point. Still, I had to give her credit. It was ballsy to remain behind the way she did.

"What's wrong?" Galen asked as he sauntered up to me. Aurora was in the middle of telling a story by the fire and I'd spent the last five minutes fishing in the cooler for a beer so I could have a better view of Judy.

"What makes you think anything is wrong?"

"Because you're watching Judy as if she's a bomb about to explode," he replied without hesitation. "What gives?"

"Oh, well ... ." I wasn't sure I should tell him, at least not now. In the end, lying wasn't something I was comfortable with, so I blurted it out. I told him the whole story. When I was finished, he looked more curious than murderous, which was a relief.

"Do you think she was looking for something specific?"

That was a good question. "I don't think she was searching for the heck of it. But I have no idea what she was trying to find up there. It's all books and potions basically."

"No, it's more than that." Galen's hand moved to the small of my back. "It was May's sanctuary. She spent a lot of time up in that room. I'm betting she has a few other things hidden up there that you haven't stumbled across yet."

That was a weird thought. "What should we do?"

"Ask her." He was already halfway across the lawn before I realized what he was going to do.

"Wait." I scrambled to keep up, but it was already too late. "Don't."

Galen ignored me. "Judy, it's time we have a little talk." He had a beer in one hand and planted his other hand on his hip. "What were you doing going through the third-floor library?"

"What?" Booker, who was sitting next to Lilac and having a good time despite the presence of his crabby mother, nearly fell off his chair. "You were going through Hadley's things?"

"I most certainly was not." Judy straightened her shoulders. I had to give her props. She was the one in the wrong, yet she still managed to look haughty. That was an impressive feat. "I can't believe you would accuse me of something like that, Booker. I mean ... really."

Booker's eyes flicked to Galen. "What did she do?" He seemed resigned that she was guilty of something, which I found very telling.

"Hadley went inside to use the restroom," Galen replied. "She heard noises from above. She found your mother going through the books on the library floor. When she asked her about it, she denied being up to anything and said she got lost going to the bathroom."

Booker made an incredulous face. "That doesn't sound likely. There's no bathroom on that floor."

Judy's eyes filled with intrigue. "You've spent time in the library? I don't suppose you've seen anything interesting?"

I was beyond confused. "What are you looking for?"

"I didn't say I was looking for anything." Judy recovered quickly. "I told you. I was using the second bathroom because someone was in the first and I simply got turned around."

Galen cleared his throat, annoyance obvious as it flitted across his handsome features. "You couldn't tell the difference between up and down? That's what you're saying."

"I was confused." Her eyes blazed. "I don't think I like what you're accusing me of."

"And I don't think I care," Galen shot back. "What were you doing in the library ... and don't bother making up another lie."

"I don't have to sit here and take this." She made a big show of hopping to her feet. "I have never been treated so poorly in my entire life. Your manners and hospitality leave much to be desired."

"Sit down, Mother." Booker came out of nowhere and surprised me when he muscled past Galen and put his hands on Judy's shoulders, firmly pressing her back into the chair. "This conversation is nowhere near over."

The look Judy shot her son was straight out of a horror novel. "You don't want to push me, Booker. You won't like what happens if you do."

"Oh, really?" Booker was having none of it. "What are you going to do to me? You've already done everything that can be done. I'm not afraid of you."

"I can do more."

"No, you can't." Booker vigorously shook his head. "These people are my friends. I'm loyal to them. And, before you ask, I'm more loyal to them than I am to you. You can pout all you want about that – all day if you like – but they've done more for me than you ever have ... including actually listening to the words that come out of my mouth. I'm certain you've never done that. You only hear what you want to hear."

"Really, Booker, is now the time for such theatrics?" Judy suddenly found something fascinating about her fingernails and stared at them. "You get that from your father. I'm not the dramatic sort."

"Yes, you're a regular ray of sunshine on a cloudy day, and you never overreact," he drawled. "Look at me." When she didn't immediately acquiesce, he yelled at her. "Look at me!"

Judy's eyes momentarily swam with loathing for her own son before she regained control of herself. "What?"

"What are you looking for?" Booker gritted out. "Don't bother lying. We know you're looking for something. You might as well tell us what it is and be done with it. You're not leaving until you do."

She huffed and raised her eyes to the sky, as if imploring some higher power to explain how she ended up with such a bossy son. Finally, she shook her head and held out her hands. "I'm looking for the St. Valentine Seal."

Whatever he was expecting, that wasn't it. "What?" Booker's eyebrows flew up his forehead. "Why would you possibly think that Hadley has the seal?"

"Wait." Galen stepped forward. "What is the St. Valentine Seal?"

"It's some mythological talisman," Booker replied. "Supposedly it can open a door between worlds. The way it's described in our history books makes me believe it actually opens a door between planes, but I think it's all fairy tales and nonsense anyway, so I never really paid that much attention. It's also supposed to enhance power for some elementals, including cupids."

"It is not a fairy tale," Judy hissed. "It's the real deal ... and it's important. You shouldn't be sharing information with these people. They're not like us."

"Whatever." Booker shook his head. "The seal was supposedly created by St. Valentine before he was martyred in the third century. Not much is known about him — and that's by design — because he was trying to hide his true identity. He was a cupid."

I was taken aback. "Wait a second ... are you saying that St. Valentine was a real person? Oh, and that he was a cupid?"

Booker was clearly amused despite the serious nature of the conversation. "That's exactly what I'm saying."

"Why was he martyred?"

"For his faith," Judy replied. "He was a true believer."

I was curious about the change in her tone. She almost sounded reverent. "A true believer in what?"

"That is none of your concern."

Booker pressed the heel of his hand to his forehead. He looked to be struggling to remember. "It was a long time ago, but I remember something about this," he started. "Valentine was known to proselytize to the masses in Italy. This was before Christianity was the ruling religion.

"There was some judge who had him locked up and then demanded that he perform a miracle," he continued. "That miracle consisted of curing the blind. I believe it was the judge's daughter. Valentine — who was actually Valentinus, but we'll stick with Valentine because it's easier — actually pulled it off. It was a big deal; the judge exalted him and freed a bunch of Christians from prison. Valentine kept up his shtick and was sent before the prefect of Rome. He tried to turn the prefect, who refused, and declared he either deny his faith or be killed. He was killed on February 14th, 269."

My mouth dropped open. "How do you remember all that?"

"It was ingrained in my head as a child." He pinned his mother with a dark look. "Valentine was a big deal because, while he was proselytizing about Jesus Christ, he was also spreading the word about the splitting of the elementals. Not everyone was for it at the start. People wanted reunification for centuries ... but that was ultimately ended by a strong contingent of people."

"And rightly so." Judy shifted on her chair. "The split was the best thing that ever happened to our people. We're much better than the sea-dwellers ... and the ground people." Her gaze was dark when it landed on me.

"Am I supposed to be one of the ground people?" I asked, confused.

"I told you. Witches were the earth elementals," Galen reminded me. "Technically, you're Judy's sworn enemy." He almost looked amused at the prospect. "As fascinating as that whole story is, why would you be looking for this St. Valentine Seal here ... and why is it important?"

"That's none of your concern," Judy sniffed, averting her eyes. "It's a relic of our people — our people!" She emphatically gestured toward her chest. "We're the top tier of elementals from the split. That seal belongs to us."

I remained confused. "I think she might be crazy," I offered after a beat. "Maybe she has religious euphoria or something. I read that's really a thing."

"No, she's just playing with you." Booker looked disgusted as he stared down his mother. "That seal was thought lost at the time Valentine was martyred. You probably don't know this — mostly because the cupids have purposely kept it secret — but the air elementals got the upper hand in the split because of the seal. No one knows how it was created, but it was present the day they decided to split the factions, and there was a power struggle over it. Air elementals weren't called cupids back then. That came about later, thanks to Valentine's sacrifice. The seal was thought lost with him."

"You said the seal could open a door between worlds," Galen pressed. "How does that work?"

Booker shrugged. "Nobody knows. People think they know, but they're all talk. Nobody alive has ever seen the seal ... at least nobody who knows what it can do. Plus, back then, nobody understood that we had millions of planes stacked on top of each other. It was believed there was one reality, so this seal was supposed to be especially powerful.

"Now we know that traveling between planes isn't as difficult as originally thought," he continued. "Pixies open doors all the times. Dwarves made their own keys. There are other creatures, too, although they choose to remain on their sides of the doors ... and I can't blame them."

His gaze was thoughtful as he focused on his mother. "I have a serious question for you." He hunkered down and rested his hands on his knees so he was at eye level with her. "Do you have anything to do with the incubus that's been running around?"

Judy was scandalized ... or at least she put on a good show. "How can you ask me that? I'm your mother."

"That's why I'm asking. I'm familiar with your work."

"You are the worst son ever," she spat, fury emanating from her. "The fact that you would say anything of the sort to me just proves that you're worthless as a son."

The harsh words propelled me to step forward. "Don't say that to him."

"It's fine, Hadley." Booker waved off my concern. "I'm used to her crap."

"That doesn't matter." I was firm. "Booker is a good man. He's saved me several times. He's saved other people. He puts his neck on the line to help others ... and he's a valued part of our community ... and he's a really loyal guy. You raised a tremendous human being. You should be happy about that."

Judy smirked. "Oh, please. I want a son who is loyal to the cause, who falls in line. He's my first born. That means he's supposed to take on a leadership position with the council. He won't even visit the conferences any longer. Why do you think I had to insist on the conference being held here?"

I was glad to hear there was a reason for the decision. It still didn't make much sense to me, though. "Why can't you just be happy that he's a good person? He doesn't want to play your cupid games. I think that makes him a better person than you and your brethren."

Judy shot back, "He's my son. I'm the top person in the cupid world now that Hank has died. That means everyone bows to me. As my son, they should bow to him, too. He refuses to play the game correctly. Do you have any idea how embarrassing that is?"

Pity stirred, and not just for Booker. I felt it for Judy, too. "It's too bad you're wrapped up in this status stuff above all else," I noted, making a tsking sound as I shook my head. "I can see that you won't change. It's a waste of time to try to get you to see what's right in front of you."

"It certainly is," Judy agreed. "Now that we're agreed on that, I'll be on my way." She stood again, but Booker immediately pressed her back into the chair.

"No, you're not going anywhere." His tone was no-nonsense as he folded his arms over his chest. "I want to know why you think the St. Valentine Seal is here. You must have a reason."

"I was just playing a hunch."

She wasn't convincing with this particular lie. "A hunch?" I moved closer to her, something occurring to me. "I guess I could try looking in her head to see if she's telling the truth."

Galen slid me a sidelong look. "I thought you weren't comfortable with that."

"I'm not, but we need answers."

Judy squirmed in her chair. "Don't even think of trying to invade my mind. I'll kill you if you try."

"If you hurt her in any way I'll rip your head off," Galen warned. It was obvious he was serious, because the heat blasting off him was enough to wilt the snottiest woman.

Judy shrank from him. "Booker won't allow you to hurt me."

"I wouldn't put your faith in that," Booker shot back. "I've had it with you. Besides, I'm just a waste of space, right, Mother? Why would I want to help you?"

I felt back for him and stroked his arm. "I think you're great," I enthused, causing Judy to sneer. "As for invading her mind, I think I should at least try. We need answers and she won't give them. That means we have to take them."

"Then give it a try." Galen jutted his chin in Judy's direction. The woman was getting smaller and smaller in her chair as we continued to talk. "This is a good idea."

I wasn't sure I agreed, but I didn't see where we had much choice. "Okay. I'll give it a shot." I moved closer to Judy, who pulled back as far as she could manage without tipping over the chair.

"Stop. Stop. Stop!" Her voice was unusually high. "You don't need to do that. I'll tell you why I think the seal is here."

Galen and I exchanged smug looks.

"Then tell us," he ordered. "Your story had better be convincing."

"I tracked it here," Judy explained. "I found a story in one of the records of the time. St. Valentine was allowed a visit with what he thought was a priest right before his death. He was able to turn over all his worldly possessions. The thing is, it wasn't a priest. It was a wizard in disguise."

The story did nothing to clear my confusion. "I don't understand."

"I tracked the man." Judy licked her lips as she gave in to the story.

She was clearly relishing her part in all of this. "He changed his name, but I found him in a village in northern Italy. Then I tracked his family tree through the ages. It led to May."

Oh, well, that explained everything. Or not. "That doesn't mean May has the seal," I argued. "She might not even know what it is ... or where it is."

"If May had the seal, I'll bet she recognized it," Booker countered. "She loved history books. We talked about St. Valentine several times."

"Okay, but that doesn't mean the seal wasn't sold or given to someone else at some point during the centuries. I mean ... we're talking 1,750 years here."

"We are." Booker turned thoughtful. "But it can't hurt to look."

Judy looked hopeful. "I agree with my son. Perhaps he's a genius after all. We must look."

I wasn't feeling as upbeat as they were, but I saw no reason not to try. "Okay, but I want someone with Judy at all times. I don't trust her."

"I'll handle that." Booker's glare was pronounced. "I'll make sure she doesn't touch a thing."

"You really are a thankless child, Booker," she spat. "I don't know where I went wrong with you."

"Oh, let me count the ways," he lamented.

"We'll break into teams," Galen insisted. "Hadley's with me. Booker has his mother. Lilac, you're with Aurora. If the seal is here, you guys are probably as interested in it as we are."

"I'll say." Lilac rubbed her hands together. "Where should we start?"

There was only one answer to that question. "The third floor. I doubt May would've stashed the seal anywhere else."

# TWENTY-SEVEN

*L*ooking for the talisman turned into a fruitless endeavor until Galen suggested calling Wesley. I wanted to smack myself for being so daft. While waiting for my grandfather to show up, I found a message in my email from Cillian. He'd identified the compound as complex pheromones. That's the most he could give me, and explained that pheromones this dense could be used in a number of ways, including to seduce someone.

"Cupids," Booker supplied. "We exude pheromones. That's how we do what we do. I'm betting an incubus has a double dose. This just keeps circling. The compound is a dead end. It's not telling us something we don't already know."

I was frustrated but agreed. The compound ultimately reinforced the theory we'd already landed on. Ah, well, at least I got to talk to Aisling. That was worth chasing our tails.

When Wesley showed up, he was confused about why we were ripping the lighthouse apart. After we told him what we were looking for, I expected him to laugh. His reaction was something else entirely.

"What does it look like?" He directed the question to Judy, who was busy pouting because Booker had been watching her every move.

"Are you talking to me?" She raised her eyebrows.

"Yes, Robert DeNiro, I'm talking to you."

"I only know from the descriptions I've read," she replied. "It would be a flat disc, copper in color. It is engraved with depictions of the original four elementals."

I tilted my head. "And what would those engravings look like?"

"The creatures the elementals shifted into," Galen supplied. "All of the original elementals could shift. I told you how the air elementals look like freaky hyenas, right?"

"Not hyenas." Booker made a horrified face. "Griffins. They have the bodies and tails of lions and the heads of eagles."

I wasn't sure that was better.

Booker narrowed his eyes. "I know what you're thinking and no, I won't show you."

"We'll talk about that later." I closeted off my curiosity and reminded myself we had a specific task to accomplish. "What about the others? What about the earth, fire and water elementals?"

"Water would be a hydra," Wesley volunteered. "It's like a serpentine creature with multiple arms."

I made a face and turned my eyes to Aurora. "Lovely."

"I don't turn into that," she protested. "I'm a siren. The lore doesn't apply to me."

I had no idea if she realized Booker could shift like his elemental ancestors, but I decided to let it go for now. It wasn't my secret to tell. "What about the others?"

"Earth would be a harpy," Booker explained. "I've never fully understood that, but that's how it ended up. The fire elementals would be represented by a phoenix ... at least if the talisman is true to the history we've been taught."

I made a mental note to research harpies later and turned my eyes to Wesley. "Does that item sound familiar to you?"

"Actually, it does."

His answer surprised me. "Are you serious?"

"I'm pretty sure I saw it a time or two. May used it as a candle holder for one of those big pillar candles up in the library. Did you look under the candles?"

"She used it as a candle holder?" Judy was horrified. "What was she thinking?"

"Probably that it looked nice with a candle on it," Wesley replied, shrugging. "I never asked her about it. I just remember commenting that it was ugly a time or two."

"Well, that's ... interesting." Galen dragged a hand through his hair. "We went through everything on the tables and shelves up there. There were no candles."

"Then it might be in her secret hiding spot."

I arched an eyebrow. "She had a secret hiding spot?"

"She did."

"Where is it?" Judy barked, her voice cracking. "Tell us where it is right now."

I shot her a quelling look. "You need to calm down."

"Yes, Mother," Booker drawled. "Calm down."

I kept a speculative eye on her while grabbing Wesley's hand and dragging him far enough away that she couldn't overhear our conversation. Galen followed, but he looked more conflicted than anything else.

"Where is the secret hiding space?" I asked quietly. "Can you tell me? This talisman seems important."

"Yeah, and if Judy knows it's here ... maybe someone else does, too," Galen added, his expression unreadable. "I'm starting to wonder if the incubus was sent because someone believed it could get information on the talisman from you. Maybe you weren't targeted for your magic at all."

For some reason, that made me feel better. "Where is the secret hiding spot?"

"Upstairs," Wesley replied. "In the bedroom. There's a secret closet behind the dresser."

Galen furrowed his brow, surprised. "How can that be? I think I would've seen that before. I sleep in that room every night."

Wesley made a face. "Do you want me to help or smack you around?"

I chuckled at the banter before turning serious again. "We really do need to know."

"I don't know what to tell you." He spread out his hands and shrugged. "There's a closet behind the dresser. It's small ... and magically cloaked. It was her private area."

"Maybe we should call her," Galen suggested.

"I haven't seen her all day," Wesley replied. "I think she's recharging. She usually pops up when she's done. She's not as strong as she would like to be yet. She's still getting used to her new reality."

"Then we'll have to find it ourselves." I was grim. "We should keep Judy out of the room when we do it. She won't like that, but ... I don't trust her."

Galen nodded as he stroked his hand down my back. "I agree. We'll put Lilac and Aurora on her. They'll keep her out of trouble."

I wasn't sure they were powerful enough for that – Judy seemed to be a determined old bird – but we had other things to worry about. "Then let's do this."


**GALEN, WESLEY, BOOKER AND I** ventured into my room. Aurora and Lilac were more than happy to play babysitter to Judy. Aurora almost looked giddy at the prospect. Judy, however, was not happy about the turn of events, and the fit she pitched was something I hadn't witnessed since I was hanging around with toddlers, back when I was one myself.

"I don't know how you deal with your mother, Booker," I announced as Galen and Booker went to work moving the dresser. It was heavy, so they both had to put their backs into it. "I always dreamed of meeting my mother. After meeting yours, I'm wondering if I'm not better off."

"Bite your tongue," Wesley admonished me. "Emma was nothing like that woman. I know she never got a chance to raise you, but I believe she would've made an outstanding mother ... and I'm not just saying that because she was my daughter."

I shot him a grateful smile. "Thanks. Do you think she would've been disappointed in me?"

Booker spoke before Wesley could answer. "Are you asking that because my mother is obviously disappointed in me? If so, let it go. Everything I've heard about your mother makes me think she was the exact opposite of my mother. That's why my mother hated her."

"Emma was sweet but fierce," Wesley offered. "You're a lot like her. She would've loved you."

"I don't think I'm all that sweet."

"Nonsense," Galen grunted as he and Booker finally slid the dresser to the side. "You're very sweet ... when you're not pouting to get your way, that is."

"Ha, ha." I frowned when the wall came into view. "There's no closet."

"Nope," Galen agreed.

"It's magically cloaked," Booker reminded us, his eyes sparking as he ran his hand over the wall. "I can feel the magic pooling here. She put a lot of effort into this charm."

"She did," Wesley agreed, folding his arms over his chest. "She wanted to make sure she was the only one who could access it."

"If she's the only one who can access it, how are we going to get inside?" I asked.

"You're going to do it." Wesley's tone was no-nonsense. "May left the lighthouse to you. That means she left its contents to you."

I wasn't convinced. "Maybe she never wanted me to find this thing. That could explain why she never told me about it."

"Or there's something else in there she wanted you to discover at a later date." Wesley fixed me with an expectant look. "You have to be the one to enter."

"But ... how?"

"Just feel your way around. You should be able to slip inside."

He sounded so sure of himself I decided the best thing to do was give it a shot. "Okay. I don't know that I believe this is going to work, but it can't hurt to try." I headed for the wall, but Galen grabbed my arm before I could get too close.

246

"Wait a second," he argued. "What if there's something in there?"

"Like what?" Wesley's eyes flashed with amusement. "Do you think May was keeping magical creatures in there for sport? That's where she put her most prized and dangerous items. If she still has that talisman — and I doubt she would've gotten rid of it — then it's in there. It's a closet. There no dragon waiting for her."

Even though I knew he was joking, my heart gave a small jolt. "Dragons aren't real, are they?"

"Not the way you think," Galen replied calmly. "Although ... they're kind of real. We'll talk about that later." He leaned over and pressed a kiss to my forehead as he released me. "Be quick. I don't like the idea of you being in a place I can't enter."

I faked bravado for his benefit. "I've got it. Don't worry about me."

"I can't help it. Worry goes hand-in-hand with love."

"Oh, geez." Booker and Wesley made twin sounds of disgust.

That was enough to make me smile as I hunkered down and tentatively reached out my fingertips. They slipped through the wall easily into ... nothing. Well, I was sure there was something on the other side of the wall. I just couldn't see it ... or apparently feel it.

"Weird." I snatched my fingers back to stare at them. They were perfectly fine. "I think there really is a door there."

"Of course there's a door there." Wesley made a derisive snort. "You'd best get to it."

"I'm going." With one more look at Galen, I poked my head through the wall and into darkness. I found myself in a weird little room that looked to be lit by fairy lights.

The room was sparse. There was a small leather chair in the corner, what looked to be an altar table with books stacked on it and a small shelf with a variety of trinkets spread across it. One of those trinkets was copper in color and it was the item I immediately went for.

"I think I found it," I called out, my fingers wrapping around the disc.

The second I made contact with the item my head started to pound and my vision went fuzzy. Warmth coursed through me, and I was positive it came from the disc. I tried to drop it, but it was already too late. I fought the darkness threatening to overwhelm me, but I wasn't strong enough to regroup and escape.

Even as I leaned away, I tumbled into the abyss ... and I didn't stop falling for a very long time.

**I LANDED IN ANOTHER WORLD.**

That's all I could think when I finally managed to open my eyes and found myself sitting in front of a huge bonfire. Around me, various people dressed in odd clothing talked among themselves, arguing fiercely.

"The split is necessary," one of the women announced. She had long gray hair that fell past her shoulders and she looked determined. She reminded me of someone, and it took me a few moments to put my thoughts in order. She looked like Judy, which I found interesting. They weren't twins, but they shared the same fierce eyes and narrow nose.

I glanced around, confused. "Um ... excuse me." No one looked in my direction. "I don't want to bother you," I started, hating that I sounded so timid. "I'm not sure how I landed here, but if you could tell me how to get back to Moonstone Bay that would be great."

They ignored me. It was as if they couldn't see or hear me. Then another familiar face popped into existence to my left and I almost jumped when I realized who it was ... and that she appeared to be corporeal.

"May?"

My grandmother smiled at me. She looked more amused than upset. "I knew you would eventually find the closet. I just thought it would take you longer."

I poked her arm, curious. "Are you really here?"

"As much as you."

The enigmatic comment wasn't comforting. "What am I doing here?"

"You're bearing witness to a very important moment in history," she replied, folding her arms over her chest and watching the beings — who all looked ready for a fight to the death. "I've watched this scene numerous times over the years. It's the first time you're seeing it, but I can sum it up for you."

I opened my mouth to argue, but the Judy lookalike was yelling. "I don't care what the rest of you think ... or feel! This is what's supposed to happen. This was always how things were supposed to go."

"Not all of us agree with that," another voice volunteered. I couldn't see the source, but it came from the darkness behind us. "Some of us believe we're supposed to remain together. That's when we're strongest."

"I don't happen to believe that," the woman shot back, her eyes flashing. "We've debated this a hundred times over. Opinions won't change. It is what it is."

I was confused and wanted to take May up on her offer. "That would be great ... and then I want to get out of here." Even though I appeared to be invisible, which was an odd feeling, I wasn't keen on remaining. The moon looked red and it cast an ominous pall over the proceedings. "Did I travel through time?"

"Not quite." May laughed at the notion. "You traveled into a memory. It's something trapped within the talisman. You have to witness the moment, want to use the talisman in the appropriate manner, and then come out the other side to wield it."

"How do you wield it?"

"I don't know. I never had a reason to wield it. For a long time I thought it was a candle holder."

"Wesley told me. Judy Pitman is appalled by that, by the way."

"Judy is exactly the sort of person who should be kept away from the talisman," May warned. "She wants to use it for a dark purpose."

"Is that her ancestor?" I inclined my head toward the gray-haired woman. "They look a lot alike."

"That *is* her ancestor." May moved her jaw, her gaze darkening. "You're in Greece right now. Greece of the past, but still Greece. You can understand what they're saying thanks to the magic of the talisman. It's trying to explain the scene to you to the best of its ability. This is the moment when the elementals split and forever changed their future.

"What followed was war, famine and endless killing," she continued. "The elementals almost wiped each other out. That's what some of the factions wanted to do to the humans."

"And what's that?"

May pointed. "Look over there. That man standing next to the air elemental, he's the fire elemental. He's as evil as Judy's ancestor. He thinks they're working together to enact a plan."

"What plan?"

"They're going to create an army of super elementals to go after the humans, essentially creating air and fire elementals without souls who will seduce humans and bend their wills. They want to enslave them."

I was dumbfounded. "You're talking about incubi. I thought the air elementals created the incubi by accident."

"That's the lore, but it's far from the truth."

I tilted my head as I listened to the fire elemental make a speech about why splitting their factions was in everyone's best interests, how it would allow for the preservation of culture and a new step forward.

"We cannot function as one species," he warned. "We must become four separate species ... even if those species aren't always equal." His eyes gleamed at the prospect and caused my blood to run cold.

"The water and earth elementals don't seem so keen about it," I noted as I stared at the two individuals in question. They were both women ... and largely quiet. They sat on a bench and watched the proceedings with dispassionate gazes. "They look resigned to their fate."

"I've watched them so many times I feel as if I really knew them," May admitted. "I believe they realized the air and fire contingencies had a plan and wanted to steer clear of it. They sensed trouble and wisely took a step back."

"The fire elementals turned into demons," I said. "That means they went full-on evil, right?"

"Not all of them but a large contingent did."

"I don't understand." Frustration flowed through me. "Why didn't you tell me all this before?"

"Because I'm not the May you know. I'm the May who visited here before."

If she thought that would clear things up for me, she was wrong. "Weren't they the same May?"

"I'm an echo," May explained. "When May left, a small part of her remained. I'm that part. I'm aware of what happened in her world, but I'm forever trapped in this one."

That was a little sad. "Did she leave that part of her here on purpose?"

"No."

"When I leave, will a part of me remain behind?"

"Yes, but you've nothing to fear. It's just a memory within a memory."

"Okay." I tapped my bottom lip and turned back to the argument. "There's something important to see here."

"There is."

I watched the fire elemental slam his hand on a stone table. He seemed to be annoyed that anyone would dare question his wisdom. "I'm not here for further debate. The decision has already been made. You know the vote won't go your way. You can't force us to stay with you."

The earth elemental spoke for the first time. At least, I assumed she was the earth elemental. She was dressed in muted browns compared to the blue the other woman wore. "This is a mistake," she supplied, her tone grave. "Our gifts complement each other. We are meant to act in accordance with each other, balance each other. No force on this earth can fight us when we are together."

The fire elemental sneered. "Some of us feel that way about our own factions. You belong to the weakest faction, so it makes sense that you would want to act as anchors around our necks. We don't want that."

The earth elemental sighed, the sound long and drawn out. "You don't see what's right in front of you. I pity you for that. By the time you realize this was a mistake it will be too late to piece things back together."

"We won't need things pieced back together," the air elemental barked. She had Judy's imperious attitude. "We're going to transcend what we were designed to be and become greater."

The earth elemental merely shook her head. She was defeated and she knew it.

"Is it the collusion between the fire and air elementals?" I asked finally. "I mean ... the cupids pretend that they didn't purposely create the incubi. They maintain it was an accident and boast about how they try to control their mistakes, destroy them, when they're made aware of the situation."

"Do you believe that?"

"I ... ." That was a good question. It was also timely. Something about the situation had been bothering me for a long time. "The incubus we're dealing with here, it was created for a specific purpose. They want this talisman for more than just the power they think it holds. They want to make sure the truth doesn't get out."

"Just because they say one thing doesn't mean they've abandoned the plan they hatched thousands of years ago," May pointed out. "It might've taken longer than they imagined, but the plan is still on the table."

"And they need the talisman to enact the plan." That's when the final piece of the puzzle slipped into place. "They need the talisman because it has the power to allow them to do ... something. I'm not sure what that something is, but I'm betting it's not good."

"The talisman is full of power," May agreed. "The power was meant to be used for good. The cupids want to use it for evil. That's always been their goal. You can't allow that to happen."

"So I have to leave it here, keep it hidden."

"No. You have to take it with you. You'll probably need it."

I shook my head. "If they can't get their hands on it, that's better."

"Except you'll need it for the battle to come. I don't know everything, or even all that much, but I do know that. No matter what, you can't let the cupids get their hands on it. That goes for the demons as well."

"What about the sirens?"

"The sirens are another story. They have their own issues. I'm sure you'll figure that out eventually. It's not important now. They're allies in this as far as you're concerned."

"So ... what?" I was at a loss. "I should take the talisman with me and then do ... what? I don't know what to do."

May's smile was kindly. "You'll figure it out." Her nose wrinkled when the fire elemental jutted out his hand to strike an agreement with the air elemental. "The incubus is an immediate danger. You have to destroy it. The majority of the cupids can't be trusted either ... except Booker. You can always trust him. He's different from the rest."

I was grim. "How do I get out of here? I need to go back."

"You do," May agreed. "The final battle is waiting for you. I just wanted you to know how the pieces were stacked against you before you waged your war."

That didn't sound promising. "I don't understand."

"You will ... and soon." Her eyes filled with sympathy. "Don't lose hope. You're stronger than you think." With those words, before I had a chance to question her further, she pushed me as hard as she could.

I flew through time again, the disc clutched in my hand, and this time when I landed I was back in my bedroom ... and it was empty. Everyone was gone and I was on my own.

## TWENTY-EIGHT

"*G*alen!"

I called for him first because I knew he wouldn't simply leave the bedroom when I was traveling beyond his reach. He was the type to sit on the other side of the door, gnaw his fingernails and worry until I re-emerged. Then he would proceed to kiss me until my lips were raw and tired. He would most certainly not simply walk away from the door.

"Galen!"

My heart skipped a beat as I moved out of the bedroom. There, in the hallway, three of the paintings that had been displayed on the walls were missing from their regular spots. They'd been knocked to the floor.

My stomach twisted when I saw a drop of blood on the hardwood floor. I stopped long enough to touch it, terror momentarily sweeping through me, and then I collected myself and descended the stairs.

The living room was an absolute mess. The coffee table had been overturned. Some of the couch cushions were shredded. Several knickknacks May had on the shelves were broken. It looked as if a typhoon had swept through the room.

"Hadley, what are you doing here?" May appeared in the open

doorway, fear lighting her eyes. "Why aren't you running away? You can't stay here."

"I have the talisman," I said dully. "You gave it to me. Or, the other you gave it to me." I felt lost and didn't have any idea what I was supposed to do. "Who took them?"

"There was a big group." May was matter-of-fact despite her fear. "They didn't go down without a fight, but they were outnumbered."

"Are they ... ?" I couldn't finish the question. I felt sick to my stomach.

"They're not dead," May offered reassuringly. "They've been taken to the shack on the beach, the one next to the new hotel. I followed to make sure they were okay before coming to check on you."

I was in shock. I recognized that. Shaking the fog from my brain was easier said than done, though. "I just saw you when I touched the talisman. It was a different you. You were ... solid."

May furrowed her brow, confused. "I don't understand. What talisman?"

"The St. Valentine's Seal. You had it in your special room. Now I have it." I held it up by way of proof.

"Oh." Realization dawned. "That's what they want. They'll want you to trade the seal for your friends. You can't do that."

The look I shot her was withering. "I won't let them die."

"That's not what I'm saying." May's steady gaze never wavered. "They're your friends, your family. Of course you can't let them die. But you have to be smart about this."

"Who is it?" I looked around to make sure I hadn't missed anything. "Is it Judy's people?"

"It's Darlene's people," May corrected. "I'm pretty sure Judy isn't a part of this. She seemed as confused as everyone else. That doesn't mean she won't turn and join her sister if she feels the wind is blowing in a certain direction. You can't trust her."

"I don't trust her." I dragged a hand through my hair as I considered my options. "In the memory, you said I had to keep the seal hidden, to make sure they didn't get it until I was ready to wield it. What happens if I use it?"

May arched an eyebrow, confused. "What memory? I don't understand."

I told her the story quickly.

"That's interesting," she noted after digesting the information. "The talisman obviously directed the memory fragment how to respond."

Frustration bubbled up. "Meaning what?"

"Meaning that the talisman understands things are not as they should be. It doesn't want to be used to help one faction crawl on top of the heap. But that doesn't mean it can't be used as a weapon to stop that from happening."

"How does that help me?" I was running out of patience. "How am I supposed to deal with this? How am I supposed to save my friends?" Galen's face ran through my mind. I knew him. He was strong. He would've put up one heckuva fight, which meant that he could be in serious pain right now ... or nearing death. The mere notion gave me a stomachache. "I have to get moving. I can't leave them to their captors for too long. Galen will be desperate to get away, to keep me from coming. I have to get to them before he gets hurt a second time." Or before they realize he's more trouble than he's worth, I silently added.

"That's what Darlene wants," May chastised. "She expects you to act with your heart instead of your head."

"Then maybe I should give her what she wants." I considered my options. "Galen says my strength comes from inside. He says I react without thinking, and that's what's been keeping me safe as of late. Maybe I should just react."

"You'll be outnumbered. I suggest going to the water and getting Aurora's brethren to help. Perhaps try to get an audience with the DDA. They'll send soldiers if you can convince them."

"That will take too much time." I didn't like her suggestions in the least. "I need to get to Galen now ... and Wesley ... and the others. They need me."

"And what happens if you try to fight this battle alone? I'll tell you what happens. You'll lose."

"I'm not going to lose." I had an idea. "I need the talisman." I headed back for the stairs. "I think I know what I have to do."

May wasn't backing down. "You have to get help. You can't do this alone."

I thought of the faces around the barbecue. "I won't be alone. I have my own army ... and they'll already be there. I know what to do."

The memory fragment had given me a few ideas. Fear for my friends had filled in the holes. It was time to fight.

No. Scratch that. It was time to win.

I DIDN'T BOTHER HIDING MY approach. I didn't see the point. They would be expecting me. May volunteered to return to the captives, tell them I was coming and try to keep them calm. I knew how well that would go over. If Galen was able to, he would renew his fight. His instinct to protect was often overwhelming.

There was nothing I could do to curtail his emotions, so I simply nodded.

The property looked empty when I arrived, but I knew better. I could feel, maybe almost even hear, a bevy of people reacting with bated whispers when I exited the cart. The emotions were varied. Some broadcast fear, others pain, and still others excitement.

Darlene was the first to walk out from behind the shack. She was alone, but I knew she had backup waiting for her to signal. There's no way she would face me without a plan in place.

Well, I had a plan, too. I wasn't sure how I was going to make it all happen, but I definitely had a plan.

"Hello, Hadley." Darlene looked smug. "I bet you're surprised to see me."

"Not so much. I knew it was you."

"Oh, really? And how is that?"

"You're not as smart as you think." I glanced around. Her soldiers remained shrouded in shadow, which I found disconcerting. "You don't have to hide your people. I know they're all here. I know my people are here, too. I want them back."

Her lips curved into an evil sneer. "I want something, too. Do you know what I want?"

"You want the disc." I saw no reason to play games. "How did you know I had it?"

"My sister conducted exhaustive research. I don't like to give her credit — well, for anything really — but it seems she knew what she was talking about. She had you in her sights from the very start."

"And so did you." I rubbed my hands over the front of my khaki capris. "I didn't even know I had it until earlier tonight. It's fascinating that you knew more about me than I did."

"We knew more about your grandmother," Darlene corrected. "She discovered the seal. Then she died before she could tell you about it ... or find a way to dispose of it. She never should've had it in the first place. It always belonged to us."

"Why?" I decided to keep her talking in the hope she would make a mistake. If she focused on me, that meant my friends were probably okay. There was always a chance May could make good on her boasts and find a way to free them. "When the elementals split, there were four factions. The seal was created to represent all four."

"And yet only one faction mattered."

"You think the air elementals were above the others," I said. "The thing is, they were all considered equals when it came to creating the seal. I know. I was there for its forging."

"You were there?" Darlene snorted. "I believe that was thousands of years before you were born."

"And yet the talisman showed me its creation." I decided to go for it. In delaying, I amped up my own anxiety. "I saw that the fire and air elementals joined together and thought they were putting one over on the earth and water elementals. That wasn't true. They knew what would happen but were helpless to stop it. I saw that the fire elementals misjudged how duplicitous the air elementals were. I saw it all."

I'd also seen something else in the vision that she didn't understand. But I kept that to myself for now. "You're not as strong as you think you are," I added. "You're not smarter than everyone around you. You haven't outsmarted the other cupids as you believe. You must realize that."

Her snarl reminded me of a rabid cat. "You don't know anything about me."

"No? I know you've been creating incubi behind the scenes. I know exactly what sort of leadership role you want to play in the cupid council. You think the incubi will give you a leg up, let you rule more than the cupids. You want to enslave humans and force them to do your bidding."

Her eyes narrowed. "How can you possibly know that?"

"The talisman knows. It showed me everything."

"The talisman is an object, not a person."

"And yet it remembers. It also feels things, like disappointment. That's what it feels when it looks at you."

Irritation washed over her features. "Listen, I don't need a lecture from the likes of you. If you're angry about the incubus, well, I'm not going to apologize. He had a job to do ... and failed. He'll get his own form of punishment for failing, so you don't have to worry about retribution. I'll take care of that.

"What's important is that you have something I want, and I have something you want," she continued. "All you have to do is give me the talisman and I'll return your friends. It's a simple trade."

She was lying. If I handed over the talisman now she would kill the others ... and me. Intent flowed freely from her. She didn't even try to hide it.

"I hate to break it to you, but I'm not an idiot." I remained calm even though terror threatened to bring me to my knees. "I can read your thoughts."

She stilled, surprised. "I wasn't informed you were a mind reader."

"Yes, well, the detective you hired couldn't possibly know everything about me. I'm still learning things about myself. New powers pop up every day. It's been a whirlwind of activity."

"What do you want?" She folded her arms over her chest. "What compromise will make you willingly hand over the disc?"

Something clicked in the back of my head: ownership. The

talisman belonged to me. That meant she couldn't master it unless I openly, and without reservation, relinquished it.

"I want my friends back."

"All of them?" Darlene let loose a chortle that was empty and hollow. "You think I'm just going to hand over all your friends without something in return? You must be mad."

I was getting there. "I want to see all of them." I was firm. "I won't hand it over until I see they're all okay."

She ran her tongue over her lips, considering the demand, and then nodded. "Fine. You can see them." She turned to the shack. "Bring them out. Keep them on this side of the line, though. Don't let them near her."

My anticipation ratcheted up a notch when I heard cursing and fighting inside the shack. Eventually, everyone was dragged to the small clearing where Darlene and I stood. I took a moment to study each in turn, my heart lurching when I realized Galen was unconscious. He looked as if he'd taken a beating ... and then some. He dropped to the ground with a thud when they dragged him out, and didn't move a single muscle. He was so still it hurt to look at him.

"He's okay," Booker volunteered, as if reading my mind. His left eye was closed and bruised, his hands tied behind his back. "He's just unconscious. They went after him hard ... and he didn't take it well."

"He fought well," Wesley agreed. For the first time since I'd met him, he looked old and frail. Blood trickled from the corner of his mouth. "It's a wonder they managed to take him at all."

I briefly locked gazes with Lilac and Aurora in turn. They couldn't read my mind, but I wanted them to know I had a plan. Lilac's hair was already glowing red and she looked as if she was about to explode. She had some sort of rope wrapped around her wrists. It was different from the rope used to tie the others, and it seemed to be giving her fits because she kept struggling against it and glaring.

"As you can see, they're all fine," Darlene offered. "Now give me the talisman."

I knew better than that. "Where is Judy?" I didn't particularly care about the woman, but Booker did. "Where is your sister?"

"She's been moved to the hotel. She'll remain there until I get the talisman. When I'm in charge, she'll have the opportunity to bow to me or die. My sister is a survivor. She'll bow to me."

"Right." I licked my lips. "I'm not handing the talisman over until you free at least three of my friends. They're still too vulnerable."

Darlene shrewdly ascertained I had something up my sleeve. "No way. I'm not giving you any of them. You'll try to fight instead of doing the smart thing and giving me what I want."

"I'm not giving you the talisman unless I get three friends. That still gives you two to use as bargaining chips."

Darlene stared at the assembled people again. "Let me guess. You want your boyfriend and grandfather to be among the three. I won't do that. They're the most valuable ones in this little group. I'm keeping them with me."

She could never know it, but she'd just been played. I sent a specific image into her head as if it was fact — one that was based around Galen and Wesley being able to help me — and she'd fallen for it. She thought it was her own idea and that she'd outsmarted me.

I acted as if I was upset, shaking my head before nodding. "All right. Then give me the others."

Darlene nodded to her men. "Transport the others to her. She won't be able to remove the demon's ties anyway. She'll be of no use to her."

Booker's speculative gaze never moved from my face as he was led across the field. When he was positioned in front of me, curiosity got the better of him. "What's the plan here? Are you really going to give her that talisman? She'll kill us anyway."

"I know." I forced a smile for his benefit. "But I couldn't just leave you out here."

"At least you'd be alive." Booker was the pragmatic sort. "I'm kind of glad Galen is out so he doesn't have to see this. She's going to kill you the second you hand that thing over."

"Well ... ." I didn't get a chance to finish because Darlene cleared her throat to regain my attention. "You have your friends. I still have your boyfriend and grandfather. All you have to do is hand over the talisman and you'll get them back. It's as simple as that."

She was still lying. Even though she knew I could read her mind, she continued to play the game. It would've been comical under different circumstances.

"Fine." I heaved out a sigh and switched my gaze to Lilac. "Do you want to play a game?"

The friendly neighborhood bartender and half-demon's eyebrows drew together. "Game?"

I reached into my pocket and withdrew the talisman, causing Darlene's eyes to gleam and a collective gasp among the cupids. With the talisman, though, I also withdrew a small knife. It was also in May's storage closet, and she told me about its magical properties before she disappeared to help my friends. She knew I would need it.

I saw her now, kneeling between Wesley and Galen. She'd appeared when the cupids lost interest in them and fixated on the talisman. She was a ghost, but she was strong, loyal and true. I hoped to be just like her one day.

"We must be fast," I announced. "The talisman is meant to be used when all four elementals are represented. Do you understand what I'm saying?"

Booker's eyes flashed with acknowledgment as Aurora broke into a wide smile.

"Stop talking," Darlene snapped. "Give me the talisman."

"We understand," Lilac volunteered. "But I can't use my magic until I'm free."

"Then get ready." I sawed the knife over Lilac's restraints first. Her hands were tied in the front. She immediately turned and shot fire out of her hands, causing the cupids grouped close to Wesley and Galen to flee in every direction.

Booker and Aurora turned so I could attack the ropes behind their backs. My fingers were surprisingly deft despite the fear coursing through me. They were free in seconds ... and then we were a group of elemental offspring ready to attack.

"You shouldn't have gone after my friends," I growled, extending the talisman. "You shouldn't have tried to be better than the others either. The talisman wants the four races to work together. It never would've given you what you wanted, no matter how you tried to wield it."

"That's mine!" Darlene screeched and stepped in my direction.

Instead of trying to cut her off, Booker, Aurora and Lilac instinctively reached for the talisman at the same time. They understood the plan ... mostly because I'd placed the idea into their heads at the same moment I'd freed them.

"Now!" I ordered.

Three fingers touched the talisman at the same time, causing the metal disc to heat in my hands. Bright light — it was almost as if the Fourth of July was happening in the center of our small circle — erupted.

For the first time since I'd met her gaze across the darkness, Darlene looked fearful. The other cupids wisely took off running, their only goal to escape the light. Darlene, though, was rooted to her spot.

"What are you doing? That's my talisman!" Even now she couldn't see the truth.

"It was never going to be yours," I argued as magical versions of four creatures swooped in her direction. I recognized them from the engravings on the talisman. They were the spirit animals of the elementals ... and they wanted vengeance. "You couldn't give the talisman what it wanted so it was never going to give you what you wanted."

"And what did it want?" Darlene raised her hand to fight off the furious magical phoenix and protect her face. "Stop!"

"Cooperation," I answered simply, closing my eyes when the magical – and completely ticked off – ethereal animals took over Darlene and started destroying her. "The elementals were never meant to be enemies. They were always meant to be allies."

Darlene's screams were enough to turn my stomach. I didn't look away, though. I couldn't. I was meant to see this. It was a warning, and it would spread far and wide.

## TWENTY-NINE

*I* wasn't sure how to explain Darlene's death to Galen's deputies, but Booker took the duty out of my hands and told them everything. They scattered quickly to track down the other cupids, and Booker left me to wait for the ambulance, taking Lilac and Aurora with him on an incubus hunt.

"The incubus still needs to be eradicated," Booker explained before he left. "Stay with Galen. Check on Wesley, too. I think his arm is dislocated."

I had no intention of leaving either of them. "You don't need me to help you kill it, do you?"

"No. I've got it. Between the three of us, we're more than capable. We've got to collect my mother, too."

I'd almost forgotten about Judy. "I'm sure that will be a pleasant reunion."

"Oh, we've got a lot to talk about." He gave me a hug and then pulled back. "We'll come to the hospital when it's finished. Look after Galen. He's your main concern."

He most definitely was.

At the hospital, they wouldn't let me back with Galen while they worked on him. I thought about pitching a fit, but it wasn't dignified

... and I was smart enough to realize I was a woman on the edge and they might be within their rights if they tried to bar me from the hospital altogether. They had a job to do. They would let me know when they were finished.

Wesley wasn't as bad off, so I was allowed to sit with him. He complained bitterly, as they popped his shoulder back into the socket and then forced him into a sling. I was ordered to make sure he didn't overdo things the next few days. I figured that was a battle I wasn't ready to engage in.

Before they finally allowed me into Galen's room, they told me he would be fine — after listing a litany of broken bones and injuries that made my stomach hurt — and then left me alone to sit with him. One of Wesley's men took my grandfather home, even though he'd offered to stay. I sent May with him, figuring a doting ghost was better than nothing, and then sat in the dimly lit room and waited for Galen to wake.

He still hadn't stirred after four hours.

"Hey." Booker had a new bruise on his cheek when he entered. He took a long look at Galen and then grabbed another chair and sat next to me. He looked grim. "Everything is taken care of."

I arched an eyebrow. "The incubus is dead?"

"It is. Darlene had been hiding it — I mean *them* — for a long time. There was more than one. That's what took so long. We had to take out four of them ... and they were a little different from the incubi we were used to. They fought hard for their lives."

My heart rolled. "I'm sorry. That's a lot of killing in one evening."

"We didn't have a choice, Hadley. There's no fixing an incubus. Once they're turned, there's no going back. These incubi might've been different – which is why everyone was having such a tough time with their scent – but they were as dangerous as we believed and had to go."

"Awesome." I dragged a hand through my hair and shifted so I could slide my fingers over Galen's still hand. "He's still out."

"He'll come around ."

"I thought he had superior healing or something. Isn't that a shifter thing?"

"It is. But he was beaten pretty badly. Even after I heard his ribs crack he kept going. He was desperate to keep them from you."

I didn't want to cry. It wouldn't help anything – or anyone – but I couldn't stop myself. "He should've let them take me."

"Oh, don't do that." Booker made a face. "Don't cry. That'll drive me crazy."

"I'm sorry." His words only made me sob harder. "I just ... can't ... stop ... myself."

"Oh, geez." Booker looked as if the last place he wanted to be was close to me. Still, he slid his arm around my shoulders and offered as much comfort as he could muster. "You're okay. Galen will be fine. After a few hours of sleep, he'll wake up and be the cranky sheriff we all know and love. Well, I don't love him, but there are times I almost like him."

Another sob shook me.

"Stop this right now. Galen wouldn't want you crying over him."

"He certainly wouldn't," a slurred voice said from the bed.

I snapped up my head and almost cried out in relief when I realized Galen was awake. I stood over him, squeezing his hand. "Try not to move. The doctor said you're in bad shape."

"I'm fine." As if to prove it, he squeezed my hand. "Don't cry, honey. Just ... don't. I can't take it."

"Listen to him," Booker prodded. "He's an invalid. You can't argue with an invalid."

I buried my head on the bed next to him and allowed the emotions I'd been holding back for hours to wash over me. Galen couldn't do much but pet my head, which he did as Booker filled him in on everything he'd missed. When he was finished, Galen looked relatively happy, which threw me for a loop.

"It's not funny," I protested.

"It's a little funny." Galen's fingers were gentle as they brushed the tears on my cheek. "Please stop crying. I'll be good as new in about eight to twelve hours. The crying hurts worse than the head injury."

"How do you know you have a head injury?"

"Because they hit him, like, five times in the head," Booker answered. "His head is too hard to crack, so I knew he would be fine."

I shot him a quelling look. "It's not funny."

"Stop poking her," Galen ordered as his fingers moved through my hair. "Everything is just catching up to her now. She'll sleep like the dead tonight. That's good, because I don't know how long I'm going to last before I pass out again."

"Then go to sleep," I urged. "You need your rest. I'll be here next to you all night."

He chuckled. "Isn't that what I usually tell you?"

"Well, now I'm the one in control. I get to be the boss."

"I'm pretty sure you're always the boss." He made a face as he shifted on the bed, making room for me. "Come on." He patted the bed, inviting me to join him, but I balked.

"You're injured. You need to be quiet."

"I can be quiet with you."

"Oh, I don't think that's true," Booker countered. "I've never once heard her be quiet."

"Shut up." I jabbed a finger in his direction. "I can be quiet."

"Come over here and prove it," Galen insisted. "If you expect me to rest, I'll need you close to my side so I won't have nightmares. You're the only thing that will keep them at bay."

I narrowed my eyes. "That's low."

"That doesn't make it untrue. Come on." He patted the bed again.

I really wanted to feel close to him, so I acquiesced. I was careful as I slid into the bed, making sure I didn't accidentally jar him. His body was warmer than usual. He once told me that was a sign he was healing. I hoped he was right about being back to himself the following day. I wasn't sure how much fretting I could take.

"There you go." Galen pressed a kiss to my forehead and then focused on Booker. "What about your mother?"

"She was at the hotel suite with the incubi. She swears up and down she's a victim in all of this, that she had no idea Darlene was purposely creating warrior incubi. I'm not sure I believe her. I think she had the same plan as Darlene. She just never got to put it into play."

"What will that mean for the election?" I asked. "She won't become president, will she?"

"I doubt it. I've already dropped an information bomb on the other council members. They're well aware of what happened. They're also aware of my mother's plan. She was calling me a filthy liar when I left the council chambers to come back here."

"What else did they say about the incubi?" Galen asked. "We know they were purposely made, but I still don't understand the endgame."

"They were. Darlene planned to make more as soon as she could. Most cupids don't have the stomach to give up their souls, but some do. These incubi were essentially the worst of the worst cupids. Whenever someone got in trouble, threatened with jail time, she would interview them in an effort to see if she could bring them to her cause. She didn't care what she was doing to them. Her only goal was to build an army."

"Well ... at least they're gone."

"They are. We killed them and dragged the bodies to the medical examiner's office. They'll be disposing of them there."

He talked about it so clinically that I felt uncomfortable. Of course, I understood the rationale behind his thinking. They weren't people to him. Perhaps they had been at one time, but if they had the capacity to turn then they were probably never good people.

"What about the rest of Darlene's people?" Galen asked. "What happened to them?"

"They scattered when we used the talisman. Your deputies are rounding them up. They've halted boat and plane traffic on and off the island. I gave them a list of the people I recognized. I'm sure they've got it all in hand."

"I'll double-check in the morning."

"You will not," I argued. "You're spending the day in bed."

"Hadley, I'll be fine in the morning; maybe a little sore. In two days it will be like nothing ever happened. You won't even remember."

I thought of the way he'd hit the ground when Darlene's men dragged him out of the shack. "I won't forget."

"Oh, geez. You're going to be trouble, aren't you?" He kissed my forehead again. "You need to unwind. A good night's sleep will do us both wonders. You can stay in here with me."

"I doubt the doctors will allow that."

"You let me worry about the doctors."

Booker's chair scraped against the floor as he stood. "I think it's time for me to call it a night. I'll check back in with you tomorrow. I'll keep an ear to the ground about the cupids until then to make sure nobody gets away."

"I appreciate it." Galen extended his hand for Booker to shake, the two men grinning at one another like idiots. "Thanks for making sure she wasn't hurt. I owe you."

"You don't." Booker was matter-of-fact. "She came to the beach by herself, in a purple golf cart, and she took down Darlene."

"We took her down together," I corrected. "That's what the scene I saw in the memory told me was necessary. We all had to work together because we are ancestors of the four different branches."

"You still did it by yourself." Booker didn't back down. "You were amazing. If you were afraid, I didn't see it. You probably would've been smarter to call Galen's deputies for backup, but I can't argue with the outcome."

"That's probably smart," I noted. "I'm not much in the mood to argue."

"That makes two of us. Tomorrow is another day, though."

Once he was gone and it was just Galen and me, I looked up at his face. He was sleepy. Bruises lined his cheeks and neck. He'd obviously put up a tremendous fight.

"You should sleep," I whispered. "I'll stay awake to make sure nothing gets us."

"No." His eyes were closed. "We're going to sleep together. Exactly like this. All night."

I had my doubts. "I don't think I can sleep."

"You can. Just let the worry from the day fall away." He tightened his arms around me. "The incubi are gone. I guess we know why they were going after both men and women. There was more than one creature hunting on the island."

"What if there's still one out there?"

"I could get my handcuffs."

I was confused. "To do what?"

"To make sure you stay right here all night. I could handcuff us together."

That sounded a little freaky. "Or you could just sleep and I'll watch you all night to make sure you're okay."

"Sure." He moved his mouth to mine and snuggled closer. The warmth of his body and the steady beat of his heart was enough to lull me. "Are you asleep yet?" he whispered, causing me to giggle.

"No. Not yet."

"Probably need another minute." He exhaled heavily against my forehead.

"I thought of a name for Wesley's horse," I volunteered out of the blue. "It happened tonight when you were hurt."

"Oh, yeah? What's the name?"

"Potter – after May. She took care of you and Wesley. I owe her."

"I don't believe she feels the same way, but we can argue about it later. I think Potter is a fine name."

"Yeah." We lapsed into comfortable silence.

"How about now?" he asked suddenly, causing me to laugh. "Are you asleep yet?

"No." His voice was so soft I found my eyelids drooping despite the kiss he planted on my lips. "Hey, Galen."

"Hmm."

"I love you. We're going to talk about your self-preservation instincts tomorrow, though."

He'd said something along those lines to me multiple times, and hearing it repeated back caused him to snort. "I can't wait."

"Goodnight."

"Goodnight. Oh, and I love you."

"I know."

"We'll have our official celebration tomorrow. I'm thinking we'll move to your bed once I'm sprung from this place, and you can dress up like a naughty nurse and take care of me."

"I can probably be persuaded to do that."

"That's exactly what I wanted to hear."